ANGELFIRE

BOOK ONE

BY:

LUKE VALEN

Published 2018
First Edition
Printed in the United States of America
ISBN: 978-1-7327366-0-3
Library of Congress Control Number: 2018910473
Cover design by: Luke Valen
Cover layout by: Luke Valen
Wing design: Mr.SuttiponYakham/shutterstock.com
Snow vector: Ya_blue_ko/shutterstock.com
Pine forest: Grop/shutterstock.com
Title Font (modified) by: SDFonts/dafont.com
Interior design/Typeset by: Gessert Books

Scripture taken from the New King James Version®. Copyright © 1982 by Thomas Nelson. Used by permission. All rights reserved

For more information or book orders please visit:
www.lukevalen.com

To my queen and two angels. You are powerful beyond measure. The gift courses through your veins like liquid fire. Spread your wings and spark the embers. It's time to fly.

CONTENTS

Sixteen years after the First Event

CHAPTER 1

HOMECOMING

Knock. Knock.
Who's there?
A boy and a girl.
A boy and a girl who?

"All right, everybody. Settle down, settle down," Mr. Allan announced as the class came to an end and the restless teens began to lose interest. "It's time to go over this week's writing assignment. The one I'm sure you *all* completed."

I heard the voice drift out the open classroom window as I walked nearby, taking a drag of my cigarette. I glanced over, my eyes making out the details. Mr. Allan stood there in his khaki pants, blue short-sleeve button-up shirt stretched to the limit from his extended stomach, tie loosened, hair a mess and large spectacles, with a distasteful look on his face...yet a twinkle of hope in his eyes.

And then I saw *her*.

Abigail Li'ved—AngelFire's very own princess—was drawing in her notebook next to the classroom window. So beautiful, sunrays seemed to dance around her soft blonde hair, like a flower blossoming for the first time in spring, swaying in the breeze. Keeping my distance, I hid under the tall oak tree in the yard just below the classroom. I hadn't been in one of those in years, just the word made me shudder—*class*. I had hoped she wouldn't notice me, though as fate would have it, just as I found myself staring, so did she. She saw me looking up at her wide-eyed and all. I tried to play it off and act cool; I took a drag on my cig, let out one last puff of smoke, flicked it in what I perceived as slow motion, lifted the collar of my long black peacoat…and walked away.

I wondered what she was drawing.

Mr. Allan's voice drifted through the open window behind me. "Abigail!" Mr. Allan snapped. "What are you drawing there? Would you like to share it with the class?"

"Nothing, Mr. Allan. It's nothing."

I glanced over my shoulder just in time to see as she slammed the notebook shut. I stopped, curious what would happen next.

"*Mmmhhhmm.*" Mr. Allen folded his arms, not believing her for one second. "Well then, maybe you can tell us about our assignment's subject. What is love to you?" The weight of this question was that of a rocket scientist being asked how he plans to land on the moon July 16th, 1969. This question was the Apollo 11. Buzz, Neil, Michael…your answer please…

I smirked, shaking my head at the grandiose.

Abigail squirmed slightly. "Love to me is…"

All eyes were on her, ears perked, as the class transformed to a conglomerate of focused minds all wondering what love was to her. Something they could feed off of and construct into a weak variation of their own, since no one bothered to actually do the assignment themselves.

Abigail straightened, meeting the teacher's eye. "Love to me is patient. It is something that is selfless and perseveres through all hardships. It is hope and protection. It's like the story of Odysseus and Penelope. He was called to war to protect the one he loved the most. Out of selflessness and patience, and the two never gave up on one another, knowing that the hope in their hearts was strong enough to reunite them once again."

A successful landing. Perked ears became pencil to paper as the ideas began to flow.

Fully expecting her to disappoint him with an answer like, "I don't know," Mr. Allan was at a loss of words with the beauty and justice she had brought to his question.

Approved.

"Hmmm, well okay then. Very good. Class, take note. This is what it looks like to come prepared."

Ring, Ring, Ring.

The end-of-class bell, although sharp and quite annoying, was always a joyful pain in a kid's ears.

"Okay, class, make sure you read chapters seven through nine of your textbooks and have your assignment on my desk Monday morning!" he tried to say over the ringing bell and the rustling of backpacks and sliding desks.

Abigail slowly collected her books and then stopped for a second and looked out the window once again, possibly even with a slight hope that the mysterious me was still out there.

"Abby!" Cherry shouted from the open hallway door, class books held close to her chest.

Oh, Cherry, what a delightful young lady. I say that with a slight touch of sarcasm. And it is *CH-erry*, not *SH-erry*—she's very sensitive about that. She's the one who always seemed to be on top of all current gossip going around school, partly due to the fact that she started most of it. This redheaded, freckled, five-four (and a half, according to her) girl, was for some odd reason Abigail's best friend and cocaptain on the cheer squad.

"Abby!" she shouted again, cocking her head in frustration.

"Hey, Cherry. What's up?" Abigail looked back out the window.

"Abigail, come on, let's go! We're going to be late for the pep rally." Cherry stopped and stared out the window as well. "What are you staring at?"

"Hmm?" Abigail smiled and turned from the window. "Oh, nothing. Let's go." That old oak tree was a saving grace, hiding me from her sight.

THE MUSIC FROM the band began to play as the cheer team came out from behind the bleachers, waving their pom-poms and kicking their legs in the air. Abigail, front and center. Balloons and streamers hung from the walls and ceiling, all the school pride filling the room like the oxygen itself. The football team took up the first three rows of the bleachers in their jerseys rolled at the sleeves and puffed-up egos. The cool guys. Among them was Chase Andrews.

Chase Andrews wasn't always a bad guy—he actually used to be pretty nice. I remember about ten years ago, six-year-old me was getting bullied by a couple of older kids at the local park when Chase came up and stopped them. They would make fun of me saying, "No one loved you—that's why they left you."

Savages.

Chase used to be good guy. Then puberty and football happened. Now *he's* the one kicking people down and doing all the bullying. I don't know why all the girls like him.

Oh, yeah. He's captain of the varsity football team.

I don't like social events—the illusion of friendship and eternal youth did not faze me. The only reason I went was to see *her*.

The way she drew me in felt almost instinctual. Like breathing. From her halo of blonde hair to the lilt of her voice. Even the way she walked was musical in essence, each step in perfect harmony with the other, whose causality was that of the surrounding world to follow her beat.

I stayed hidden in the shadows of the corner bleachers, just close enough to the exit. *Shhh.* Principal Watkins is about to speak.

"What an amazing year, wouldn't you say, class?"

The crowd cheered and roared.

"This has truly been a year for the books. I have had the pleasure of seeing all of you young kiddos grow into such mature and intelligent young adults over these years. And to you seniors, I believe you are ready for the next step into adulthood," he said into the microphone as paper airplanes crowded the gymnasium skies. Having no air traffic control meant there were midair collisions and improper landings into a few of the teachers' hair. Balloons popped and fart noises echoed like explosions. This was no pep rally—this was World War High School.

"Don't even think about it, Charles," Principal Watkins said without even having to look up to see Charles Ratowski in the rafters holding a watermelon-sized water balloon ready to drop on the principal's freshly ironed suit and tie.

Charles, obviously disappointed he no longer had the element of surprise and deprived of the sense of victory, tucked away his prized claim to the high school prank fame.

"As I was saying, it's been an honor educating you all, and I can't wait to see you all at graduation. Go Hawks!"

The music rose once again as the band entered into their final hoorah. Principal Watkins waved and exited stage left. Great act.

"Abby," Cherry whispered in between fake smiles, arm waving, and leg kicks. The girl might as well have been yelling, I could hear her a mile off. Though I had always been able to hear more than most, probably because my sense of feeling was nearly non-existent. One learns to numb their senses after enough has occurred to justify the off switch.

The cheer squad seemed to be a herd of stuck-up cookie-cutter girls who thought they were better than everyone else. But not Abigail. She was different.

"Abby, what are you always thinking about?" Cherry poked.

Abigail turned to answer, her eyes instantly locking with mine. Shit. She saw me again. I quickly hid behind the bleachers. She would think I was stalking her for sure. I wasn't.

"Nothing, what's up?" Abigail bobbed her head around Cherry's.

"Please tell me you are going to Chase Andrews's party after this." Cherry was so excited she was bubbling with zeal, awaiting Abigail's answer.

"Oh. Yeah. I didn't know he was having a party." Abigail fabricated a smile.

"Okay great, I'll pick you up at nine o'clock, okay?"

"Yeah, sounds good. Hey, Cherry, do you know who that guy is?"

Shit. She was pointing at me now.

"Who?" Cherry turned to see what was on the end of Abigail's finger. "That creepy guy hiding in the corner? Does he really think no one can see him? Yeah, that's Dean." Cherry frowned, her disgust obvious.

"Dean? Dean what?" Abigail asked.

Cherry smacked her gum obnoxiously. "He doesn't have a last name. I think he is like some kind of orphan or something. I think he used to go here but got kicked out for fighting a lot. I don't know, why?"

"No reason. Just wondering." Abigail's eyes darted back to Cherry.

"Okay, weirdo. Well, yeah, so tonight. Nine o'clock. Don't forget…Abby!"

Abigail was burning a hole in the back of my head—I could feel it.

"Oh, yeah, yeah, nine o'clock. Perfect." Abigail smiled as Cherry ran off.

Abigail turned back to see if I was still there. Just the blackness of the shadows cast from the bleachers. "Hmmm." She muttered as she turned to leave. Something lingered in her mind with a seemingly relentless annoyance plastered on her face. As if she could not shake the feeling that we had met before, that I was important. Or maybe that was my self-inflated ego projecting my own lingering thoughts onto another.

So elegant and beautiful, it's as if all the decorations were there just for her. *Do I know her?* What had she been drawing in her notebook? That was my last thought before I turned to leave. It would be getting dark soon and I needed to get home. I've always hated what comes with the dark.

What had she been drawing?

THE ALLEY AROUND the corner was a cesspool. The brick walls dripped with wet spray paint from the local gangs taking claim of their territory. The ground was covered in blood and sweat leaked from junkies duking it out for one last hit. Exposed needles littered the ground like weeds fertilized by human feces. No one ever bothered me. I kept to myself, as did they. The poor, lost souls.

So why were they looking at me today?

They never looked at me. And they were *staring*, not just looking. What is going on?

Keeping my head down, I tried not to make eye contact with them. Lying there half alive like zombies who couldn't decide if they wanted to live or die. Fifty more feet, I was almost out. Twenty more feet. The rattling of glass bottles rang throughout the narrow alley as I accidentally kicked one after the other, speeding up my step, no longer attempting to be guile and slow. Why were they looking at me? Their gaze pierced my soul, as if begging for help, begging to end their miserable lives. Ten feet…

That's when I saw it.

Eyes. One pair. Ripping into me. Eyes a red so deep they resembled the planet Mars floating as twins side by side in the dark void of alley space. I froze, a numbness overtook my body like a tidal wave taking the shore. I couldn't move. These eyes drew me in closer and closer to a shadow blacker than black. Even space wasn't this black.

What is that? The eyes floated, staring, menacingly. Eight feet…Seven feet…

Fight it. Leave. Get out of here. *GO!*

I wriggled my mind free of the fear, and my eyes away from the locked gaze. Run. Breathing in deeply to fuel my quick motion, I ran, the smell of human bile and waste burned my nostrils as my senses returned.

I ran as fast as I could. One leg in front of the other. Repeat. Fighting the overwhelming urge to turn around, I kept my eyes focused on the road ahead. Trying to shake the sight from my brain, the thought of *her* entered my mind. Calming me just as I approached home.

The gentle glow of remaining photons slowly left the sky. From purple, to dark blue, to gray and black. It was almost dark—what time was it? Covered in a cold sweat, I looked down to check my watch. 8:47 p.m. How could that be? How long had I been in that alley? Two extra hours is not normal. The streetlamp flickered on as I rounded the last corner, releasing all my worries.

The sight of home warranted a large sigh of relief. "Ahh. Home, sweet home."

To many, it would look simply like a beat-up, abandoned church. Boarded up from head to toe, this old girl had seen better days. It was abandoned back in '97 when the Asian financial crisis gripped the world with fear of a worldwide economic meltdown due to financial contagion. Long story short, people got scared, stopped giving as much, and the church just couldn't survive.

Good thing for me though. I found this place just after turning thirteen, after being kicked out of my latest foster home. For some odd reason I had always had a peculiar sense of safety in this place. More so than our flawed foster system. I would have been a good kid if the "parents" were good "parents." From rules so strict I couldn't breathe at a certain volume unless I wanted to "run a mile!" to getting that weekly beating to keep me "strong." Things just didn't work out.

This was the only place I ever truly felt at peace, like I was supposed to be here.

Surrounded by a yard of yellowing grass, dead weeds, and an old willow tree hanging on to its last branch of life, it was beautiful. The tall, oversized double doors creaked as the wood splintered a little each time I would open them, almost as if to greet me home. My grand entrance was a disheveled, dark red carpet that once was glorious and bright. The pews to my left and right were covered in dust, like a blanket of their own. I sifted through the air populated by dancing particles made visible by rays of light passing through the mosaic glass windows that lined the walls. The mixed smells of dirt, wood, and old carpet were things of beauty.

"How's your day been, J.C.?" I asked the giant statue of Jesus that was sitting front and center. My roommate. "Anything exciting happen today?"

He never answered me.

"No? Well, guess what—I saw that girl again today. Except something felt different. I felt like I had something to say to her, but I don't know what."

The thought of her invaded my mind once again. Only to be overtaken by the image of those eyes. Those piercing red eyes among the infinite black. Snap out of it. I shook my head in an effort to reset the rogue thoughts, like the white flakes in a snow globe landing to the bottom at rest.

I needed to see her again. Tonight.

But where?

—§—

Ding-dong.

The bell echoed throughout the empty caverns that was Abigail's house.

Ding-dong.

"Coming!" Abigail responded, tucking away a large leather-bound book underneath her bed and putting down her pencil from where she had been meticulously scribbling in her notebook. "One second! Almost there!"

Cherry stood on the front step impatiently waiting as Abigail opened the front door.

"Dang, Abby. Making me wait like ten years, geez! Hey, do you have a different dress I can borrow? My mom made me wear this hideous creature." Cherry kept rambling as she pushed her way past Abigail.

Decorated in gold and ivory, the white marble floors glistened as the two made their way through the immense complex. Ceilings so high the only way to tell where they stopped was by the hanging crystal and diamond chandeliers. Glass cases filled with ancient artifacts furnished each room, and Abigail often wondered if she lived in a house or a museum.

The two made their way up the spiral staircase into Abigail's room. Just like any other sixteen-year-old girl, it smelled of roses and hope. Although, rather than having walls covered in pink paint and posters of boy bands, hers were lined with books upon books. A library of sorts. Big books, little books, new books, and old books.

"Abigail, you nerd. Do you actually read any of these or do you just like to pretend?" Cherry leafed through a book before tossing it onto the bed. "Dumb question. Of course you read them. You're Mr. Allan's favorite student."

Abigail pasted a smile on her face. Was it wrong to read books? Was it really such a crime to prefer diving into a juicy story, be it fact or fiction?

"What's this?" Cherry asked, grabbing Abigail's personal journal and sitting on the Egyptian-spun bedding.

She lifted the soft brown leather book, the edges worn and wrapped in a rope like piece of its own leather. Just as Cherry was about to unravel it, Abigail noticed. "Stop!"

"Huh?" Cherry paused in a moment of confusion. These two shared everything with each other, even if Abigail didn't necessarily like to share everything.

"I mean...Please, don't. It's just...it's nothing." Abigail stumbled on her words as she reclaimed the journal from Cherry's curious clutch.

Cherry shrugged. "Sure. Whatever. Anyway, about the dress?"

Cherry's puppy eyes were honestly repulsive, but Abigail felt herself relenting. "Oh, yeah. Just grab whatever you want from my closet."

Cherry stood up and made her way to the vastly oversized walk-in closet—a closet that could easily have been a second bedroom. Abigail clutched the journal with only one thought running through her mind: *Never let anyone see what's inside.*

"What do you think of this one?" Cherry emerged, wearing a bright pink cocktail dress that was obviously one size too small for her. "I love the way it makes my boobs look."

"Yeah, totally," Abigail lied. "Go with that one."

"Okay. I have what I'm wearing." Cherry turned slowly from side to side, checking herself out in the mirror. "What are you wearing?" A hint of judgment tipped her words.

"This." Abigail shrugged, looking down at the plain red V-cut T-shirt and navy blue denim jeans she wore. "I figured the party wasn't gonna be too formal or anything."

Abigail was an oddly humble and conservative girl, considering her father was the richest man in AngelFire. No one really knew what he did other than being a businessman.

"You're going to wear that? Didn't you wear that to school today?" Cherry's look of confusion warped into a frown as she examined Abigail. "You've got this never-ending closet and you choose that? Ugh, I'll never understand you."

Abigail shrugged, letting the comments roll off her. Just like all of Cherry's comments. She didn't mean anything by it. Not really.

Cherry sighed. "You *cannot* wear that."

"Why not?" Abigail asked, genuinely confused.

"Because Chase Andrews. That's why not."

"You say that like it means something."

"It does mean something, Abigail. Chase Andrews is only the most popular, cutest, sexiest guy in school."

"So?"

"So? So! Ugh, fine. Whatever. We're going to be late, so let's just go. You can wear that…I guess. Ugh." Cherry stormed out of the room and down the stairs.

Abigail stared after Cherry and then glanced back over her outfit. What was so wrong with it? She felt good. Comfortable.

"Let's go!" Cherry yelled from somewhere down the hall.

Just as Abigail was lacing up her red-and-white tennis shoes, an odd feeling swept over her. As if someone were watching her. Her eyes darted from side to side, like an estranged animal searching for its predator, checking every corner of the room.

Nothing.

This wasn't the first time she'd felt like someone was watching her. Fear engulfed her soul—something felt off tonight. Like it was a comfort blanket, she reached for her little brown journal, tucked it away in the pocket of her red leather jacket, brushed off the eerie feeling, and finished tying her shoe, trying to ignore her unsteady fingers, and then headed out the door.

"'Kay, ready. Let's go!" She paused, looking back to examine her room one last time.

Still nothing.

Always nothing.

CHAPTER 2

REALITY CHECK

A CONSTANT POUNDING of music could be heard from the house as Cherry and Abigail approached the party. The two-story cabin was lit up by black light. A purple haze emitted from the windows and the muffled sound of chatter escaped the cracks of wood. Tucked away in the forest hills, the house was secluded. Only the trees and stars could lay witness that a party ensued. Making their way through the sea of red cups that cluttered the steps, the two drew near to the door.

"Okay, just don't act, ah…just be normal, cool?" Cherry said in the kindest way possible as she reached out her closed fist to knock on the door.

Knock. Knock. Knock.

The two stood there awkwardly awaiting their knock to be answered and invited to join in on the festivities. Twiddling their thumbs, looking straight ahead, not at one another. Finally, after what seemed like a lifetime, the door swung open.

"Hey." Chase answered the door himself, looking from girl to girl, analyzing them for a moment before recognizing the two.

Cherry smiled from ear to ear, gawking at his beauty. Abigail forced a smirk.

"Um…Cherry right? And Abigail. What's uppp? Come on in, ladies. Join the party!" Chase waved them in with a big smile, swinging the door completely open.

"Thanks, Chase. Sorry we're late. Abigail couldn't decide what to wear!" Cherry lied as she became spellbound by her host.

Leaving the quiet serenity of the surrounding forest, the two entered the wild jungle. Human animals running rampant, fueled by poison water. All trying to impress the other, the males puffing their chests, the females doing the same. Performing acts of strength through arm wrestling, songs with guitar, or dance in order to find a potential mate.

Let the breeding rituals begin.

Cherry disappeared quicker than a bad magician at a nightclub in Vegas. Abigail, confident on her own, felt none the different—it was actually a sigh of relief. She proceeded to move through the masses packed together like cattle. The deafening music made yelling the only way possible to be heard ever so slightly when asking, "Excuse me. Pardon me."

She was too kind. Everyone said as much. But she couldn't seem to stop it, or even tone it down. The kindness just popped right out, before she could even think.

There was that feeling again. It hit her as she was cutting her way through the thickened jungle floor. Someone was watching her.

The hair on her arms stood to attention as the bumps rose from their slumber. The room fell silent. All around her, silence, despite people's mouths moving and their bodies dancing. Like someone had hit the mute button. No music. No singing. No talking. Abigail's eyes once again darting from side to side.

"Hello?" She heard her own voice, loud and clear. "Excuse me." She attempted to move past a partygoer, yet he continued his conversation, leaning forward to flirt with the girl and proceeding to block more of the doorway.

"Can I get past?" she asked, louder.

Neither of them looked at her. Abigail looked around. No one else moved—no one looked at her. It was as if she were invisible.

"Hello!" She snapped her fingers and waved her hands. The snapping echoed throughout the room. No other noise. Not a sound.

Nothing.

Nothing. Nothing. Noth…

The sound of slow, heavy breathing filled her ears. The noise was as clear as day. All the people continued to move, to dance, like nothing was happening. Like they couldn't hear what she heard. The wheezing air—inhaling and exhaling.

Where was it coming from?

Passing through the hallway, there it was. A creature of nightmares. In the other room beyond the archway it stood, looming. Its hair long and black, covered in what looked like hot tar. Its sunken-in eyes blazed with a crimson glow. Its skin was burnt and scarred, its legs bent backward at the knees like those of an ostrich, and long, bony arms with fingers the length of rulers; it stood threatening, drool falling from its snoutlike mouth.

Its eyes locked on Abigail, and she could feel his gaze entering her very soul.

Petrified by fear, her legs took root. She couldn't move.

She tried to break her stare away from the creature—she tried to run but only squirmed, like a helpless ant under the flames of the child's torturous magnifying glass. The creature advanced, taking a step. With all her might, she tried to scream. Nothing came out. Not a single noise.

Another step forward. It grew closer, never breaking eye contact.

A heat filled the room as drops of sweat formed on her forehead. The smell of charcoal entered her lungs. With each step toward her, a burning red print was left in the creature's path.

In that moment, Abigail realized she was alone. The people around her all seemed to have disappeared. Her head locked into place, she darted her eyes around as she looked for her friends to help. No one. Nothing.

Closer it stepped. Another step. Closer. Abigail's lungs burned with each effort to scream, with nothing more than the sound of air dribbling off her lips. With all her strength, she fought to rip her legs from the ground and run.

Its arm slowly rose as it reached up for her and—

"Abby! What the heck are you doing, just standing here?!" Cherry fell in from out of nowhere, spilling some of her home-made cocktail on Abigail.

The mixture of music and loud voices flooded her ears just as quickly as it had vanished. A second later, the people around her seemed to reappear, as if they'd never been gone.

"What?" Abigail turned to Cherry, feeling the sweat dripping down her forehead. Then, she turned back to where the creature was, her eyes searching frantically.

"What the heck are you staring at?" Cherry looked into the archway where people played drinking games or stood laughing or dancing. "Are you sweating? I told you not to act weird—you're going to ruin everything for me!"

"Cherry! You didn't see that?" Abigail grabbed Cherry by the shoulders and pointed.

"See what?" Cherry didn't even try to hide the disgusted look on her face.

"That thing! It was right there! It was all black and drip-ping oil and had red eyes and..." Abigail pulled Cherry to the middle of the archway.

People were beginning to stare.

"Abigail! You're acting crazy! What did you smoke?" Cher-ry laughed, playing it off. "You bitch, holding out on me! Come on. Chase wants you to meet his friend." She grabbed Abigail's hand, dragging her through the halls. Everyone went back to their mating rituals, no time to waste on a crazy girl.

Abigail looked back, trying to find the creature as she was pulled through the house.

What had happened? What was that?

Had she been dreaming?

Her mind ran wild.

LIKE I SAID, I hated social gatherings.

The thought of having to interact with another human be-ing nauseated my innermost core. Yet, I had this overwhelm-ing feeling that I had to go—I *had* to see her. Somehow, I could feel that something was off. That she needed me.

The cold night air tickled my nose, the crisp smell of icy wind creeping into my nostrils. Winter was beginning. The cabin drew closer with each dragging step. The only thing moving me forward was the revolving thought of her face and the feeling inside.

The night sky had only been illuminated by soft starlight, and the front door had been left ajar as I made my way up the steps. The music was drowning, and the people ran rampant. Wild animals, the lot of them.

She has to be here somewhere, I thought to myself. Making my way through the zoo, I got those eyes again. As if they knew something about me that I didn't. Judging. Condemning. The whites of their eyes glowed in the purple haze of the black light.

"Cool peacoat, Neo!" someone yelled from the masses as the hyenas laughed.

I paid no attention. I was here for one reason only. Stop looking at me. She isn't here. I should just—what was that?

Passing through the crowd of mindless adolescents, I stopped. It couldn't be what I thought it was. Out of the corner of my eye, I had caught a glimpse. Backtracking, I took a couple steps in reverse. Kids bumped into me left and right, jostling for position, trying to get to the watering hole. Real slow, I made my backward approach, keeping my eyes facing forward.

Stopping at the opening of an archway just to my left, I looked over. I had seen exactly what I thought I saw.

The same blazing crimson eyes I had seen in the alleyway. This time, the creature was in plain sight. It wasn't hiding in the darkness of shadows.

Am I going crazy?

With its long, snoutlike face, it leaned in closer to one of the jock boys it was standing next to. Seeming to whisper something into the football player's ear. Just as the creature finished whatever it was saying, it stood back to position, and the guy began pulling something from his jacket pocket.

Did no one else think this was weird? That some non-human creature was just casually standing in the middle of a high school party? What kind of crazy stuff were these people into? This was exactly why I hated social gatherings. Put a freaking monster in the middle of the party and no one cares!

A pill. The jock pulled a small white pill from his pocket. He was standing next to Cherry when he did it—I would recognize that girl anywhere. The guy had no idea I was watching him the whole time. He waited for her to look away and dropped it in her drink, trying to be slick. What a sack of dirt. I'm gonna kick his—

"Hey!" I stormed past the archway into the room, fully focused on the trash bag of a jock.

Their eyes turned to me. As did his. The chatter came to a halt. Music still blaring. All eyes were on me. The creature shifted ominously. Staring at me with a deep intensity as if wanting to lunge.

"What do you think you're doing?" I yelled, shifting my focus to the creature, its head twisting curiously. As if confused I could see it.

The mumbles of the crowd buzzed in the silence. Someone had stopped the music.

"Who is that?"

"Who is he talking to?"

"Seriously, what's his problem?"

"…the homeless kid…I've seen him around town. What a freak."

Its head turned ever so slightly without breaking its gaze. Analyzing me.

"Yeah you—I'm talking to you!" A burning anger grew within me. Every nerve, every muscle, every cell was under my control. A feeling unknown to me, it felt…good.

The creature seemed confused and growing impatient. Like it couldn't get the information it was looking for as it attempted to penetrate my mind. Steam and smoke billowed from its body as it filled its lungs.

I stood my ground. "You think I'm afraid of you?"

The fury grew. My eyes filled with rage.

The emotions in the room were split into two: fear and laughter. The hyenas were at it again, cackling in mockery. Could they not see…it? That massive *thing* standing smack in the middle of the room. How was that possible?

The creature's focus shifted quickly, twisting its head. It was looking at my arm—no, my *wrist*.

My wrist was burning. It felt like it was on fire.

Just for a brief second, I looked down to see what had it so curious. The place that my birthmark had been was now visibly burning red hot. Quickly, I returned my sights to the creature. Giving me one last look of frustration, it vanished. Gone. Just like the snap of the fingers.

"Hey!" I jumped a little more into the room. "Get back here!"

It was no use.

I felt someone grab my arm, their grip tight, and turned to see Chase.

"Okay, psycho, you gotta go," he said.

Had none of them seen this creature? Was I really the only one?

"Hey you!" I directed my attention to the dirtbag jock who had dropped the drugs in Cherry's drink. "You think it's cool to drug girls?" I pointed to the drink.

The fizzling of the opiate persisted.

Looking down, Cherry took the cup and hurled it all over the lowlife jock. "You ass!" Surrounding partygoers dodged the collateral damage as the piece-of-trash child-boy stood there, dripping on the floor and wiping his eyes. I was at least five feet away, a good enough distance not to worry about getting wet.

Cherry stormed off. Out of the room and into the hallway, where she grabbed Abigail.

Abigail.

I noticed her for the first time as my attention followed Cherry's exit, wondering how I'd missed her. She was just standing there, in the hallway behind me, staring. Her eyes were different than everyone else's—she wasn't judging me.

In fact, she seemed to be looking at me with curiosity. Maybe even compassion.

"Hey, asshole, what's your problem!" The now wet bag of dirt—the mud bag—yelled.

So the space monkey can talk.

"I asked you a question, asshole!" The guy moved closer as Chase held me where I stood.

"You're my problem, bud," I said, trying to wrestle free. "You jocks think you can get away with anything just because you throw a ball around."

The fire inside was returning.

Briefly, I looked over at Abigail. I saw the way she was looking at me. A sense of fearful compassion came from her eyes.

These two weren't worth it. "You know what? You're not worth my time," I said, breaking free of Chase's grip.

I turned to leave. Dirtbags. Not but a second later, all I can remember was something hard hitting me in the back of the head and my face bouncing off the ground. Pieces of a broken beer bottle scattered around my face.

"I say when you can leave," Dirtbag said, standing overhead. "Now get up."

The room burst into excitement.

"*Get up,*" a deep voice echoed in my mind, silencing the cheers of the crowd, as I flashed to a bright place—too bright—so bright I couldn't see.

It spoke again. "*Get up.*"

The brightness vanished. My mind was floating in darkness. I quickly opened my eyes, and the sound of the hollering animals returned.

Feet. All I could see was feet.

Get up, I told myself.

"I said get up," the kid said again, grabbing at my jacket.

Nobody touches my jacket.

In one swift motion, I jumped to my feet. Just as I did, he was ready with a fast right hook. This time I was ready, too. Something was different. I could see his hand coming at my face, as if it had been recorded and played into slow motion. Grabbing his fist, a gasp came from the crowd. His eyes: bewildered. My eyes: bewildered.

Throwing him across the room was easy work. His body felt as light as a feather.

Her eyes flashed into my mind.

He slammed into the wall with such great force that a human-sized hole appeared where there had once been a complete living room. Dirtbag's legs dangled from inside the hole, not moving. The animals were silent, observing the damage.

I think I can leave now.

The silence of the crowd was broken by hysteria as people began to scream and shout, running in every direction to escape, in fear they had just witnessed a murder. How did I...

A broken bottle entered between the caged bars of my ribs with brute force. I could feel every inch of it ripping through my body.

"AHHHH!" I let out a bloodcurdling cry as the bottle slid from the depths of my body, spewing scarlet red blood as if a faucet was turned on inside me.

I had forgotten about Chase—he must have been pissed I'd ruined his party, not to mention the crater I'd created in his parents' cabin.

I dropped to my knees in pure agony only to get pummeled by his annoyingly meaty fists.

"Stop it!" Her voice came piercing through the chaos. "Stop it, Chase. You're going to kill him!"

Kids were running around, left and right in a rampant madness. Like buzzing bees whose hive had been attacked.

At this point, I was getting my face pounded like raw meat on a butcher's table as I lay bleeding on the ground. Cheap shot.

"Chase, stop it! Stop!" Abigail pulled at his arm.

Through all the havoc, I looked up with swollen eyes and noticed a scrawny, four-eyed kid with his video camera. So captivated by all the action that was taking place he had decided to record it, rather than I don't know, *HELP*. What a jerk.

I knew this kid—how did I know him?

MY MIND FLASHED to nine years old. It was a bright spring day in a local neighborhood.

I had fallen off a bike that I lifted from some kid who'd taken my lunch the day before. That's when Four Eyes came running from his house where he'd been playing catch with his dad.

"Hey, are you okay?" the kid asked. "I saw you fall. That looked pretty bad. You're bleeding."

He was there on both knees with a hand on my shoulder.

I looked down. My knees were scraped and ingrained with asphalt and dirt. Ouch.

"Here, let me help." He ran back inside and came out moments later with a towel and a Band-Aid. "Here." He helped clean my knees, bandaging them up. "My name is Bryon. That's my dad." He pointed to the man standing in the yard, watching proudly as his boy helped some helpless child. I watched as he smiled widely at his dad.

Before the kid could turn back around, I was gone.

I didn't need any friends.

—§—

BRYON. THAT'S HIS name—I knew I'd known this kid. He probably didn't remember me. Or maybe he did? Maybe he held a grudge all these years for running off on him after he'd tried to help me. Maybe that's why he was recording my imminent death with no signs of helping. Look at him, standing there in his Vans, blue jeans, and pink salmon shirt. Still as geeky as I remember.

This time he would let me bleed.

My face began to feel like a pumpkin, swollen and fat. Blinding migraines swept like waves with each pump of the old heart.

The sight of blue and red lights painted the room. Sirens on top of screaming teens tore through my ears. Blood covered my face and spewed from my side. The pain was unbearable, even considering the adrenaline that pumped through my veins like a powerful hydrant. Someone had called the cops. Chase must have been scared off by the sight of the police cars because my face was no longer bouncing off the floor.

"Agh." I attempted to move.

Looking up, I saw her. Kneeling right next to me, just staring. Her eyes were even more beautiful up close. I had hoped to see her on better terms—this was the last way I'd wanted to meet.

Scratch that. Yelling at a seemingly imaginary creature and being beat down by two worthless punks hadn't really crossed my mind in the line of scenarios leading up to meeting Abigail.

"Fun party, huh?" I slurred out of a bleeding mouth and swollen lips, trying with all my might to crack a smile.

Fun party—that's it? That's all I could come up with? Idiot.

"You're really hurt," she said with the most angelic voice I had ever heard. Maybe it was the ringing in my ears, or maybe I had never heard it this close before, yet it was as if her voice alone had begun to heal my soul.

"I'm okay," I said stubbornly as pride filled my being.

"Let me help you." She reached for my hand to help me up.

Something happened. She stopped before she could grab my hand. My wrist, it was on fire again. I looked closer, and so was hers, only different. Hot. Hot—no, not hot...*cold*.

My wrist was so cold, it felt *hot*.

A blue glow emitted between the proximity of our nearly touching bodies. Scared—confused—I somehow gathered my strength and rose to my feet. Abigail stood quickly, taking a few steps back. I stared, searching her eyes for an answer, as if they could speak to mine.

Time stood still. It was just her and me, standing there. Alone. I no longer felt pain. I felt...alive. For the first time in my life, I felt a sense of purpose. I felt comfortable. As if we knew each other. Really *knew* each other. She stood there, staring back at me as if trying to understand what my eyes were saying to hers.

The blue and red flashing lights our only company. The earthquake in my chest measured a ten on the Richter scale as she moved closer. Less than six inches apart. I could feel her breath on mine. My mind was blank as we stared into each other's souls.

Slowly, she reached out for my still-illuminated wrist, curious.

"Everybody, stay where you are!" yelled a hefty cop.

I realized a police force was entering the home.

Time sped up, as if trying to catch up for the stolen time Abigail and I had shared. Everybody was running for their lives, cups and bottles thrown, vases and art broken and smashed in the stampede of fleeting teens.

Distracted by the chaos, she turned, as if aware of where she was once again.

The pain returned instantaneously. "Agh." I gripped my side, fighting to stay standing.

"Who are you?" Abigail asked.

She must have felt it too.

"Abby, come on! What are you doing? We have to get out of here!" Cherry loudly interrupted, grabbing Abigail by the arm and dragging her out of the mess of drunken teens and excited cops.

"Wait! But..." Abigail kept her eyes on me as she was dragged toward the exit.

"Let's go!" Cherry pulled harder.

Taking a second to gather my strength, I took my chance to exit while the cops were busy putting others in cuffs. A slow, painful exit, but an exit nonetheless.

With everyone making their way out of the whirlwind of madness, the only person who seemed to not be leaving was Bryon. This was magic for him and his cinema camera. The kid actually carried around a fully equipped shoulder rig camera. The Steven Spielberg of AngelFire. I spotted him in the corner of my eye just before I stepped out. Bryon was running throughout the house, putting the camera in as many faces as he could. "Oh man, this is magic. This is going to go viral for sure!" I could hear his excitement.

"Hey! Get over here! Give me that camera, kid!" A rather large officer grunted as he wobbled toward Bryon, stumbling over bottles.

"Shit." Bryon turned the camera on himself "This is Bryon Stockton live from—"

"Gimme that camera, boy!" The officer could be heard in the background of the video through the mess of yelling teens.

"I've got to go! See you next time, YouTube! Remember to subscribe for more awesome content!" Bryon signed off as he bolted. The officer in pursuit huffed and puffed, but it was no use. The kid was like the Energizer Bunny. Dropping his hands to his knees, the officer digressed. I took my leave.

The night fell silent as the muffled sound of dragging feet and shutting doors echoed throughout the air. Blue and red lights flashed one at a time through the rows of trees and the hum of the police cars faded away into the night.

CHAPTER 3

TWENTY-ONE QUESTIONS

M Y BREATHING WAS slow and heavy as I limped back to my sanctuary. Streetlamps lit the way for me as if guiding me in my broken state of being, blood dripping from every orifice of my body. How was I even moving—how was I still alive? *Keep going. Keep going,* I told myself through the overwhelming sense of pain and need for rest. My vision was becoming blurry. The streetlamps began to glow with round halos and rays of light encompassing my sight.

Almost there, I was almost there. Just one more block. I can see it now. My love, my church, my home, there she stood looking just as beaten and broken as me. So beautiful.

Each step dragged on. I could feel my strength leaving me. I'm not going to make it, my feet felt as heavy as a ton of bricks. With one final effort I reached for the gate... My fingers grazed the handle just as my physical body had reached its limit. As I hit the ground, I lay there, looking up at the streetlamp that guarded my castle thinking, *This is it. This is how I die.*

Darkness swept over me as my eyes began to shut.

—§—

"WAKE UP," A deep voice echoed in my mind.

I know that voice.

"Wake up."

"Wake up," a soft voice now, her voice. Mom?

"Wake up." I had to see this voice. With all my might, I struggled to crack open the lids that caged my eyes. Holding tight, as if opening them was inexcusable, I managed to get them open ever so slowly. The warm glow of candlelight awakened my senses. Her silhouette was all I could see against the dancing flames. That smell of old wood and dust was more than comforting as I inhaled life.

"What happened?" I asked, half alive. Looking around, I felt the familiar rough carpets of safety. I was inside the church. How did I get here?

"You were bleeding pretty bad," she said as she came into my proximity of vision. The light now illuminated her flawless face. Abigail.

"How did you find me here?"

Wow, she was even more beautiful than before.

"Like I said, you were bleeding pretty bad." She pointed to a trail of blood leading in through the great doors and down the narrow aisles of my wooden shelter. Fantastic. Those bloodstains are never coming out of the carpets. "So your name is Dean, right?" she asked bluntly.

How did she know my name? What is going on? Is that my name?

"That's what I've been told," I muttered.

It actually was what I've been told—I'm not sure if that was really my name or if the foster care system assigned me the first name that popped up in the lottery of abandoned baby names.

Clang!

A loud metal noise came from the back-right corner of the church where offerings used to be taken.

"Sorry about that." An old, raspy voice came from the corner. "I was trying to be as quiet as possible to give you two lovebirds a moment. Guess my old hands ain't what they used to be." The skinny old man reached down with one hand on his knee for support and picked up the metal cup. "You know, Dean, you're going to have to stop coming home in pieces. One of these days, I won't be here to put them back together."

"Uncle Homer." I pressed up onto one hand, the other still gripping my side. Abigail knelt by my side, looking at the old man. "I didn't know you were here," I said painfully.

"How could you? Your eyes look worse than mine."

What a jokester.

Uncle Homer isn't actually my uncle. He was just the groundskeeper of the church. Why he has never left, I couldn't say. But I'm glad he didn't. He's been the one person I knew I could always count on. When I first found this place, he tried to help find me a proper home. Though when he saw how bad the system had been treating me—one black eye after the other—he decided to let me stay. So long as I didn't join a gang, do drugs or any other stupid thing that could get me in trouble, or worse. The man was as skinny as a malnourished skeleton and wore clothes two sizes too big for him. Always a gray button-up shirt buttoned to the very top and tucked into his baggy brown pants. His long, white beard and clean white comb-over seemed to give him a sense of wisdom and class.

"You know that isn't going to come out of the carpet, right?" he said, pointing at the bloodstains.

I gave him a mean, sarcastic glance.

"You're lucky your friend came along," he said. "I wouldn't have been able to pull you in all by myself in this cold weather." He pointed his bony finger at Abigail. "Too pretty for your ugly butt," he mumbled under his breath.

"What?" I'd heard him. I always did.

"Nothing," he said quickly. "Just saying I'll let you two talk. I'll go grab some hot water for us." Uncle Homer waddled off into the old kitchen.

Turning back to Abigail, our eyes met.

"I'm Abigail," she said softly. "It's nice to finally meet you, Dean. Your uncle is very sweet."

Abigail reached to shake my hand. I attempted to do the same...

"Ahh!" Gripping my side in agony, I couldn't complete our first formal greeting.

"Suck it up, you're going to be just fine." She pointed to the cut in my shirt pulling it aside. There was nothing there—no gash, no blood.

"How did you do that?" I asked in disbelief. My eyes saw it, but my mind didn't know what to make of it.

"I have always been really good at helping people. My dad wanted me to be a businessperson like him, but I've always wanted to be a nurse. It's always just felt...natural. To help people, that is."

Not exactly the scientific answer I was looking for, but it would do.

"Well, thanks." Struggling to stand, I forced myself up.

"Don't push yourself. You need rest." Her gentle hand touched mine. The warmth that surged from her hand into my innermost being was unreal. As if being touched by a furnace warming me from my very core.

"I'll be okay. Thank you for your help." I quirked my mouth up into a smile. "I can handle myself from here." I made my way down the aisle as I gripped the splintered pews to support the weight of my body. Good old J.C. stood there front and center. "Hey, buddy, looks like you had a better night than me."

Abigail stood. "Who are you talking to?"

"No one. It's nothing. Shouldn't you be getting home now? I'm sure your family is worried." I stopped, wincing in pain.

"My dad works late every night. Sometimes he doesn't even come home. I'll be okay."

I could sense a hint of sadness from the tremble in her voice.

"Oh, I think you dropped this at the party." Abigail reached into her pocket and pulled out a tiny leather booklet with the initials "D.M." carved into the cover.

"Where did you get that?" I asked frantically.

"I told you, it must have fallen out of your pocket at the party when you were getting your face beaten in." She extended it out.

"Give it here." I reached for the booklet.

She quickly pulled it back. "What's the M stand for?"

A small sense of frustration came over me. More of an annoyance. "Just give it back."

"Well?" she persisted.

"Michael," I forced out.

"Is that your last name?"

"I guess so. I don't know. Can I have my book back now?" I reached again for it. She pulled back once again. My patience was wearing thin.

"Why are you so grabby over this little book?" She folded her stubborn arms. Right around the book.

"Just give it here, okay? Please." I put on my nicest smile. Blood still lined my teeth.

Please? That was the last word I wanted to use at this point.

"I'm just curious. You seem to be following me around at school." She smirked a little. "I feel like I have some right to know things about you, too." Abigail began to unwrap the book.

I snatched it out of her hands quicker than a frog snatching a fly right out of the sky.

"Hey!"

A quick victory smirk appeared on my face almost to say "HA!" just before my body realized the speed at which I had just moved and the pain surged throughout my entirety. I didn't show it.

"Whatever. I'll remember that next time I have to save your life." She stood to leave. Even when upset, her face still glowed. She whipped around and stormed off. Smart. Quick. Feisty. I like her.

I turned quickly away from her and began making my way down the aisle and closer to what was once the priest's private quarters, now my self-named bedroom. A bedroom that did not consist of the average bedroom items. A small, dusty couch was what made up my bed, a few statues of Jesus, and desks made of books lined the walls. The only source of light came through a tiny cracked window at the top of the small room. At this time, it was moonlight. Just before I made it to the entrance of my room, I turned in time to catch Abigail making her way out of the old church. Why had she been so kind to me? Why couldn't I have played it cool and been nicer to her? She was only asking some harmless questions.

I was alone again.

I turned one last time, took two more painful steps, and dropped down onto my bed of a couch.

"I got that hot water…" Uncle Homer had returned with a tray of three waters to an empty room. "Well, more for me, I guess."

Exhausted. The sound of the creaking wood standing strong against the restless waves of wind lulled me to sleep. The candlelight seemed to dance throughout the night so elegantly to the sound of the wind and the orchestra of crickets, warming the cold and cracking wood that held the walls together. The gold and red accents of drapery and artifacts shined with a brilliance that could not be described.

My eyes, heavy, began to shut as I slipped into a deep and healing slumber.

—§—

CLICK, CLACK, CLICK, *Clack.*

The sound of typing came from Abigail's upstairs room.

"Where did you run off to the other night?" Cherry asked, sitting cross-legged on Abigail's gold-and-white Egyptian-style bed as she painted her nails a bright pink.

"Huh? What are you talking about?" Abigail asked, not concentrating on the question. She was too distracted by her online search for "Ancient Languages." Her hands glued to the keyboard and her eyes to the screen.

All her life, Abigail had been very intuitive. She was not one to simply take things for what they were. She had to know how and why things were what they were. Her determination and hunger for knowledge was what had propelled her to the top her class. A rare breed, indeed.

"Umm, duh. At Chase's party. You just ran off and left me after I saved your butt from getting arrested." Cherry's tone was more than offended, though she continued to paint her nails.

"Oh, yeah. I wasn't feeling too good, so I just went home." Abigail's face got closer to the screen.

"Why didn't you tell me? I would have driven you." Cherry finished off her left hand.

"I didn't want you to worry or to ruin your night," Abigail lied. "I mean, I saw how you and Chase were talking with each other. I figured you would want to go and find him to make sure he was okay."

Cherry perked up, blowing on her left hand. "OMG. I know! He was like a little puppy dog, just begging for it. Ahh, he's so cute."

"Where are you…" Abigail muttered under her breath, looking back at her online search. Images of ancient relics passed through the screen.

"Huh?" Cherry asked.

"Nothing. Nothing. So are you going to give him the goods or what?" Abigail wasn't even slightly interested, but it helped to keep Cherry talking.

"No way! Well, I mean, not *yet*. He's got to work for it. Take me on dates, buy me lunch, you know—wine and dine me. Make me feel like the princess that I am." Cherry flipped her hair and batted her eyes.

Abigail clicked on an image. "If you like him so much, why don't you just tell him?"

"You can't just tell a guy you like them, Abigail! It's against the rules! That's like relationship suicide. Duh."

Abigail swiveled in her chair, listening now. "What rules?"

"You know, girl rules. If you want a guy, you have to play hard to get." Cherry seemed to know everything about relationships.

"Oh yeah?" Abigail said sarcastically, knowing full well that Cherry has never even gotten close to having a boyfriend. She returned her attention to the computer.

"Yeah," Cherry said matter-of-factly.

"Seems you're not the only one playing hard to get," Abigail said to herself as she found a familiar image on her computer.

Abigail inspected the image, curiosity sparked. The image seemed to match the birthmark on Dean's wrist. Though in the artist's rendition, the image itself was smaller than that of a mustard seed on what was a fuller image of the Arch of the Covenant. Was that the *exact* same symbol? Abigail couldn't tell for sure—the image was too small. Every time she would try to enlarge it, the image would pixelate, making it impossible to tell.

"Hmmm. Very curious. Very curious indeed," Abigail said, again to herself.

"Huh? Why are you talking to yourself? Are you, like, going crazy? What are you looking at anyway, just a bunch of lame old drawings?" Cherry asked.

"It's nothing. You want to go shopping or what?" Abigail offered just to get Cherry off her back.

"Ugh, I thought you'd never ask!" Cherry hopped up like a bunny on Easter. "Let's go!" She was out of the room faster than Abigail could blink.

She turned back to the image. "Daddy hasn't mentioned this one. Ever…" She stared at the image for a few more seconds before shutting off the monitor and leaving the room.

CHAPTER 4

TRAINING DAY

A FEW DAYS had passed, and I hadn't left the church yet. The images of that horrid creature haunted my mind. I hadn't slept much, and the times that I did were filled with nightmares. Nightmares so real I could swear I was there again. I would wake in cold sweats with those burning red eyes staring into mine. Something about the way it had looked at me made me feel like I had seen those eyes before—like it knew me. The smell of burning charcoal lingered in my nostrils, making it hard to breathe.

Some of the nightmares would take me to other worlds. I would be floating in a dark room, so dark not an ounce of light could exist. I would try to yell for someone time and time again, yet nothing would come out, try as I might. Then, the red eyes would appear as big as planets looming overhead, piercing my armored thoughts, listening. I felt as if they were still there even when I woke, watching my every move. Calculating and learning.

What was it looking for?

Back at the party, when I had gotten angry, it had turned its head and its gaze had shifted. What was it looking at? My wrist. That's right; it shifted to see what was happening to my wrist and then vanished. What was that—did that scare it off? But why? How did that happen?

I was talking to myself, pacing up and down the aisle of an abandoned church—I am officially going crazy.

I have so many questions, but I can't talk to anyone about this. Everyone already thinks I *am* crazy. This would put me in a psych ward for life. I would be there in a white straitjacket, telling everyone of the invisible dark creature with red eyes that follows me and listens to my thoughts. I would be deemed the crazy guy of AngelFire and left to rot till maggots ate out my eyes, alone and scared. And Uncle Homer, well, Uncle Homer is pretty crazy too. He might believe me, but I don't know where that would get me. Two crazy guys talking about nonsense.

No. I will not let that happen. I will get down to the bottom of this.

I know what I saw, and I know what I feel. Something is going on in this town. I needed to prepare. First thing's first, I needed to figure out how to control myself. I put a guy through a wall the other night—that's not normal. Given he deserved it…Okay, here we go.

I hopped to and made my way out of the castle-like doors that protected my inner sanctum. The light from the morning sun blinded my virgin eyes as they had been hidden away for days in a darkness only lit by candle. The smell of fresh pine needles filled my senses along with the fresh dew from the night before. The air was clean and new, crisp and welcoming.

"Where you going, boyo?" Uncle Homer's voice came from the front yard. He was already awake and covered in dirt.

"Uncle, how in the world are you so dirty already? It's on-ly"—I checked my watch—"six-thirty in the morning."

"It's already six-thirty! The day is almost gone! Back when I was a youngster in the army, we had to wake up before we went to sleep. I remember this time in Baghdad, me and the boys had to go out and search for—"

"Tell me later, Uncle! I have to go! The day is almost gone!" I had to cut him off or he would go on rambling for hours about his time in the service.

"You're right, my boy! Go on now—get moving, soldier! You come back tonight before supper, and no more black eyes. Keep those hands up. Defend yourself, you wuss." Uncle Homer yelled with his hands up, as if he were ready to fight.

I walked past the statue. "All right, J.C., I'll catch you later. Hold down the fort till I get back—we both know the place would burn down under Uncle's watch! It's training day," I jokingly yelled back to the statue of Jesus Christ that stood tall in the front of the stage.

Uncle shook his fist at me and then waved goodbye with a playful smile.

Maybe I was already crazy, huh? At least I wasn't the only one.

WALKING DOWN THE sidewalk alone in my long black pea-coat, I noticed families playing in the parks as I passed. So happy, so content, so…loving. I wished I had had these memories. The children would play in the falling autumn leaves, laughing and throwing them in the air. Surrounded by pine trees and mountains covered in snow, they were wrapped head to toe in mini coats and large hats. The orange and golden flakes would fall to the ground as the children reached out their hands, covered by oversized snow gloves, in efforts to catch one of these alluring creations of nature. The sound of their laughter was pure and joyful, something I longed for.

Their smiles reaching from ear to ear as their mothers picked them off the ground and spun them in the air.

Making my way down to the old junkyard, the thought of my parents came to me. This was something that haunted my every waking moment. The thought that they didn't want me, that they'd abandoned me. Why would anyone abandon their child? All I ever wanted was to ask them why? Why didn't they love me enough to keep me?

The feeling of jealousy stroked my heart. Who were my parents? Maybe if I knew them—or where I came from—I could find some answers. Answers to what is going on inside of me. What a cruel joke. Something I know will never happen yet I long for with each passing second. With every atom in my genetic molecular makeup, I seek them.

I am the hidden heartbreak.

Abigail. Her smile flashed before my eyes. The feelings of jealousy and sadness left me only to be replaced by a warm hope. I didn't notice it at the time, but making my way down to the junkyard and passing all the love that filled the air and joy that filled my eyes, my body was reacting. My wrist was cold—it was so cold the veins that lined my arm were a road map of icy blue lines. I thought nothing of the cold. The air itself froze my breath with each exhale of air heated from within.

A couple more yards down the road, I turned the corner, just passing the local drugstore advertising one-dollar blocks of wood. There it was, Old Man Pete's Junkyard. The smell of rusted metal, leaky oil, and rotting garbage was a dead giveaway. A gentle breeze wafted the smell into my nose like a mean joke.

No one dared to enter Old Man Pete's Junkyard. As a matter of fact, no one had ever actually seen Old Man Pete. It was rumored that he had died protecting his plot of land sixty years ago when a group of teens came onto his property and tried to steal his prized possession—a small, black box that crowned the top of a pile of trash. A pile so big it could have been a New York City skyscraper. A rusted, sharp-edged, dirty skyscraper. Some said that his heart was kept in that box and anyone who found it could control his spirit. Others would say that it was Pandora's box and that all Hell would be set free if anyone were to ever open it.

Being that this was a small town, rumors spread and the attempts to snatch this small, black box began. Yet every attempt ended in failure.

The two that everyone knew of are the Gilliam brothers and good ol' Johnny Lefty. They called him Johnny Lefty because he was always looking left. It must have been a birth defect or something, poor guy.

THE GILLIAM BROTHERS attempt was doomed before it even started. They were known around town for being the most stubborn, clumsy pair of knuckleheads that walked these streets.

When they arrived at the junkyard October 2, 1999, the night was cold and dark. The moon lit the yard, as the two approached the fence, they stopped in confusion.

"Has this fence always had barbed wires at the top of it?" Tommy Gilliam said to Timothy Gilliam. His thick Southern accent could only be understood by his equally thick-accented brother.

"Shhh! You're going to get us caught, you dummy!" shouted Timothy.

"Me! You're the one who's yelling, dummy!" Tommy yelled back.

"Who are you calling a dummy, dummy?" Timothy said, enraged.

"You, dummy!" Tommy fired back. With that the two went after each other, dropping to the ground wrestling it out like a couple of amateur WWE superstars. The silver celestial spotlight lit their stage. After what seemed like a lifetime—really only about one minute—Tommy had put Timothy in a chokehold.

"Say uncle, dummy!" Tommy squeezed his arm around Timothy's neck.

"Nev...errrr..." Timothy struggled to get out of the death hold.

"Say uncle!" Tommy squeezed harder.

". . . uncle...uncle..." Timothy managed to say through his almost-crushed windpipe.

"Ha! Who's the dummy now?" Tommy released his brother, throwing his hands in the air victoriously.

"Whatever, jerk. Let's just do this." Timothy stood, rubbing his neck.

The two pondered the fence, coming up with less than ingenious ways to get over it. Finally...

"All right, I got it." Tommy bent down to the dirt, pulling Timothy by his shirt collar to join him. "Here's how we are going to do it..."

Tommy began to draw an intricate plan in the dirt, pointing at key elements all while calling Timothy a dummy.

"Got it, dummy?" Tommy asked.

The look of confusion was strong on Timothy's face. "Yeah, yeah, I got it," Timothy lied with profound confidence.

Long story short, the two were seen running for dear life, screaming words of terror and gibberish about six minutes later as they ran past the drugstore around the corner. To this day, the two will still not step within two miles of that junkyard, swearing the devil himself lived there.

As for Johnny Lefty, the story goes that Johnny was seen entering the junkyard on a warm summer day of 2001 but was never seen coming out. That's it. No one has seen the poor guy since. Short and anticlimactic, yet intriguing nonetheless.

All the other attempts usually ended before they began, either out of sheer fear or simply from being stopped by the local authorities for trespassing on private property.

As time went on, the junkyard had lost a bit of its fear factor and became the hangout for some local thugs and druggies.

I HAD BEEN coming here for a year or two now, just to break the old routine. There was a large gaping hole in the side of the fence that had once been used to keep vermin like me out. Ducking down and pushing past the sharp, pointed metal, I made my way in. As I looked up, the yard had a certain majestic glow to it this time of day. The sun bounced off the scrap pieces of metal and trash with an ambiance fit for a king.

As the sun broke through a hole in the tower of garbage, it touched my face, warming it. I could feel my strength return as if manna from heaven was nourishing my very soul.

The ground was muddied from the melting snow, and the air was thick with the aroma of gasoline and trash as I searched for my first victim. Each drudging step was a struggle. My feet were sucked into the ground, as if the earth were trying to claim my boots as its own.

There it was, victim number one. That old Coke machine had been in the same spot, untouched, as long as I had been coming here. Let the training commence.

Facing off with the machine, which stood an arm's length away, I took my stance. Legs a bit wider than shoulder width, slight bend in the knees for nimbleness, fists balled up like mini-sledgehammers...Concentrate.

With all my might, I swung.

Ding.

My hand bounced off that unfaltering solid block of metal like a rubber ball.

"AHHHH!" I screamed, cradling my throbbing fist. "What the heck was that?! It didn't even move! Not even a dent! AH-HHH!"

Doubt was instantaneous. Did I imagine that whole night? Maybe I had actually just gotten my ass kicked and imagined all the other stuff when I was lying unconscious on the floor.

No. I know what I saw. I know what I *felt*. And I know what I did.

Again.

"Focus, Dean." I lined up my target and swung. "AH! AGAIN!"

I am my own hype man. *Swing. Swing. Swing. Swing!* Right, left, right, left. My eyes filled with tears of frustration. I know what I did—why can't I do it now? Right, left, right, left. My vision blurred through the watery agony. The Coke machine was relentless and unforgiving. While it had little more than dents to its body, my hands were bloody and bruised.

What was I doing wrong?

I looked at my archnemesis one last time, lined up, and took my shot.

I swung as hard as I possibly could, putting all my will and force behind this deathly blow and...nothing.

The damn thing didn't even budge. The only thing that happened was a possible fracture across all my knuckles. Grasping my hand, I dropped to my knees. Did I really imagine the whole thing?

I am the humiliated. Anger and frustration swelled throughout my being.

"AHHHH!!!!" I screamed as I picked up the nearest rock, throwing it as hard and far as I could.

Not more than two seconds later, I heard, "Ah. What the hell? Who the hell is throwing rocks?!" A man's voice came from the other side of the junk pile.

"Oh, shit." I stood up and began making my way toward the exit as fast as possible.

A group of gangsters came running around the pile—three guys to be exact. Dressed in black and gray plaid button-ups, matching bandanas, and sagging khaki pants, they posted up.

"Hey, pendeja, are you the one throwing rocks?" the larger one yelled from the middle of the trio, his bald head reflecting the sunlight.

I turned the opposite direction and began walking. *Just keep your head down and keep moving.* My confidence was broken after I couldn't even defeat the traitorous Coke machine—how was I going to fight three guys? I kept moving as fast I could, not looking back. One step, two steps, almost there. With fifty feet to go, I was almost home free when I slammed into one of them like a brick wall. He must have run around the other pile while I was looking down. Reluctantly, I raised my eyes to meet his. He stood there, menacingly, shaking his head no.

"You think it's fun to throw shit? Didn't your mommy ever teach you to not throw rocks?"

This guy again. My patience for people was really, *really* thin.

"Mommy wasn't around much." I looked around at the other two and back to this guy. The two were just standing there, about twenty feet away, near that indestructible Coke machine.

"Ah, pobrecito. He don't have no mommy. Maybe we should teach him not to play with rocks then, ¿que no?"

This guy was starting to piss me off.

The group began to close in on me real slow. I kept my eyes on the one in front of me.

Sling.

My ears perked as I heard a knife pop out from one of the guys behind me. Believe it or not, that was not the first time I had heard that familiar sound.

"Listen, I'm not looking for any trouble." Yet, somehow, maybe I was. The next words slipped out faster than I could think. "Why don't you just run home to Mommy before you get hurt?"

Shit. Why did I say that?

"You guys hear that?" The thug broke into laughter, pushing me a step back. "We got a tough guy here."

The others drew in closer. I could feel my blood begin to boil. They were within reach. All three of them. Like hungry animals.

I turned as fast as I could, swinging with all I had left from the beating I had taken earlier. It wasn't quick enough. I missed. One of the thugs dipped my right hook and threw his own punch. The only difference between us is that his connected. Like a freight train hitting the side of my face. I fell to the ground, catching myself on my hands and knees.

Her face flashed in front of my eyes.

Why now? Why did I keep seeing her?

Shake it off, Dean.

With a furious rage, I swung from the ground up, connecting with the chin of the thug who had knocked me down. A trail of dust followed my fist. Faster than anyone could blink, he was soaring through the sky and over the towering piles of scrap and trash like a rocket launched into space. The sticky mud claimed his boots.

Dumbfounded, the two remaining guys took a brief step back, watching their *hombre* go flying through the sky. The two looked at each other in silent fear, as if saying: "What should we do? Do we keep fighting?" The look on their faces was priceless, like a baby who just discovered a hot stove top. A dumb baby reaching out to touch it again. After their intimate and silent conversation, they turned back to me and charged.

"AH!" the one on the left yelled.

The quieter of the two ran, wielding his switchblade as he lunged at my core. I parried, causing him to stumble past. The leader took this opportunity and crossed me with a strong right hook. My neck twisted ninety degrees as if on a swivel. Turning back, eyes fluttering, somehow I caught his next attempt at a left hook. Looking this lowlife thug in the eyes, I saw genuine fear. Nonetheless, I threw him across the yard like a rag doll.

Something caught my eye. My wrist—my birthmark—it was burning again.

"I'm doing it!" I blurted out in excitement.

Distracted by my own self-appreciation, I had forgotten the third guy who'd slipped past earlier. Taking this brief moment of contingency to charge at me with brute force, the sneak picked me up, slamming me into a rogue piece of sharpened steel projecting from the surrounding scrap.

"AHHHH!!" I coughed up, simultaneously front-kicking the clown in front of me.

He flew through the air faster than a Formula One race car, heels gliding the ground with a cloud of dust cycloning around him as he came to an immediate, bone-crushing halt, hitting the unmovable pile of cubed cars a hundred yards away.

The sharp, swordlike object was at least seven inches inside my back. I could feel it touching my intestines. Sliding my body off the piercing piece of metal, blood dripping, I strutted my way over to the talkative thug lying face down in the mud. "Pobrecito, didn't Mommy ever teach you not to pick a fight you can't win?"

Blood dripped from my broken knuckles as I proudly stepped over the unconscious body, into the golden beams of the setting sun that elegantly graced my exit. Numbed by pride, I hardly noticed the fissure of flesh that was once my complete back as it oozed the scarlet liquid that filled my veins.

Life was about to get very interesting.

"I don't know, Abbs. This Dean guy seems like bad news if you ask me," Cherry said as they entered Abigail's house, returning from school.

"Something about him is different though," Abby said, ascending the tall, seemingly endless spiral staircase. "I can't explain it."

As she had finished her sentence, the doorbell rang, echoing throughout the chambers of the castle that was her home.

Abigail turned to Cherry. "Can you get that? I'm going to run up and check something on the computer real quick." Abigail didn't wait for Cherry to respond—she was already running up the remaining steps.

"Sure…why not?" Cherry reluctantly said behind her. "You're welcome!"

Abigail heard Cherry head down the staircase. "And stop talking about weirdo Dean and these creepy old symbols!" Cherry yelled up as she made her way to open the door. "That's all you've talked about for the past three days! Freak," she muttered the last word as she swung open the ten-foot-tall door.

"Hey, is Abigail here?"

—§—

CHERRY'S JAW DROPPED in obvious disgust and confusion.

My breathing was shallow and my face was pale. I had lost a lot of blood and the adrenaline had since stopped pumping. Not to mention the walk from the junkyard was over two and a half miles, draining me of any remaining strength. Trying to keep from passing out, I worked up a smile. In my mind, it was a nice, soft, inviting smile…to her it was probably the creepy smirk of a murderer.

Cherry sneered back a charitable crack of the lips.

"Umm…" She didn't take her eyes off me, as if fearful I may pounce. "Abby! Someone's here to see you."

I held my smile. And my side.

"Who is it?!" I heard her voice from the top of the stairs as she came running down in excitement. "Oh, Dean…hi."

Not knowing whether to be excited, confused, or scared, she stopped a few steps from the bottom. Her body language was all over the place. I gave a half wave and a painful smile.

"Ummhummm, I should be going." Cherry moved toward the door. "I have to go watch my little brother. Are you going to be okay?" Everything about her posture screamed that she wanted to get out of there as fast as possible.

"Yeah, I should be," I responded.

She gave me a confused look and then looked back at Abigail. Stupid. She wasn't talking to me. Why would she be talking to me?

"Yes, I'm fine. Thanks, Cherry." Abigail flashed a quick smile.

"Okay…be careful," Cherry said—as if I didn't have ears. She looked me up and down, then looked back to Abby with concerned.

I widened my murderous smile as a thank-you.

Cherry left quickly after the awkward encounter.

"What are you doing here?" Abigail asked, coming down the stairs the rest of the way.

"Can I come in?" I was about to pass out right there on her gold-engraved marble steps.

"Oh, yeah, I'm sorry. Come in," she replied.

I made an attempt at the second step with no success. As I stumbled forward into the doorway, she caught my fall. As she removed her hand from my lower back, she noticed the red organic paint that now coated her palm.

"Oh my gosh! What happened? Did this just happen? Come upstairs—I have a first aid kit." She quickly reached to help me up.

Ha ha. Funny girl. She thinks I can make it up the stairs when I couldn't even get up one measly step. Good one.

I looked up into her deep blue eyes etched with concern, and she stared back into mine. The pain seemed to vanish as I floated in the essence of her gaze. It *seemed* to vanish. It didn't. Trust me, it did not.

But it seemed to.

"Come on, let's go." She put my arm over her shoulders and began to walk me up the stairway. One slow step at a time, we made our way up.

The seemingly endless staircase finally gave way as we summited the mountain. At the top of the staircase was a rather large painted portrait of a blond-haired, blue-eyed man in a suit with a red power tie. Her father was the obvious guess.

She caught me looking. "My father," she said. "He's not home, don't worry."

I must have had a worried look on my face.

Countless doors lined the arched hallway on both sides. Thankfully, we stopped at the first on the right.

"Come." She opened the door. "Sit."

We entered her room. I was in too much pain, fighting the urge to pass out, to notice the details of her library of books and the artifacts that populated her private quarters.

She helped me over to her bed. Did she not know I was dripping blood? Her nice bed is going to be ruined. I sat anyway.

"Just can't seem to keep out of trouble, can you?"

I wanted to laugh, but all that came out was a grunt. "This is just not my week for first impressions, is it?" I am funny.

"Mmmm…you made a pretty good impression on Bobby's face the other night," she said, rummaging through her desk drawers.

"What do you mean?"

I had a feeling I knew what she was talking about.

"I mean, it's all over the internet already. The video has like over three million views on Facebook." She found what she was looking for: the first aid kit. "You kicked some serious ass at Chase's party, don't you remember?" She seemed somewhat enthralled as she set down the first aid kit and reached over for her laptop. Pulling up the viral video on YouTube uploaded by Bryon Badass—ha, Bryon—she handed the laptop to me.

"I need to cut your shirt off, okay?" she said as she began cutting, moving from the bottom to the top of my shirt, not waiting for my approval. I didn't mind. Her hands worked so earnestly. As she removed my shirt and pulled it from sticking in the gash on my back, she did it so tenderly. Distracted completely from the laptop, I couldn't stop watching her beautiful, shining blue eyes, focused and hard at work. She slowed, her fingers traced the scars that lined my body like ridges on the horizon. Troubled, she looked up into my already lost eyes, only to lose her own. Tension rose as an awkwardness entered the room like an elephant dressed for a dinner party. She seemed intrigued.

The butterflies in my stomach multiplied into millions. Flapping around in a frenzy of emotions. This time the pain really did vanish. Every time I looked into her eyes, this seemed to happen. This must be what they talked about in all the movies and books. I could see she felt the same. Her eyes searching for something, something deep. As I wished this moment could last forever, the pain began to return, releasing me from love's hypnosis.

Breaking eye contact, I hit the play button on the video. She quickly went back to work, pulling out a needle and thread. Watching myself slam a kid through a wall was fascinating. I had never seen anyone do anything like this before—I didn't think this kind of thing was possible, especially from me. I tried to spot my birthmark, but there was too much commotion; the camera wouldn't stay still long enough.

"Ahh!" I pouted as she jabbed me with the needle.

"Oh, calm down, you big baby. You're almost done," she said sternly.

Almost done? Liar! Like the dentist when they say they'll pull the tooth on three and always pull on two!

She was tough, though. I liked that.

I resumed the video.

"Shit…This has been Bryon Stockton live from…"

"Gimme that camera, boy!"

The video came to an end. I still couldn't believe it. Doing it and seeing it were two completely different feelings.

"All right, you're all done," she said as she bit off the last piece of thread.

"Thanks," I said, getting up to leave. I was truly grateful, but I was also so excited and confused as to what all was happening, I didn't know what else to say.

"Thanks? That's it?" She seemed upset.

"Thank you…*very* much? What else do you want?" I stopped and faced her. If I stayed any longer, I would only get hurt. The fear of letting someone in only to be abandoned was real. Being left at birth and tossed from family to family was not too reassuring when it came to my trust.

"Umm, we can start with an explanation." She held up the bloody bandages and sewing kit.

I had stood too quickly. That dizzy feeling was coming back. I couldn't let her see.

"I slipped, okay?"

I don't like reliving painful moments.

"You slipped. Just like you slipped onto that guy's knife?"

Who ever said it was a knife?

She was beginning to frustrate me, so I motioned for the door. "I don't have time for this."

She cut me off and blocked the door. "I have saved your life *twice* already."

"I didn't ask for your help the first time. I would have been fine."

Her arms stretched out, blocking both sides around. "You came to *my* house. I deserve an explanation. How did you even know where I lived?"

Reaching into my dirtied jeans pocket, I pulled out a ripped yellow page from a phone booth that had her last name and address on it.

"Okay, fine." She seemed dissatisfied. "At least explain this to me." Abigail went over to her desk and pulled out a sheet of notebook paper with doodles all over it. Except these were not typical doodles, it was…my birthmark.

"I don't know what that is."

Liar. Yes, I did. Now I was the dentist.

She snatched my wrist faster than I could think to move it. "Oh yeah? It's on your little book you keep hidden too."

Her grip was impressive.

"Who do you think you are?" I asked. "So you saw my birthmark and drew it—so what?" I didn't have the energy for this. My weak knees were knocking like a joke. I pushed past her to leave as she reached into my pocket like the little pick-pocket she was and stole my journal.

"What are you hiding in here, huh?" she tormented as she began unraveling the rope around it.

I grabbed for the book with a quickness. But her grip was tight. "Let. Go. Of. The. Book."

A tug of war broke out between the two of us. She was a lot stronger than she looked. Or I was still weak from being impaled earlier today. Vexed, I pulled harder, as did she. My levels of annoyance rose. As they did, the mark on my wrist once again began to illuminate with a bright red glow. Abigail noticed, and hers began to illuminate the same, only hers was a bright and beautiful white essence.

Out of pure shock, we released the book, dropping it to the floor. The silence in the room was thick as the bounce from the old leather journal could not be heard. Amazed and bewildered, I grabbed the book as fast as it had fallen and ran out.

"Don't expect me to be there for you when you get shot next time!" she yelled as I stumbled down the staircase and slammed the front door behind me.

"What the hell was that?" I muttered to myself as I ran down the street as fast as I could, making my way back to my safe place. To my sanctuary.

If I wasn't so distraught, I may have noticed the hooded figure that was looming in the trees, ever so guile. Just watching. Listening. Its gaze like that of a sniper, unwavering as it stared up into Abigail's towerous window. Watching her standing there, angry and confused, it took pleasure. The town lay silent. Not even the crickets made a noise.

"What is going on?" Abigail whispered to herself, making her way to the window. She stood there just staring at her wrist, flipping her hand up and down.

Abigail stopped—she could feel the eyes burning a hole in her back. Looking out the window, she searched the dark void of the surrounding forest. The night breeze pushed the treetops from—side to side. Something was off, but she didn't know what. She closed her blinds for the night. Just as she did, a shiny, new, silver Bentley pulled into the drive with a license plate entitled RED. The door swung open and a black Italian leather shoe took its arriving step out. A man in a blue pinstriped suit emerged from the depths of the car.

"Abigail. I'm home," the voice echoed as the figure entered the castle.

CHAPTER 5

DISCOVERY

I'D TAKEN THE night and most of the next day to rest and recover. My body seemed to heal itself quickly, knowing it may be under attack again soon. With a tornado of thoughts whipping around in my mind, I couldn't stay stagnant another day. I put on my coat to brave the weather and was off.

Uncle Homer must have been out getting supplies. I didn't see him when I had gotten home. Good thing—he would have lectured me about how back in his day...*Blah. Blah. Blah.* The old man had so many war stories, they all seemed to melt into one.

Leaving the warm confines of my church, the cold brisk air crashed against my exposed face like the waves of an ocean hitting the shore. I ran as fast as I could, the thought of her was both intriguing and irking.

I am the deep blue annoyance of love.

Making my way through the frigid streets, the smell of burning firewood warmed my soul. Looking into the small cabin houses as I passed, the families all seemed so happy.

Like a fishbowl of humans, just living their lives, unaware of my existence. Unaware of my fleeting envy.

As I neared my destination, the golden rays of life peeked over the mountains as the sun dropped behind them, exchanging watch to the moon. The marshmallow clouds that lined the sky like blankets of the earth were now a mixture of pinks, oranges, and reds. As if God himself had painted a masterpiece. Just because.

The smell of firewood was overtaken by that of freshly ground coffee beans. My sign that I had reached my final destination. The cybercafé.

Living in an old abandoned church has its ups and downs. One, no one ever bothered me, and two, I could do whatever I wanted, whenever I wanted.

Well, mostly. Uncle did have tendency of making me do chores and follow some of his outdated rules. The most annoying of which was having to burn a bushel of sage in every fire, every night. The burning wasn't the annoying part. The remembering to always bring home some sage from town was. Crazy old man said he learned it in the war from some local natives, said it warded off evil spirits.

Overall, living in the church wasn't too bad.

Though one of the only downsides to living off the grid was no electricity. Hence, no computer or internet connection. Thus, the cybercafé.

I had to see that video again. Maybe it could give me a clue as to what is going on and how these…powers…are triggered.

Dingle-ling.

The little brass bell rung from above the door as I entered the lounge. No one batted an eye, they were all so concentrated on their screens, like zombies fueled by reality stars, seven-second videos, and photos of cats with little hats on. This is what has become of humanity. The degradation of the mind through flashing lights and viral videos. Okay, time to go watch *my* viral video.

"Hello, sir, welcome to Forest Café," the barista said with his fake prescription glasses, man bun, and wooden bow tie.

The poor soul, he was genuinely happy to greet me. I gave a charitable nod. I was too focused for small talk.

Jumping on the first computer I found, I began the search. Okay what do I search…

Guy… gets… thrown… through… wall…

Let's see if that works.

"Wow. That was easy." There it is—got it. *Play.* The sound of cheers and screams exploded into the peaceful café as the video commenced.

"Sir! Sir!" the greeter yelled as he ran to my desk. Frantically searching through all the symbols and buttons, I found the mute button and smashed it. "Sorry about that."

I actually was sorry. It had scared me too.

"Sir, this is a silent café in courtesy of those trying to read or write in peace. If you would like to watch videos, you are going to need to check out one of our headsets." He pointed to the front desk with a basket of headsets sitting on top.

I nodded. "Okay, yeah. Sure."

"Okay, sir, if you would just follow me up to the front desk, I can help you with that," the man bun said as he made his way back to the desk, coaxing me to follow suit. I stood and followed.

"All right, how much?" I asked, pulling out some loose change and a couple lint balls from my coat pocket.

"Oh no, sir, there is no charge. Just sign here and you're all set. Just remember to return them before you leave." He pointed to a clipboard and smiled.

How trusting of him.

Confused, yet mostly indifferent, I grabbed the headset. "Thanks."

The eyes from the café patrons had been glued to me from start to finish, all the way back to my silent seat.

Just as I sat back down and pressed play—"Hey, hey, you're that guy!" The voice had come inching in from the back of the room with an excitement that again broke the silence.

All eyes were back on me.

"I don't know what you're talking about," I said without breaking my sight from the playing video. "How did I..."

"*That* guy!" he repeated as a skinny finger came pointing in from over my shoulder and onto the computer screen.

I had no other choice than to turn and look at who was addressing me as "That guy."

Bryon.

I tried to turn back to the screen as fast as I could, hoping he wouldn't notice I had recognized him. That would only escalate his excitement.

"Dude, that was so badass, the way you flipped that jerk and then threw the other one through a freaking wall! Bro, I mean, how much do you lift?!" He couldn't catch his breath, he was filled with so much excitement. "You must work out every day! Everyone is talking about you. You're the man."

He keeps saying that like it meant something to me. I looked around—the eyes of the room were on me once again, only this time they came with a different, unfamiliar emotion. The energy in the room had changed. The eyes were wider, more alive than before. As if the trance of virtual reality had been broken by actual reality.

Groups of two and more began to form, and whispers could be heard.

"That's him."

"No it's not."

"That's the guy. That's the one from the video."

I heard as their eyes darted from me to computer screen, back to me and back to the computer screens.

I had to get out of here.

Leaping out of my chair, I tried to ignore how the room began to buzz with an excited and curious commotion. The hipster tending to the front tried to regain control. "People. People. Please, lower your voices. There are others that are trying to concentrate."

No one was trying to concentrate on anything other than the freak who had thrown another human through a solid wall.

I crossed the room before the hipster turned his attention to me.

"Sir, sir. Your headphones…I need those back!"

The headphones were still draped over my shoulders and around my neck as I ran toward the door. Shoulda charged me. I didn't stop.

"Yo. Where are you going?! You gotta teach me some of those moves! I didn't even catch your name!" Bryon shouted over the buzzing bees and disgruntled employee.

His words fell short of my ears as the bell rung again—*dingle-ling*—punctuating my exit.

"So. Abigail. How was your day?" Her father's deep voice echoed throughout the dining hall. The smell of rich mahogany and caramel occupied the residence.

"It was fine," Abigail quickly answered.

"Anything exciting happen today?" Mr. Li'Ved removed his suit jacket and placed it over his chair.

"No," she lied. "Not really. Nope. Nothing I can think of. How was your day, Daddy?" Abigail twiddled her thumbs in her throne-like dinner chair. The table couldn't be big enough.

"Just another long day of business. Headquarters was very busy today. Numbers are up." He loosened his tie and sat at the dinner table. Food of every country and a palette of colors lined the table. The smell of freshly baked bread and roasted chicken gently wafted through the air. Candles lined the table, lighting the food so elegantly.

An awkward silence filled the room, so thin a pin drop could be heard a mile away.

"When can I visit you at HQ? I think I'm old enough now." Abigail spun the grape juice in her gold-lined glass and took a sip.

"Abigail. We've discussed this. You know you can't come down there," he said, cutting his steak and taking a bite. The sound of firewood crackled from the fireplace at the end of the room.

"I know. I just figured—"

"So. Are you excited for graduation?" he asked, leaning into the question. His eyes focused on his daughter.

"Yeah, I guess so. But, Daddy, there was actually something I wanted to ask you about. I think something is happening to—"

A cell phone started ringing, and the Bluetooth device began to flash on his ear.

"Hello…What can I do for you, B?" Holding up a finger to Abigail, he gestured that it would only take a brief moment.

Looking down to her now-tasteless food, she knew that was the end of their conversation.

"No! No! We have gone over this!" he yelled into thin air. Leaning over, he said, "I've got to take this, baby. I'm sorry." He kissed her on the forehead and walked out of the dining hall, the echoes giving way to his annoyed tone. "I thought I told you to take care of it."

Under her breath, Abigail muttered, "Well, that was another great conversation, Dad. Love you too, Dad. Thanks for the dinner, Abigail. Oh, no problem, Dad." She played with her food, forking it left to right.

Sadness became her. Although this was the life that she knew and the father that she had grown so accustomed to, Abigail had never given up hope that one day she and her father would have that connection she longed for. The kind that existed in the movies, where a father would come home, smiling and happy, sweep her up off the ground, spin her around, and tell her how much he loved and missed her. Dreams could be melancholy. No matter how much she did or what she achieved, it always seemed short of impressing her father. Her sadness was personified by the self-playing piano in the living quarters. "Nocturne in A Minor" by Chad Lawson sang the notes of sweet, sweet sadness. Alone again in this castle, she was beside herself. To live a life that she was not happy with, yet she still must put on the smile she was known for. Her dreams danced around her mind of a father, a mother, a family. A loving family.

Something she would never have.

They disappeared with the final notes of the melody, like ghosts of smoke from a life never lived. Only dreams of her nocturnal mind. The pounding of her heart, returning back to her routine beat. With the final keystroke of the piano—

DING-DONG!

The doorbell rang loudly throughout the complex. A rude finale to the solemn piano.

"I'll get it!" Abigail exclaimed, as if her father would have even come in the first place.

Abigail ran over from the dining hall, through the marble-laden floors, reaching the front door.

As she opened the door, to her surprise, yours truly was standing there once again.

"What are you doing here?!" she whispered loudly as she stepped out of the doorway, closing it behind her just enough to block their conversation.

"You want to talk? You want to find out what is really going on?" I asked with a directness that could not be beaten around.

"Who is it, Abigail?" Mr. Li'Ved asked from somewhere inside the house.

She ignored the question, looking back into the house and back out.

"Well, I do too. I want to figure out what is happening to me, and for some odd reason, I think you may be able to help," I continued.

"No one, Daddy! Just a Girl Scout selling some cookies."

A Girl Scout, ha. Who does she think she was fooling?

"You have to go," Abigail said, giving me *the look*. That look that meant she was not playing around, that it was time to leave or maybe this time it would be me that would get thrown across the room.

"A Girl Scout? This late?" her father responded once again, his voice still coming from somewhere deep in the house.

I could see obvious confusion on Abigail's face, as if questioning why he was so concerned, and I quickly whispered, "Meet me at the church at midnight tonight when your dad is asleep."

Abigail turned her head inside the doorway and lied through her teeth to her concerned father, yelling. "Ummhu-uuhh!" She looked back at me, whispering. "You mean sneak out? I can't do that—my dad will find out! And if he finds out a boy is here, even this late, he will kill us both!" she whispered back at me.

"Just do it, okay? I know you know something is going on here too. It's not just a coincidence what happened in your room." I turned and disappeared into the dark of the night.

What was I doing? What was I thinking, involving sweet, innocent Abigail in all of this? If she didn't show up tonight that would be for the best. I would prefer it. She did not need to be caught up in all of my craziness.

I don't even know what is going on.

"WELL, DID YOU buy any?" Abigail's father said from directly behind her. He peered out the door.

"Ahh! Daddy, you scared me. I thought you were on a business call. No. I didn't—they didn't have the ones I like." Abigail snuck under his arm back into the castle.

"Ahh. That's a shame. I love those Trefoils." Mr. Li'Ved gripped the door handle. "Abigail."

She stopped quickly.

"Was there something you wanted to talk to me about at the dinner table?" he asked.

"It's okay, it can wait," she lied again. Lies. Lies. Lies. "Why?"

"Oh, it's nothing. I just thought you wanted to ask me something." He remained in the doorway about ten feet away. "Everything is okay? Nothing I should be concerned about? Nothing I need to handle?"

"Everything is fine, Daddy." Abigail walked up to Mr. Li'Ved and kissed him on the cheek.

"Okay. Did you read that book today?" he asked.

"Yes, Daddy! I'm almost done—you can test me later. I promise." She wasn't lying this time.

"Okay. Good. Sleep well, princess. I've got some more work to handle. I'll see you in the morning." He leaned forward and kissed her head.

"Night, Daddy!" Abigail smiled and ran past her father and up the stairs to her bedroom. Just when she was all the way up the stairs, Mr. Li'Ved leaned out and glanced through the tree-studded front yard with a look of suspicion painting his face. Trust was not his strong suit.

As THE CLOCK approached midnight, Abigail paced her room, contemplating whether or not she was going to betray her father's trust and sneak out, like Rapunzel from her solitary castle guarded by the sleeping dragon.

Her mind was a whirlwind of thoughts. *Should I? I do want to know how he did what he did. But should I? It doesn't concern me, I helped the guy, and that is that. I was being a good person. It's not like I like the guy or find him attractive. I mean, he is kind of attractive. No no, Abigail, focus. If you do this, there is no going back. You will have lied to father and that is that. Maybe it will lead nowhere, and it will all be okay? Yeah, it's all just been a coincidence. Yeah. Okay. Just this once, I'll humor the guy.*

She had made up her mind as she threw on a red fur snow coat. The lower-than-freezing weather was unforgiving at best. She sneaked down the stairs and out the front door the wind hit like a frozen truck. Two steps out the door, Abigail stopped. She could feel that familiar feeling of being watched.

"Beth!" Abigail yelled into the snow, "if that is you, you better stop! You know what will happen if I tell Daddy."

She pulled up her hood and walked off down the rock driveway.

THIS TIME OF year was especially cold for me. Being that there was no electricity in the church, I had to make do with the makeshift fireplace that Uncle Homer had crafted from the dislodged bricks from around the premises. It was a humble fireplace, one that would not heat the entire room but was good enough for just me and him to sit and sleep in front of during the cold winter nights.

I used a lot of the old and flaking wood that used to be pews. The place where people would come to kneel and pray was now the answered prayers of myself: warmth. Uncle never condoned this method of fire making, but he also didn't contest it. Especially on nights like this. Just as I was stoking the fire for the night, my watch had reached midnight. *Beep Beep. Beep Beep. Beep Beep.*

She wasn't coming. Good. I can figure this out on my own—I didn't need her.

I am a transient woe.

Creak...

A long creaking noise emerged from the front doors.

"Uncle?"

No response. Normally the old man would crack a joke. Something like, "Who else would it be, dummy?" I sat in silence—I could hear his snoring from the other room, so it couldn't have been Uncle. I turned to look, fists balled, adrenaline being pumped as fast as my heart could beat. I was prepared for anything. A shadow emerged through the cracking door from the streetlamp that stood outside. Snow and ice came swooping in with the night breeze like a small, white tornado.

I took my stance. Even then, I wasn't prepared for what came next...

"Ugh, it's freezing out there!" Abigail came in through the front door. "What are you doing?" she asked as she saw me standing in full defense mode.

"Sorry, I thought you were someone else." I loosened my grip.

"Who?" She shook off snow from her shoulders and dropped her hood.

"It doesn't matter. Close the door—you're letting in all the cold," I said as my growing fire began to dance wildly in the wind, close to extermination.

Closing the door, she made her way into my life once again. I am enigmatically ecstatic.

"You're late," I spoke as she approached.

"Do you want me to go back?" She stopped and pointed at the door. "Because I can. I don't even want to be here."

She was tough.

"It's fine." I returned to my fire, placing another log down for fuel.

Abigail joined me, standing close for warmth. "Okay, so what did you want to talk about? You seemed very adamant about everything earlier."

"This," I said, reaching into my coat pocket and pulling out the leather-bound journal I had fought so hard to keep from her. I had never shown this to anyone. This girl was making me do so much lately that I had never done or felt before.

"Oh, so now you decide to tell me what's in this magic book of yours?" She was getting feisty.

"Do you want to see it or not?" I asked, rewrapping the leather string.

"Yes. Yes. Okay, geez." Abigail mimed zipping her mouth and throwing away the key.

"Ever since I bumped into you a couple months ago, I have been having these…dreams," I said as I continued to unravel the little brown journal.

"Wait, what?" A genuinely confused look became her.

"Don't you remember? Down at the drugstore. I was picking up some supplies and you were with that girl you always hang out with—Cherry? We accidentally bumped into each other when I was leaving and you were going in."

Why would she remember that meaningless encounter? Only a loser like me would remember something like that.

She smiled faintly, an apologetic smile. "I don't remember that."

I knew she wouldn't.

"You helped me pick up the wood and told me something about keeping warm, that it was going to be a cold one." Why do I persist?

The memory came back to her with a rushing force. It was visible in her eyes as they lit up. A little spark of happiness warmed me along with the fire.

"I remember! Cherry was upset you almost made her spill her iced mocha latte. That was you?" The room was so cold her breath was visible with each word.

I smirked. "Yeah."

"Okay, so what about that day?" she asked, ready to remember more.

"You're going to think I'm crazy or something." I had finished unraveling the journal.

This was a big moment for me. I had never shown anyone anything that was personal to me. Not even Homer had seen inside this journal, and he is crazier than me. Letting someone in was always something that frightened me to the core. Whether it be from abandonment issues from my estranged parents or something else, God only knows.

"No, I'm not. Just tell me what's going on." Her tone had shifted. She must have noticed my concern. Her voice was soft and reassuring. Safe.

"Promise me that you're not going to freak out."

"I am way past freaking out, I have seen you half dead and bleeding multiple times. I think I can handle whatever it is you're going to show me."

This was true.

"Okay..." I said nervously as I considered backing out from my decision. Finally, I breached the pages. "Look." I handed over the journal.

She took it without breaking eye contact. Finally, she looked down, puzzled. Almost as if she saw something she recognized but didn't quite know what it was.

I stood there, frozen with curiosity. What was going through her mind? What was she thinking, how was she going to react...

She finally broke the silence. "What is this? I've seen these before...when I was trying to figure out what the symbol on your wrist meant."

The fire crackled in the background, emitting a warming light, causing our frozen bodies to have shadows that danced against the inner sanctums walls, like ghosts of a ballroom.

"What do you mean you've seen these before?" I asked, as if no one should have seen these before. These were things I had been drawing since I was a kid. Before I even knew what a book or the internet was.

"I mean, I've seen these. I did an image search after I drew the one I had seen on you. A lot of these symbols were either drawn or painted or carved into some old or even ancient artworks." Abigail was holding the book and getting excited, flipping from page to page. "My dad actually has a couple pieces I found it on too. It wasn't easy to find though, most of them are hidden in the work."

The howling of the frozen wind grew as it whistled through the treetops.

"Did you see this?" I asked, grabbing the book and flipping back through the pages.

"What is th—" She stopped as she recognized it. It was the same symbol that she had on her wrist. Her birthmark. "No way," she said as she turned from the page to her own body.

"Yeah," I said, seeing the amazement in her eyes.

"So you saw it that day we ran into each other—big deal." She folded the book in one hand and offered it back to me.

"You were wearing a jacket and gloves. There is no way I saw it." She thought I was trying to pull a fast one. "This is what I see when I go to sleep. Every. Single. Night."

"Well, what is all this then?" she asked, reopening the book and flipping to the first pages. There, in bold and hard-pressed lettering, stood something of an alien-like language. It didn't look Egyptian, or Arabic, or any other recognizable language.

"I don't know," I said.

She was getting flustered. "What do you mean, you don't know?"

"I mean, I don't know. I've had this book as long as I can remember. My first foster family told me that…that it was given to them when they adopted me. I guess it was the only thing I had with me the day I was left at the hospital."

Our eyes were locked in intensity. The room felt small, as if it had shrunk to only contain her and me and nothing else. The fire had not grown, yet I was beginning to sweat—the space between us felt hot. I could see her mind reeling.

"Abigail, look at the dates."

"So you're telling me that you have had this journal since you were born, but you don't know who gave it to you or what language this is?" Her tone had shifted again, as if I were withholding information on purpose. She looked at the date. "And that this is almost five thousand years old? HA!"

"That's exactly what I'm telling you. I think it belonged to my biological parents. I've tried finding them. It's impossible. Maybe they were historians or something." I was as sincere as I could ever be. "Uncle Homer is the only family I have now, and he doesn't even know about this book."

"Okay, so then why does this concern me?" she asked even though she knew the answer. She just didn't want to admit it.

I stabbed the page with my pointer finger. "You know exactly why this concerns you. You're drawing is in there too, right next to mine and all the others."

She didn't respond. She just side-eyed the book as if looking directly at it or me would pry information out of her. Arms crossed, face stern, blonde hair glowing in the light of the fire. Even when she was angry, she was a stunning sight.

"I didn't start having these dreams or sensing these weird things until the day I ran into you. And everything that has been happening this past week—I mean, come on! I know you saw what I saw in your room the other night! And being able to throw someone through a wall, you can't tell me that didn't freak you, and the other ten million people who saw it, out. And I'm seeing these weird...*things* all over town now too!" I spouted in one long-winded breath.

She turned and looked at me. "Wait. What did you just say?"

"I said, I know this is all freaking you out too!"

"No. After that, what kind of...things are you seeing?" She leaned in.

How do I describe these ugly creatures—they were the kind of thing from nightmares. The kind that couldn't be described.

"I don't know. They have these piercing red eyes that are like glowing embers, and these tall bony bodies that look burnt or charred black and long, stringy black hair; sharp, snoutlike mouths; and tusks that—"

"I saw it too," she says quickly. Her eyes wide as if she had just seen a ghost.

"What do you mean you've seen them too? That's not possible."

Then again, I guess anything is possible at this point.

"I saw it at Chase's party that night. It was standing there in the living room—I thought I was going crazy!" Abigail uncrossed her arms and began pacing back and forth.

"You better not be messing with me, Abigail."

If she was messing with me, I was going to kill her.

"I'm not! Why would I joke about that? I saw it and tried to tell Cherry, and she said I was crazy. But I knew I saw something!" She looked at me just before taking a seat in one of the old pews. Breathing slowly, she cradled her head in her hands. "Why isn't your symbol in Daddy's book?" she mumbled to herself.

"What book? Abigail. What is going on? What do you know?" I asked as if suddenly she would explode with all the knowledge and information that I so desperately sought.

A moment passed while Abigail was in deep thought. Now staring at the fire, she looked as if she had answers to my long-awaited questions. Her face seemed focused and new questions were being formed.

"This is too weird," she said finally, pushing the book into my chest and turning to leave.

"Where are you going? Abigail!" I yelled after her.

"I have to go!" She twirled back to me and then away as she exited the front doors.

The breeze came rushing in, taking my voice with it as I tried again to yell for her to return. The force of the wind blew open the doors, extinguishing my fire, my safety. Running to the doors, holding them both, I stood there looking out into the moonlit streets to see if I could see her. Nothing. Slamming the doors closed, I ran to my now-lifeless fire and began sparking the kindling in efforts to revive it.

As the fire returned to life and the crackling began once again like the return of a beating heart, I felt it. Loneliness swept over me, accompanied by the orchestra of crickets, rubbing their legs to keep warm themselves. Sitting there next to the open fire, alone.

I am the eternal abandoned.

CHAPTER 6

FAMILY

T HE SHADOWS OF the trees lit by the moon were not alone. There was another among them, one that was equally as solid and had two legs to stand on rather than one. It watched as Abigail went running from the old abandoned church into the blizzard that came rolling in with the night air.

Taking a second glance at the church, it began its approach. As it grew nearer and nearer to the colossal wooden doors that guarded the entrance, a flicker of light could be seen from a side glass window. The shadow made its way to the colorful mosaic as carefully as it could. Covered in dirt and grime, the window was too dirty to see in.

"How could I have been so stupid?" I asked myself, sitting there next to my newly relit fire. "I knew I shouldn't have shown her anything, I knew this was going to happen." Unbeknown to me was another approaching.

Creak.

I could hear the door begin to open ever so slightly. It was as if the church and I were one—every little movement or sound was as if I myself could feel it.

"Who's there?" I shouted looking to the door.

Creak.

"Abigail, stop playing around and just come in. It's freezing outside." I turned back to the fire.

Nothing. Maybe it was just the wind?

Creak.

I jumped to my feet to go investigate. The wind would have blown the door open by now, and Abigail was the only one who knew where I lived. "Abigail…"

My steps were heavy as I made my way toward the door. My senses were heightened in their fight-or-flight pattern. I could smell the wood burning, I could hear more clearly, I could feel the room. There was a different energy coming from the doorway that I had never felt before. Something powerful. Something dark.

Just as I reached out to take hold of the old brass door handle, the two doors exploded open. Splintering the door as if it were made of paper, a monstrous shadow knocked me back down to the ground with brute force. Fear filled my body as I looked up at this shapeless figure looming over my ant-like body. The force blew out my fire once again, the room was dark. My arms and legs were weak—my mind told them to move, but they lay frozen in fear. My eyes peeled open as this being's darkness began to fill the room. Like dark sheets in the wind, the creature filled the entirety of the ceiling. Consumed by the darkness, the only thing I could make out were the two burning red eyes in the middle of the cloud-like monster.

"Stay away from the girl," it said in a snakelike voice as it drifted closer to my face. I could feel its breath on my face. Only inches away, I could see my scared reflection in its glossy red eyes.

The air itself froze as the creature spoke. The hair on the back of my neck rose like the dead from their graves as the dark voice landed on my ears. My scalp covered in goose-bumps, I could feel the beating of my heart landing each bar in my throat.

"What's going on in there, boy? Didn't I tell you to keep it down?" Uncle's voice came from the other room.

"Nothing, Uncle, just the wind. Go back to sleep!" I lifted my arm in the direction of the door next to the stage as if I could stop it from opening. The creature looked at the door and back to me.

Just as suddenly as it had entered, the creature disappeared. Just like that. A ghost in the night. A nightmare I had survived, as if it had never happened at all. The only thing that remained of it was the fear this creature had instilled in my innermost being.

Still frozen from what had just happened—what *had* just happened? It was all so fast, like a dream. I laid there on the cold wooden floor no longer in fear, but rather confusion. Ice crystals landed on my face, kissing me with their frozen love.

The wind was blowing snow into my place of warmth as if I had invited it in, whistling through the treetops like a raging choir. Rising up after minutes of utter confusion, I ran to close what was left of my entrance. I then turned and ran back to where my fire had once again been extinguished. Sparking the kindling, I began to defrost as my fire came back to life for the third time.

Uncle hadn't come out of the room. I listened in the silence…His snoring was like music to my ears. I couldn't imagine anything happening to that man.

That…thing's voice. It was so cold, colder than the icy air itself. What was that? It wasn't like the others I had seen. No, this one was bigger. This one didn't have even a body…or a face. The only thing that was familiar were the eyes, those burning red eyes. The eyes that pierced my soul, and the feeling of complete hopelessness that accompanied them. Why didn't it do anything? Why did it want me to stay away from Abigail?

With all fear and confusion aside, the only thing I could think of now was figuring out what was really going on in this town. All these things were not just coincidence, the creature in the alley, the other at the party, and now this one. Abigail saw them too, so I know I'm not going crazy.

Abigail said that she had seen my drawings before. I need to figure out what she meant. I needed to see them for myself.

Something bigger than her and me is going on. I can feel it.

THE MOON LIT up the sky as if trying its best to impersonate the sun. The castle shone bright like a city of its own, tucked away behind the protection of the trees. Abigail lay up in her room, finally asleep after overthinking her way into a deep slumber.

Down the stairs and through the intricate grid of hallways, her father, Mr. Li'Ved, sat in his brown French leather chair with a glass of the finest brandy in one hand and a perfectly rolled Cuban cigar in the other. The room was silent and smelled of rich smoke. He sat there with his feet up on a small ottoman.

Without turning to the doorway, he spoke. "Yes, Beth—what can I do for you?" His voice was smooth, enticing.

A tall, young woman stood in his doorway. "I'm sorry to bother you, Uncle." Her straight black hair was almost long enough to touch the ground.

"It's fine. You're here already. What is it?" He sounded slightly annoyed.

"It's Abigail," she continued.

"What about her—is she all right?" Mr. Li'Ved puffed his cigar.

"Yes, Uncle, she is fine. I just wanted to let you know I saw her out tonight." Beth took a step forward.

"That's impossible. She has been up in her room this whole time." Mr. Li'Ved paid little attention, flipping through a stack of papers on his desk.

"Not from where I was standing," Beth said.

He humored her. "And where exactly were you standing?"

"The old, abandoned church. She was with a boy."

Sitting up in his chair, Mr. Li'Ved placed his glass on the desk. He stood and turned to look at Beth. She seemed to wince, her tall slender body so fragile now.

"What boy?" His tone deepened as his heavy gaze locked with hers.

"I'm not sure, Uncle. I just thought you'd like to know…I'm sorry," she said as she bowed her head.

"Where is she now?" The cigar burned hot between his fingers.

"Upstairs, in her room," Beth answered with her head still down. "She is sleeping."

"Get out. And don't ever show up here unannounced again." His stern voice was solid as a rock.

"Yes, Uncle." She turned to leave but stopped, hesitant. "Uncle."

"You're still here?" He was clearly annoyed.

Her pale, white face looked to the floor and was covered by her long black hair. "Sir, something about that boy felt different. He was…just different," she said, confused at her lack of words.

"Maybe you should stop hiding in the shadows and find yourself a man. They are odd creatures to you, aren't they, my dear niece?"

She nodded once, almost to herself, and left.

Mr. Li'Ved stood hunched over his desk. His fists balled, the veins throbbing as if he were going to press straight through the solid wood. His face filled with blood and anger, becoming a dark red as heat emitted through his suit jacket. A man in total control—a man losing his grip of his own kin.

THE COOL NIGHT came to a close and the stars began to fade, giving way to the rising sun, the town of AngelFire lay in peace…

"Hey guys! Bryon Stockton here! It's another beautiful Monday morning here in AngelFire! I hope y'all are having as great a morning as I am. The sun is up, the birds are a-chirpin', and the air is brisk!" Bryon recorded himself as he made his way to school. "It seems a lot of you liked and shared my latest video, the killer brawl, from the other night. I want to just take a second and thank you all for that. Especially you, Scott_flyer97, I appreciate the multiple shares and your enthusiasm for learning more! I read a lot of your comments, now I did find out what the guy's name is, but that's about it! He is very camera-shy and doesn't seem to enjoy conversation. Though I did find out he works out almost every day! I mean, you have to in order to throw someone through a wall, huh?!"

Bryon continued down the dirt road, passing half-awake teenagers wrapped up in jackets and scarves making their slow approach to the hellhole they called high school. The ground was covered in white powder from the night before, and the air was sharp to the nostrils. White trees lined all sides of the mountain road. Bryon ran up to the first lively looking kid he could find.

"Hello, sir! How are you this morning?! I see you have a coffee from Forest Café there, can you tell my viewers a little

about your experience there, in case they ever choose to visit?" Bryon put his phone's camera in the poor soul's zom-
bielike face.

"Get that out of my face, dude." The passerby shoved Bryon's hand away.

"Okay, have a good one! See you in Home Ec!" Bryon
yelled and turned back to his camera. "Well, I'll be back on
at lunch. You have a great day, all you beautiful people." He
signed off and made his way into the zoo-like hallway of ani-
malistic teenagers, all gathered in their cliques outside of the
main entrance.

THE FRONT OF the school was newly shoveled by the early
morning janitors. Abigail could tell as she made her way to
class, tripping over the occasional kid with a roller backpack.
The school bell echoed throughout the hallways and up the
quiet streets as all the teens made their way into the class-
rooms.

Abigail and Cherry took their seats next to each other in
History as they awaited the teacher to place the daily guide on
the chalkboard.

"You look horrible, Abby," Cherry said with a scandalous
tone.

"Thanks?" Abigail said. She didn't know if Cherry was joking or being serious.

"No really, what's wrong?" Cherry was serious.

Abigail pulled out her notebook and pencil. "I didn't get
much sleep last night."

Cherry leaned in. "Oh la la—what were you up to?"

"Nothing like that. I went to Dean's place," Abigail said.

"What?!" Cherry jumped out of her seat.

"Cherry. Please take your seat," the vest-wearing, mustache-wielding teacher commanded. "All right, class. Today we are looking at ancient Israel."

"Awe!" the class collectively groaned.

"Abigail…" Cherry whispered as the teacher began his lesson, "what in the world were you doing with Dean last night? And I didn't know he had a place—I assumed he lived on the streets."

"Not quite. But it doesn't matter—it was stupid." Abigail wanted to end the conversation, she opened her notebook and pointedly began taking notes.

"You're not getting out of this that easily. What did you two do?" Cherry pressed.

"Nothing. Seriously, we didn't do anything. We talked and then I left and that was it." Abigail tried not to look over at Cherry.

"LADIES!" the teacher interjected, stopping what he was writing on the board and turning to look directly at Abigail. "Do you have something that you would like to share with the rest of the class?"

"No, sir." Abigail looked up and then to Cherry. They quickly responded simultaneously. With an eyebrow raise and stern look, he resumed his notes on the board.

"We are not done here, Abigail," Cherry whispered as she leaned back into her chair.

The curly- and gray-haired teacher continued. "Israel has been a place of conflict for nearly its entire existence." He wheeled out an outdated film projector as he spoke, plugging it in. "There has been war after war over the holy ground where the first and second temples were built. The place is said to have been where Jesus himself performed miracles." He began flashing through images of the ancient city and artist renditions of what was once a beautiful and thriving world. Abigail watched and listened in hopes that she would find a clue as to what was happening in her own world. The other students couldn't care less as they hid their phones under the tables, sending texts back and forth, while others stared off mindlessly into space.

"I know this is all just so interesting, but if you could please, class..." He pointed back to the board. "Now, there is a theory that the famed Ark of the Covenant is housed here in Israel." He clicked over to an image.

Abigail nearly jumped out of her seat when she saw it. "What!"

"Abigail, can I help you with something?" He spoke in his monotonous voice.

"No, sir, just dropped my pencil," she lied.

"Mmmhhhmm." He clearly didn't believe her for one second. "Other theologians and ancient archeologists believe the holy artifact to be hidden away somewhere in Egypt, Mount Nebo, Ethiopia, or even Southern Africa. This holy artifact, which has caused countless wars, as well as the holy ground it has touched, was the main plot for Steven Spielberg's film *Raiders of the Lost Ark.*"

Even referencing Indiana Jones, he was losing the class. Way past their time.

Everyone...except for Abigail.

"The ark is said to contain the original stone slabs given to Moses by God, along with unimaginable powers. People who controlled the ark seemed to be virtually unstoppable during their times. Some believe those in possession of the ark were given control of God's most powerful angels, thus defeating any and all known armies." The teacher went on, bored of his own lecture, wishing he had a cell phone to hide under his desk too.

There it was again. Abigail caught the flashing images like the hawk catches the fleeting field mouse.

As he flipped from image to image, Abigail noticed the mark again. The same one that was on Dean was on the Ark of the Covenant. She hadn't seen these images when she had done her search the other night.

"I've gotta go tell him," she mumbled to herself.

"What?" Cherry whispered, leaning over.

"Nothing." Abigail raised her hand. "Sir. Excuse me, may I please go to the restroom?"

"Is it an emergency?" he asked, clearly out of obligation.

"Yes, sir. Very much so an emergency." This time she was not lying. It was just a different sort of emergency.

"Fine. Take your hall pass." He didn't care for more than a split second.

"Thank you." Abigail stood up, not forgetting to grab her books, and ran out of the classroom. Making her way through the empty halls, all she could think was what everything meant. The other night, the drawings, the creature, the symbols, it was all so much coming at her all at once. Like a train of new information plowing full force straight for her life.

Turning the hallway corner to the front entrance, she plowed into a brick wall of a person. Her books went flying in every direction as she lost her footing and hit the ground. "I'm so sorry," she said without looking up, the apology more of a natural response. She scrambled to pick up her books.

"Abigail, where are you off to?" a familiar deep voice asked.

Abigail looked up from the ground, her hand on the last book. A large white hand reached down, extending out of its blue pinstriped sleeve. "Are you okay?"

"Dad?" The confusion painted her face like a kid on Halloween. "What are you doing here?"

"I should ask you the same thing. Shouldn't you be in class?"

"Oh yeah. I was just going to the bathroom."

"You passed it, baby." He pointed to the restroom sign about ten yards back.

She looked back to where her father was pointing and palmed her forehead as if she had really missed it. "Oh. Oops. I must have missed it. I really needed it."

"I was actually coming to pull you out of class to see if you'd like to go to an early lunch with your old man." He lifted her off the ground and stared deeply into her blue eyes with his.

"Really?" She smiled from ear to ear, pushing her hair behind her ear.

"Yeah, I thought it would be nice, just the two of us. I mean, they are probably teaching you something you already read about anyway, my smart little girl."

"Yeah. Okay. Yeah, that sounds nice." She smiled.

"Don't you need the restroom, baby?" her father said, reminding her of her lie.

"Oh yeah. Sorry. Be right back."

She walked into the bathroom, unsure how she was going to let Dean know what she had just seen. Yet, at the same time, it seemed to matter a lot less. This was the first time that her father had seemed to show any interest in spending time with her. She stood there, staring at her own reflection in the mirror as if she had never seen that person before. The girl in the reflection with books clutched to her chest looked happy. Just standing there, staring right back.

"What are you doing?" she asked herself softly. "You just met the guy—you don't owe him anything. Go have fun with your dad." She took a deep breath and left the restroom.

Her father was still waiting in the hall, his eyes on his cell phone as he flipped through something on the screen.

"All right, Dad, I'm ready." She came out smiling cheek to cheek in her jean jacket.

He motioned with one hand to the doorway. "Let's go."

The two left the school and made their way down to his silver Bentley parked right out front.

THEIR CHARIOT OF a car shone as it drove lonesomely down the dirt roads of their small town. Everybody knew who was in that car—the businessman himself. Mr. Li'Ved was adored by most of the townsfolk. He was known for making very generous contributions to all the schools and hospitals around town. A man who created jobs and helped support the lives of those in his community. As they drove and as cars passed, everyone would wave happily with great gratitude and respect. Mr. Li'Ved would smile and wave back to each and every one of them, as if he knew them personally.

As if they were actually important to him.

The tires bounced as they pulled into the muddy, potholed parking lot of the diner. Mr. Li'Ved opened his door and got out.

"Hey, Dad," Abigail said.

He paused, not shutting the door.

Eyes forward and still strapped in, Abigail stared at the plowed snow at the edge of the parking lot.

"Yeah, baby, what is it?" he asked.

"Thank you."

"For what, Abigail?" He leaned back in the car.

"For this. It really means a lot to me." Her tone was soft.

"Oh, baby, of course. I know I don't get to spend a lot of time with you and I'm sorry for that. But you know I love you. I just have a lot of people to take care of too. You know that right, baby?" he asked, eyebrows creased with sincerity.

"Yeah, I know," she said, receding back into herself a bit.

"Come on, let's go get us some of those pancakes you love!" He smiled brightly before shutting the door. Abigail stepped out of the car, with a smile just as big.

The diner was made of an old train engine still attached to a shipping container. Its red and yellow rusted paint shone dully in the sunlight. A locals' favorite mom-and-pop shop. A neon sign that read "Hot Cakes All Day" buzzed in the small, round window. Surrounded by snow, it seemed the diner was the shining pinnacle of a snow mountain for all to admire. Mr. Li'Ved reached for the old brass handle.

Dingle-ling.

The diner door rang as the two entered.

A woman dressed in a white-and-pink, vertically striped dress looked up from behind the counter. "Hello, sit anywhere you'd like. I'll be right with you."

"Thank you, Marg," Mr. Li'Ved said.

Elvis Presley played joyfully on the jukebox near the back of the diner. The smell of fresh pancakes wafted in the air. The duo made their way into one of the old-fashioned booths from the fifties, still just as comfortable as ever. Puffed-up red leather chairs with white stitching—couldn't get more comfortable than that. Abigail sat across from her father, just staring, admiring him as if he were a new man—a new father—the one that she had always longed for.

"What? Is there something on my face?" he asked jokingly.

She let out a tiny giggle. "Ha ha, no. I'm just looking. I love you, Dad."

"I love you too, Abigail."

Marg approached the table, menus in hand. She set them on the table and pulled out her notebook. "Well, aren't you two just the cutest? What can I get y'all to drink?"

Her father answered for both of them. "I think we will start with two hot cocoas. That's okay with you, right?"

"Hot cocoa is perfect," Abigail said happily.

Marg smiled. "Two hot cocoas it is! You look good, Abigail. All grown up! How old are you now?"

Abigail smiled back. "Seventeen, ma'am. I'll be eighteen in a little over a month."

"You better watch out, Lucien. You are going to have a grown woman in your house. Soon she will be taking over."

"We plan on it," Mr. Li'Ved said, and Marg waved her pad and pen and rolled away on her ancient skates.

Abigail smiled even bigger still without taking her eyes off her father. He smiled back.

"So, baby, how is school going?" Mr. Li'Ved asked.

"Great. Finals are coming up soon, but I think I'm going to do really well. Especially in History and English," she said with a giggle, as if she were amazed that he was actually interested in hearing how she was doing at school. This was quickly becoming one of the best days of her life.

"Good, baby. And any boys?" His voice was so nonchalant.

Abigail winced. "No, no boys."

"Your cousin Beth told me she had seen you with a boy. Was she mistaken?" He began to butter his bread while staring at Abigail.

Abigail balled her fists under the table. "Oh, yeah, he is just my class partner for a project we are working on," she said as if she had just remembered.

"I see. What is the project?"

"It's on ancient Israel. We are doing a project on some of the old archeological mysteries," she said, casually reading her menu. Smooth. She was becoming a good liar.

"That's good, baby. Bring him by the house sometime. You know how I love the past—easier times. Maybe I can help you two out."

Abigail fidgeted in her seat. "Oh no, Daddy, it's okay. I think we got it."

"Bring him by tonight, Abigail. I would like to meet this boy." His tone had changed completely. He was now very stern and direct.

Abigail surrendered. "Yes, Daddy, of course."

Marg rolled back over to their table, "Two hot cocoas for the two beautiful people," she said as she placed them on the tabletop.

Abigail grabbed her mug, warming her hands. "Thank you, Marg."

Marg nodded and rolled away down the narrow aisle to her only other table. Not many people were out eating in the middle of a workday.

"Hey, Daddy."

Mr. Li'Ved looked up from his mug.

"When you said, 'We plan on it'—on me taking over the family business—did you mean it?" Abigail asked.

"Yes, of course. That is why I have you studying all those books. When you turn eighteen, everything will change for us. You know this. We can finally be a family. We just have some business to handle first. Things are going to get very hard before they get better. That is why you must be prepared. Business is not easy." Mr. Li'Ved took a sip of his cocoa. "Being on top never is."

FOREST CAFÉ WAS quickly becoming my go-to spot. The evening was nice as the sun began its descent.

Dingle-ling.

The bell rang as I entered the crowded café. Didn't these people have anything else to do other than drink coffee all day? Today there was a different hipster guarding the register. Thank God, the other one wouldn't have forgotten that I took his headset.

I sat with my headphones on, *the ones I'd technically stolen*, at a computer screen tapping away on the keyboard…Searching aimlessly, I had no idea what I was looking for. What had she searched to find the symbols like she said? Image after image, I grew more and more frustrated when nothing seemed to line up. Short tempered, I slammed my fists on the desk, bouncing the keyboard and mouse into the air.

Everyone stopped and stared.

"What?!" I yelled.

Just as quickly as they looked, their eyes darted back to their screens.

"Hey there! You having some trouble finding what you're looking for?" A voice came from behind me.

"I'm fine," I responded, staring at my lost search screen.

"Doesn't look like it. Here, let me help." The voice grew a hand. It reached in, grabbing the mouse.

"I said I'm fine!" I turned to look at who the hand was attached to. Bryon. "What do you want?"

"Just want to help. You looked like you were having some trouble. So what is it you're looking for?"

"Nothing. It doesn't matter," I said with a defeated energy.

"Come on, what is it?" Bryon persisted. "I'm really good with computers and finding stuff."

I was reluctant to ask for help. "It's nothing, really."

"All right. Well, if you need help, I'll be over there." He pointed to his desk covered in chips, coffee, and wires. Does this guy even have a life?

Bryon began to walk back to his desk when I broke.

"All right," I said.

"All right, what?"

He was such a pest.

"All right, could you help me?" I mumbled.

"Sure!" He jumped at the opportunity with a big smile plastered to his annoying mug. "What is it you're looking for?"

"See this?" I pointed to the mark on my wrist.

"Youuu want to look up a birthmark?" he asked, as if it were a stupid idea.

"Never mind, man, it was a stupid idea." I tried to shove him off and get back to the computer.

"No, no, it's cool. Okay, let me see your arm."

"For what?"

"Just give me your arm." Bryon grabbed my arm and pulled out his phone.

"What are you doing?" I asked.

"I'm going to do an image search." Bryon continued to pull up his camera on his phone. "By taking a picture of your birthmark, I can enter it into a filtered search and find other images that contain the same image or ones very similar to it." With that, Bryon took a photo and uploaded it to his image search engine on his computer. Half a second later, hundreds of images flew onto the screen.

"Wow. How did you do know how to do that?" I asked, dumbfounded.

"I told you, I'm good with finding things," Bryon bragged.

Looking back to the computer, our eyes couldn't focus on just one thing—there was so much.

"Whoa," Bryon let out. "What is all of this?"

The images were not what I was expecting at all. As we scrolled from picture to picture, our combined curiosity grew.

"How did you get this on your wrist? You're messing with me, right? That's a tattoo, isn't it?" Bryon asked as we continued to look.

"No. I've had it ever since I was born," I said, staring at the screen. I could barely believe it myself.

Bryon leaned in. "Dude these are like…awesome."

I leaned in too. "Yeah."

Breaking out of the awe and wonder from the images, Bryan said, "Dude, I knew you were like some time-traveling superhero-alien or something!" He jumped out of his chair.

"Shhh!" I shushed him and pulled him back down by the shirt collar. "What are you thinking?!"

"I'm sorry, but, dude, this is crazy! The only pictures coming up are all from B.C. as in Before Christ! There are no current photos of this anywhere. Not to mention all of these are associated with ancient battles from like every religion." Bryon was bugging out. "Look, look at this..." The symbol was seen emerging through a ball of flames on what resembled the blade of a sword as it came down from the sky like the wrath of God himself. "I mean, dude. This is awesome. Your birthmark is on nearly every ancient crucifix and painting throughout the world."

"What does it mean?" I asked rhetorically, sitting back in my chair. Bryon stood up and leaned onto the desk closer to the computer, as if it would help to get a better look. Unaware of our building curiosity, the café patrons stayed locked onto their screens. Everything was so quiet, the only thing I could hear over Bryon's heavy breathing was the *sip, sip* of coffee all around.

"It means you're a badass. No wonder you were able to throw that dude through a wall. I mean, you're a boss," Bryon continued. "Is your dad a badass too or what?!"

That struck a chord. I looked at Bryon, a little angry, but I knew he didn't know. I stood up and walked toward the door without turning back.

"Dude, Dean! Wait up!" Bryon called after me.

I pushed the door open, my frown feeling like it was permanently etched on my face as the cold wind rushed past me.

Dingle-ling. Dingle-ling.

The door rang as it slammed shut behind me only to ring again as Bryon followed after. "Where are you going? Was it something I said? Dean!"

I whipped around to face him. "I don't know who my parents are. Okay? That's what I was looking for! That symbol is all I have of them! Those pictures don't mean shit!"

The snow fell silently on the pure white ground all around me.

I paced back and forth, packing the snow beneath my feat, unsure of why I felt like sharing. "I thought, well, I thought that if I could find out who my family is—or *was*—then I could try to find them and ask them questions about what is happening to me. I thought if I found them, I could ask them why they left me and why I'm seeing all the things that I'm seeing!"

The birthmark on my wrist began to glow a deep red. The snow around my feet began to puddle and the snow falling near to me became like drops of rain.

"Dude." Bryon stared, raising his hands, placing them behind his head, and taking a step back.

I am rage.

"You don't get it, Bryon! You have a family, you know who they are, and you know you can go to them when things are falling apart around you! I can't!"

The storm inside me grew.

"Dude!" Bryon yelled.

"What?!" I yelled back, seeing the fear in his eyes, I stopped. Looking down at the puddle of water around my feet, I noticed my wrist. Heat was emanating off my body. Bryon stood petrified, like a small boy who had just seen the monster that lived in his closet all those years. "Bryon," I said apologetically.

He didn't respond right away. "It's okay." He dropped his hands. "But wow, we need to teach you how to control your temper. That was insane! I have never seen anything like that before," he said, laughing and smiling as he ran toward me, throwing his arm around my shoulder. "Come with me. I think I know someone who can help."

"Help with what?"

—§—

WALKING DOWN THE dirt path out of town with Bryon was an odd feeling, unfamiliar at best. I had never actually walked with anyone, let alone to get somewhere together.

Looking behind me, I could see the town in the distance, with a slight fade among it from the low-flying clouds, it looked like something out of a photograph, unreal. Snow covering the ground and trees. Beautiful log cabins with green tin roofs covered in pounds of fresh, white powder. The mountains looming behind the small town with patches of green treetops popping out from the snow that blanketed them. The path was lined with open fields on both sides as far as the eye could see. With the sun beginning its descent, the golden rays shined beautifully through the rows of freshly picked alfalfa fields. It looked as if we were walking into the infinite abyss with no end in sight, the horizon untouchable.

"Where are we going?" I asked.

Mmmm. The smell of pine needles filled my lungs. That smell would never get old.

"Don't worry about it. Let's just say I know a guy who knows things," Bryon said unhelpfully. His pace was slow. He must have been taking in the views as well.

How do I know I can even trust this guy? For all I knew he could be taking me to some torture chamber to experiment on me for one of his YouTube videos.

As time passed and the sun approached the end of its daily life, a large oak tree could be seen in the distance. A solitary giant standing like a lone wolf in the field of an empty dirt lot just to the right of our path. No mountains, or shrubs, just the tree with endless horizons. We must have walked at least twenty miles by the time we grew close.

"Here we are!" Bryon said with a big smile, followed by a slight sigh of relief. "My feet are killing me!"

"Where are we?" I searched the 360 degrees of nothingness.

Bryon held up his finger and walked over to the tree. Taking a breath and moment to think, he then began to knock on the trunk of the tree. He placed his ear onto the tree with his next knocks.

Knock. Listen. Repeat.

"What are you doing?" I asked.

"Hold on…It's around here somewhere…" Bryon responded as he continued to knock on the tree trunk.

"I must have been crazy to think you could actually help, I'm going back—"

"GOT IT!" Bryon exclaimed. He pressed his fingers into the trunk. A small, hidden door popped out of the trunk. About the size of a small child, it was round and seemed to be made from the tree itself, blending seamlessly. I stood there stunned. I had never seen anything like it before. I was excited and a bit nervous at the same time. "Well, come on! Don't just stand there. Let's go!" he said, crouching down carefully and stepping into the hole in the side of the tree trunk.

Maybe this guy could help me after all. Bryon stuck his hand out of the very tiny, round wooden entrance, waving for me to come in. The sky was lit only by the residual sunbeams that bounced from the clouds as the ball of fire dropped below the horizon. Squatting down to half my height, I took hold of Bryon's arm and stepped in. There wasn't much room—actually there was no room at all. The two of us were pressed up against each other in the interior of the enclosure. I struggled for a better position. The next thing I noticed inside the old oak was the smell. Outside had been a fresh, crisp air, only to be replaced with the thick, musky smell of mud and moss. Closing the door behind me, we stood body to body in the pitch-black trunk of a tree that smelled like rot. I questioned once again why I would trust this guy.

It's a good thing I wasn't claustrophobic.

"Bryon," I said, voice monotonous.

"Yeah, I know. Gimme a second." Bryon shuffled his feet, attempting to turn around, bumping me up against the bark.

"Bryon!" I said.

"One second, geez." He continued doing circles, squashing me against the innards of the tree.

"What are you looking for?" I patted the walls. They were smooth, really smooth. Almost like glass. Odd.

"A knob—she must have moved it."

"Who moved what?"

"This!" he said. I could hear something slide together and lock, almost like a metal bolt.

The small area of ground next to our feet slid back into the trunk, revealing a spiral staircase dimly lit by candlelight.

"Whoa." I stepped back, careful not to fall in.

"Come on, we don't have all day."

Bryon began walking down the wooden staircase. It wasn't all wood; it was dirt that was shaped and packed together and held up by wooden planks. Where did this guy even find this place to start with?

"I'm going to introduce you to my good friend Jade. She is the one who made all of this. She is going to be very interested in you…not in a sexual way or anything. I just mean…Never mind, you get it," Bryon babbled. "Jade can be a little…weird, but she is a genius. She taught me everything I know about technology and research. She is into stuff like this."

"Stuff like what?" I asked carefully, watching each step.

As we neared the bottom of the stairs, a large cave-like room revealed itself. The walls and ceilings were all smooth and made of what looked like carved sand and rock, with several wooden beams along the walls, supporting the large room. The space was so large with ceilings that looked to be thirty feet tall. Everything was lit either by candle or by old oil lamps. Books lay scattered all over the wooden ground. Shelves all around the room were filled with what looked like scrolls, novels, encyclopedias, gadgets, and artifacts that reached the very tops of the cavern.

There in the corner, apparently undisturbed from our arrival, working away was an average-sized figure in brown suede pants and a white button-up shirt, both of which were covered in dust, with her back to us. She stood, looking down into a large magnifying glass at a blank piece of paper.

"Jade!" Bryon yelled.

Startled, the figure leapt from her post and landed on her butt. She scrambled to her feet to face us. She had crazy black hair sticking up in every direction and her eyes were shielded by multilayered bifocals. I think they were green.

"Oh my God, Bryon don't do that," Jade said through heavy breaths. "How did you get in here? I moved the knob." She had an accent—Spanish, maybe?

She couldn't have been more than one or two years older than us, with a petite figure and five-foot-nothing. How was this girl supposed to help? I was growing impatient.

"I noticed," Bryon said as he flipped through a book on one of the desks.

"And who's this?" Jade was referring to me as she looked me up and down, her hands on her glasses, analyzing.

"Jade! This is Dean," Bryon said, introducing us.

"Pleasure to meet you, Dean," she said, putting her hair up into a bun and turning back to her work, the words insincere. "But I'm going to have to ask both of you to leave. Bryon, you know not to bring anyone here." Definitely a Spanish accent I was hearing.

"Dean is not just anyone. He is special," Bryon gloated.

"I don't care how special of a friend he is, you can't stay," Jade said, already busy at work looking through the magnifying glass.

"Come on, Bryon. Let's just go," I said, turning back to the stairs.

"Wait." Bryon stopped me. "Jade, I think you might want to take a look at this before you kick us out."

Jade placed both hands on her desk and turned to look at us, her green eyes glaring. "What is it?"

Bryon stepped toward me, grabbing my arm. He pulled me over to Jade, revealing the birthmark that resides on my wrist. She looked closer, leaning in. As she neared, she seemed to have noticed something, her eyebrow rose, and her eyes became wide. Grabbing my wrist out of Bryon's hands, she pulled it up to the binoculars she called glasses. A moment passed as she continued to examine my mark. "Hmm." She looked up for a brief second to make eye contact with Bryon, then at me, and back down. Her eyes *were* green.

"This is incredible…Come with me," Jade said, turning and walking to the other side of her chambers. Following suit, we walked through the book-littered ground to a small wooden desk with stacks of books as tall as a person.

"I told you he was special," Bryon stated.

"You said your name is Dean?" Jade asked.

"Yes, that's right," I said.

She stopped and stared at me hard. "What is your last name?"

"I don't know." My eyes dropped.

"What do you mean you don't know?" she asked.

"I don't know because I don't know who my parents are…" I said.

"I see." She seemed to know something. Grabbing at some books, she began to flip through the pages.

"What are those?" I asked.

"These...are books. Very old books."

Apparently, we have a wise guy on our hands. Great.

Jade slammed a handful of larger books down on the table in front of us. Dust from the table and the books flew everywhere. "These books were written before the birth of Christ."

"Just like the pictures we saw!" Bryon slapped me on the shoulder with a big smile. I gave him a look that said, *If you ever do that again, I'll throw YOU through a wall.*

Jade continued to filter through the pages of one of the large leather-bound books. "Here." She stopped on a page, pointing.

Excitement filled my being as I leaned in to look at what she had found.

The image on the page was of a sword that had the exact same symbol engraved in its hilt.

"We've already seen this," I said, disappointed. I took a few steps back, placing my hands on my head, the excitement left me.

"What does it mean, Jade?" Bryon leaned in.

"This sword was said to have been wielded by an ancient creature that guarded the holy lands. It says here that this archaic being would come down in a cloud of flames wherever war would break among the holy lands." Jade was digging in, exciting herself. "There are also sightings of it near the lands of Jerusalem, Bethlehem, the Nile...The list goes on and on."

Exciting me too. I moved back in to the huddle. Leaning in, I took another look at the image, tracing the sword with my hands.

"Wait a second..." Jade put down the book and ran to her wall of scrolls.

"What are you looking for now?" I asked.

"Dude, this is so freakin' cool!" Bryon jumped and began looking through the books on the desk like a kid in a comic book store.

"I have seen this symbol in a few other spots too…Look here." Jade pulled out a scroll and blew off the dust, revealing the still-rolled parchment. There it was, the symbol on my wrist right there on the scroll. It was mixed in with a slew of other symbols.

"What is this?" I asked.

"This is a scroll straight from the pyramids of ancient Egypt. These are hieroglyphs." Jade looked at me with amazement, unraveling the papers. Her eyes the size of melons through her glasses.

"It says here that a powerful being would come down on winged horse whose feathers itself were covered in flames." She ran her fingers over the hieroglyphs. "It says it came down to protect the people in the time of Thutmose II. This was the creature that destroyed the city of Egypt during the Eighteenth Dynasty." Jade looked over at me once again. This time her sense of amazement was accompanied by curiosity. Her jaw almost slack. "This was back in the time of Moses," she said with such weight, plopping down on a chair near the desk.

"Okay, so what does all this mean?" I asked with no clue as to what was going on. "It's just a coincidence," I said after a moment. I'd learned over the years not to get my hopes up for anything. Though lately I had been forgetting that.

"Why did you come to me? Why were you looking this up? If it's just a birthmark, then why are you here?" Jade asked as she moved closer to me, staring into my eyes with a stern glare. I could feel her breath on mine.

Why was she so close to my face? Did she think it was dramatic? At least she'd brushed her teeth.

Before I could find an answer, Bryon broke the awkward silent stare. "JADE! You have to see what he can do!"

We both glared at Bryon, who seemed not to notice. Instead, he reached for his laptop and pulled up the infamous YouTube video of the fight.

How did he get internet down here?

"You have internet?" I asked.

"What? No, crazy. We are in an underground cave beneath a tree for Pete's sake. No one has internet. I shot this, remember?"

Another wise guy. Even better.

Watching in amazement, Jade couldn't take her eyes off of the screen.

"What were you looking at before the fight began?" Jade asked.

"What do you mean?" I asked.

"Look here." She rewound the video and paused it before Bryon had actually focused the camera on me. There I was, just standing there, my wrist glowing. No one was paying any attention yet. "You were looking at something. Your mark looks like it's on fire—what was it?"

"You're not going to believe me," I said.

"Try me," she said with a serious face. We stood up from the computer.

"I don't know. It was this…thing," I said, trying to describe it the best I could.

"What kind of thing?" Bryon pulled out a bag of trail mix.

We stopped and looked at him. He stared back as he stuffed a handful in his mouth.

What a gentleman he was around girls. Man, I was hungry.

I looked back at Jade, trying to figure out how to describe it. "It was this tall, burnt creature. It had long black hair that looked like it was dipped in oil, and its eyes were a deep red. It looked like some kind of a…"

"A demon." Jade said.

"A demon?" Bryon and I both said. Bryon spit out most of his chewed trail mix.

Appetite gone.

Bryon immediately began digging in his bag and stuffing his face again, watching Jade like a good movie awaiting answers.

"Yes. A demon. I have read about these creatures," Jade said as she ran to another shelf to grab a book, "extensively."

"You're joking, right?" I said mockingly. "Demons aren't real. They are just made up to scare us into being good little boys and girls." I watched her climb a ladder and search the top shelves of the bookcase.

"I'm afraid not. I have read extensively on their kind. I just have never known anyone to have actually seen one." She fluttered her fingers along the books' spines.

"Well, I've seen three," I said.

Jade stopped her search and turned to look at me. Bryon also froze midchew and looked up to me.

"Three? What did the other two look like?" Jade asked, standing on the ladder.

"One of them was hiding in an alleyway—it was the first one I had noticed. I couldn't tell what it looked like—it was too dark—but it did have those same red eyes. I told you about the second, and the third was this ghostlike thing. It was like smoke that filled the room, and when it spoke, the air felt like all the heat had been sucked out."

"Dude," Bryon said, his eyes wide with fear. The fun and games were at an end.

"It *spoke* to you?" Jade asked as she thumbed through more pages. "What did it say?"

"It just said to 'stay away from her,'" I paraphrased.

Jade mumbled something as she continued to look through her books. "Is this what they looked like?" Jade threw three books on the desk, all opened to different pages with rough sketches of creatures.

"That's exactly what they looked like!" I said.

Finally some answers. Maybe coming here wasn't a waste of time after all. My beating heart, it raced.

Jade was already searching through another book.

"What are you looking for now?" I asked.

"You said that the creature said to 'stay away from her.' Who is she? Who are they protecting, and why do they want you to stay away?" Jade asked as she tossed books to the ground left and right.

"I don't know," I said. "The only person I can think of is Abigail. She is the only one I have been hanging out with."

Bryon jumped. "Abigail?! You have been hanging out with *the* Abigail?!" Food spit all over the place from his once-again-stuffed cheeks. His heavy breathing almost choked him on his salty trail mix. "I can't breathe. She's, she's…" he said, sitting back down.

"Who is Abigail?" Jade asked with raised eyebrows.

"Only the most beautiful and incredible girl at AngelFire High! You're dating her?" Bryon said, staring hard while awaiting my answer, clearly hoping for a negative.

Jade rolled her eyes.

"No! I'm not dating her," I said defensively. "She just has helped me out a few times, that's all. I feel comfortable around her."

Bryon let out his breath and went back to eating. A sigh of relief. She was still available.

"Why are they protecting her?" Jade mumbled.

"How do we know it is even her they are talking about and not some other girl you may have bumped into?" Bryon stuffed another handful of mixed nuts into his mouth.

"She has a mark like me. Only different," I said.

"Whelp, never mind. It's her." Bryon chewed.

"What does it look like?" Jade asked, grabbing a book off the desk and flipping through the pages.

I moved to the sandy area of the ground and began drawing the image with my finger.

"Interesting," said Jade, crossing her arms and staring at the sand art.

"What is it?" Bryon asked.

"I don't know. I have never seen it before," Jade said, uncrossing her arms and adjusting her glasses. "SO! You, Mr. Dean, have some unexplainable strength that surfaces when your marking flares up and you can see demons who don't like you. Does that pretty much sum it up?" Jade asked, walking back to where we had first met. Bryon stood up off his bum and followed. I stood there, confused at how simple of terms she had put it in.

Bryon stood next to Jade and looked at me. I had nothing to say. I stared back and shrugged my shoulders. *I suppose?*

"Okay then. We have some work to do. First things first, we need to find your sword."

CHAPTER 7

DADDY DEAREST

T HE NIGHT AIR was arctic as Bryon and I made our way back into town. The snow was not falling, but the wind made it so cold that Hell itself would have frozen over. With so much on our minds, we walked in silence, our thoughts jumping from one thing to another. Although Jade had brought forth valuable information, it still seemed as if we were at ground zero. I still had so many questions and it seemed none of them were answered.

I am the lost wanderer.

The lights of the city shone through the trees as we approached town. Like stars that decided to land on earth and shine on the ground, the town was beautiful. The moon was out that night, its light shadowing the glow of the stars.

As we came upon my home, sweet home, the church looked so lonesome now. It was an odd feeling to have never had a friend till now.

"Today was cool," I said as we drew nearer to the lamp that guarded my entrance.

"Yeah, man, it was wild! I can't wait to see what we discover tomorrow!" Bryon said with such energy. Regardless of where my mind was, Bryon always seemed to be optimistic. From the little time that I had known him, I had never seen him down or heard a negative thing come out of his mouth. He was always looking to the future, a positive and bright future.

"You still want to hang out with me?" I asked. "You don't think I'm a freak?"

"Heck no—you're the coolest person I know!" Bryon smiled from ear to ear.

"Why are you being so nice to me, man? Why are you helping me?"

"Honestly?" Bryon said. "Other than my YouTube subscribers…you're my only real friend. Everyone else just thinks I'm the weirdo around school."

That was the first time I had ever felt accepted.

"DEAN!" We heard a yell from down the frozen street. "DEAN!"

Turning to look, we saw Abigail running down the street, waving her arms. She ran up next us. "Dean…" she said, out of breath.

"What is it? Are you okay? Did they do anything to you!" I caught her as she ran into my arms. I could feel my body begin to heat up. The ground around me transformed from ice to water.

"Dude…" Bryon subtly waved his hand, motioning for me to calm down.

Still holding Abigail, I looked at my burning wrist.

One deep breath. Two. Three.

It subsided.

"What? Yeah, I'm fine. Did who do what to me?" she asked, catching her breath.

"Nothing. Never mind." I released my grip and pushed her arms' length, still holding her shoulders.

"How are you so hot?"

"I, uh…" I said, letting go.

"It's freezing out here."

"So, what's up?" I asked.

"My dad and I were wondering if you'd like to join us for dinner tonight?"

"Thanks, but I'm all right. Bryon and I have a lot of work to do."

Bryon shrugged in approval of my lie, already stuffing his face with some kind of candy. Where does he store all this food?

"Oh hi, Bryon. I'm—"

"Abigail, I know. We have Chemistry," Bryon said through stuffed cheeks. "I mean Chemistry class. Not like sexual chemistry, or… anything. I'll stop. Nice to meet you."

Abigail seemed to have enjoyed that, letting out a small giggle. "You're funny, Bryon."

Bryon blushed as he took another bite.

"Is it cool if I steal your friend just for tonight? Y'all can get back to business tomorrow."

"Yeah, no, that's cool. That's cool with me," Bryon said as he began to step away. "Dean, my man, I have a lot of editing to do for another video anyway. I'll catch you tomorrow."

Abigail smiled. "Nice meeting you, Bryon."

Bryon gave a shy smile. "It was a pleasure meeting you! Don't go fallin' in love now!" Bryon said as he skipped away.

"What?" Abigail and I looked at each other. "No, no, that's—ha," we said simultaneously.

"Looks like you're free?" Abigail said, breaking the awkwardness, looking at me with those big blue eyes.

I gave in. "All right, what's the worst that could happen?"

Abigail and I began our walk from the church back to her place. Fall in love. Ha. Bryon was a crazy guy. I looked over at her. Her nose was red from the cold wind—and perfect. I mean, I guess Bryon wasn't *that* crazy.

She looked over at me. "What?" she said with a giggle.

"Nothing." I quickly looked away.

"What were you and Bryon doing all day? You're covered in dirt," Abigail asked as she pinched the corner of my peacoat and released a cloud of dust.

"Nothing." I said, eyes forward before I peeked over at her again.

She looked so beautiful. Wrapped from head to toe in layers upon layers, her beauty shone through. Her blonde hair just barely visible through her oversized knit beanie. Just walking next to her, I felt a warmth that was unlike any other. The wind blew her subtly-scented perfume in my direction. It was that of an angel.

She tried to dig in deeper. "Nothing? That's all I get after everything?"

"So what's your dad like?" I shifted.

"My dad," she said, looking forward on the path. Her face lit up as we passed under the streetlamps. "My dad is not your typical 'father figure.'"

A father of any kind must be amazing, I thought to myself. "I wouldn't know." The words rolled off my tongue.

"Oh. Sorry," she said, dropping her eyes. She didn't know.

"It's fine, I mean, look how well I turned out! I hardly get into any trouble at all," I said, smiling at her. Abigail lifted her head and smiled back. "Tell me more."

"He is a workaholic. All he does is work, and when he comes home, he does more work. I hardly ever get to see him," she said.

"What does he do?"

"He is a businessman. He deals a lot in exports, among other things. I don't know, really. It's just a lot," she said.

"What about your mom?"

Abigail stopped, looked down at the ground, and put her hands in her pockets.

"What's wrong?" I asked. "Abigail." I pulled her hands out of her pocket, very gently and held them. "It's okay, you can tell me." The wind blew past our ears, whistling in the tree-tops. Snow swirled off of the ground in an elegant dance.

"I never knew my mother," she said with a broken voice. "She died giving birth to me." Her beautiful blue eyes looked broken and sad. The tears started to swell. I couldn't bear to see her so hurt. It killed me. Without even knowing the woman, Abigail held so much hurt and feeling of responsibility it was like a billboard on her face. She stared at me with somber eyes.

"It wasn't your fault, Abigail," I said, looking deep into her eyes. I moved in slowly and wrapped my arms around her. Holding her tight, she wrapped her arms around me too. "It was not your fault."

Our bodies grew warm. Again, the ground around me—us—began to melt away. "Thank you, Dean," she said with her head on my shoulder. Our birthmarks began to glow a soft white glow. Gently pulling away and grabbing my hands, she and I looked down at our glowing wrists. "Ha ha, what is going on?" she said, breaking her sadness with a beautiful smile and laugh. I had no words. All I could do was stare and admire how beautiful this girl was.

"Come on, let's get out of the snow," I said, motioning to the road. She smiled as we turned to continue. We released hands and resumed our journey to her castle. A few steps in, I felt the soft touch of her hand on mine. Butterflies exploded throughout my body and the cold was gone. Our fingers inter-locked, and we walked.

I am the heart's beating drums. I am pure joy.

She was silent the rest of the walk, gently keeping her head on my shoulder. I walked in happiness.

Her castle came into view after a few minutes down the road. It lit up the night—it might as well have been bigger and brighter than the moon. Two stone lions guarded the gate's entrance of the drive, one on each side. How had I not noticed any of this the other times? Oh, that's right: I was dying. The castle seemed eerily quiet. More than other homes here in AngelFire. I had never met someone's dad before either. That may have been it.

Though, something felt off.

I felt off.

As we closed in on the mansion, this feeling of fight or flight swept over me. It must have been nerves. I didn't think I would be this nervous to meet a girl's dad, though Abigail is not just any other girl.

"Okay." She stopped on the front step and turned toward me. "My dad can be a bit intimidating. Don't let him scare you, okay? Also make sure to give him a firm handshake and don't break eye contact when you meet him. He is going to look for any and all signs of weakness. And—"

"Abigail, I get it. I'll be okay," I said to reassure both her and me. The nerves sparked inside me like electricity.

"Okay," she said as she dusted me off, looked in my eyes with a slight smirk, nodded her head, and turned opened the door. "Daddy, I'm home!"

"I'm in the office, baby. I'll be right out." His voice echoed from the very end of the hallway.

A fire could be heard crackling off in one of the rooms as we made our way down the marble-lined hallway. Abigail led me in. The artifacts that were housed in glass cases all looked so old. I had seen them before, just briefly the time she had sewn me up. Seeing them up close was so much different. Intriguing, to say the least. They resembled a few of the ones I had seen recently in my research. The ones from B.C. and the holy lands. How is it all rich people are interested in antiques? Everything was so beautiful, each room lined with a gold trim. I could smell the mouthwatering aroma of food wafting through the train-sized hall. We must have been nearing the kitchen.

"Abigail! Baby!" Mr. Li'Ved said about ten feet away as he turned the corner from his office into the hallway. His black pinstripe suit looked clean and freshly pressed with a small red handkerchief in his front pocket.

"Hi, Daddy." She ran up and kissed him on each cheek. "Daddy, this is Dean," she said, turning to present me to her father.

His gaze slowly shifted from his daughter over to me. His eyes resembled Abigail's, though something about them seemed dark.

As his eyes made their way to mine, something inside me was piercing. It was as if he were looking into my soul and I could feel it. Like he was searching for something. I couldn't break eye contact even if I'd wanted to. Slowly, he reached out his hand to shake mine. As I mirrored the motion, I gripped his cold, brute-like hand.

A flash of images flooded my mind. Like memories on fast forward. I couldn't pick them out as they were coming too fast. Releasing his hand I jumped back, out of breath as if I had just run thirty miles. A cold sweat brewed on my forehead. Looking up at him I saw his eyes, still locked into my soul, now with a hint of curiosity.

"Dean, are you all right?" he asked, jumping forward to help me gain my balance.

"Dean?" Abigail said, running toward me.

Taking a second to catch my breath, I said, "I'm fine. Must just be tired from the day. I haven't eaten much."

Lying was becoming a character trait. Maybe she and I had more in common than I thought.

"Well, let's get some food in you," Mr. Li'Ved said as he motioned toward the dining hall, leading the way. I straightened up and slowly followed, Abigail at my side.

"Come on, are you okay?" Abigail whispered, placing her hand on my back. She must have sensed that I had lied.

"I'm fine," I responded, shaking it off. "Let's just go eat."

She nodded as we made our way forward.

What was that? What had just happened? I tried to replay the images as slowly as I could, but I still could not make out what they were. It was all a blur. I could feel them. They weren't just images—they were memories. It felt almost as if a part of me had returned from the dead. I wish I could make sense of them. The only image I could make out was his eyes. I had seen them somewhere before. He was looking down on me surrounded by all white, like a bright light was above his head. The image was visceral.

"Dinner is served!" Mr. Li'Ved announced as we entered the dining hall, raising his arms in presentation. The hall itself was larger than the roads in town. The ceilings were lined with chandeliers and painted with what looked like art from the Renaissance. The walls were decorated with leather-bound books and artifacts to match. With a long, prestigious oak table fit for a king in the center of it all. The wood was ingrained with gold throughout. I had never seen such craftsmanship. The tabletop itself looked like a piece of art, blanketed in food of all kinds. The garnishes, fruits, and desserts were all the colors of a painter's pad. There was so much of it! More than any one family could finish on their own.

Smells of every kind entered and warmed me at the core.

"Well, are you just going to stare at it, or are you going to join us?" I heard Mr. Li'Ved from down the table as the two were already sitting, waiting on me to take my place. I must have dazed off from all the amazing smells and sights. Sensory overload. Walking the length of the table, I made it to the head. Abigail was sitting to the right of her father. Mr. Li'Ved pulled out the chair to his left just across from Abigail.

Joining the two, I took my place. "This looks great, sir. Thank you for having me."

"Of course, Dean. I had to meet this mysterious boy that Abigail has been spending time with." His smile was contagious. His teeth so perfectly square and whiter than the snow that lined the town.

"Oh, Daddy, you know we are just working on a project together," Abigail said quickly. I watched her, then I looked back at Mr. Li'Ved and nodded yes in agreement.

"What kind of project was it again?" he kindly asked, grabbing his fork and knife. Abigail, and I quickly glanced at one another as if to send Morse code with our eyes.

"It's for history class," she said, also grabbing her fork and knife. "Right, Dean?"

I nodded. "Yes, that is right, Abigail."

Maybe I wasn't as good a liar as I'd thought.

"Oh, that's right, you were doing a project on ancient Israel," her father said as he began to cut into his steak with a knife that looked like it was from the Knights of the Round Table. "You know, I have some original artifacts from Israel. Would you like to see them after dinner?"

Interested, I jumped in. "That would be great, sir. Thank you."

"You don't have to keep calling me sir. Mr. Li'Ved is fine."

"Yes, sir…I mean, Mr. Li'Ved." I cut into my steak. The juicy meat was so tender it was like cutting through butter. My mouth dribbled with saliva as I took a generous bite of the exquisite cuisine. That single bite was the most delectable thing my taste buds had ever experienced. My eyes lit up in pure joy. I cut the next pieces faster. I couldn't eat them quick enough.

"You were hungry. Slow down, son. There is more where that came from," Mr. Li'Ved said, watching me devour the plate.

"Sorry, sir—Mr. Li'Ved. It's just, I have never tasted anything like this before," I said, trying to finish a bite.

"Incredible, I know. So, Dean, tell me about yourself. What do your parents do? I may know them here in town. I do own most of the local businesses." Mr. Li'Ved took another bite and then a sip of red wine from a glass goblet trimmed with gold.

I didn't know what to say. Taking a drink of my water and looking down at my food, I said, "I never knew my parents."

"I'm sorry to hear that." He wiped his mouth.

"It's fine." A half smile curled from my lips as I looked up at Abigail. She smiled back, trying to hide it from her father.

"Well, you seem to be doing okay for yourself, son."

Who does he think I am? His son? I hate when people call me that. "I suppose so."

He had no clue what I had gone through or the wild days that had recently come to pass. Abigail sat there, so quiet she was either really enjoying her food or trying to make it through the dinner alive—I couldn't determine which. Either way, she didn't want her dad to find out anything about what she had been up to with me, I could tell.

He broke the silence. "What is it about ancient Israel that you two are working on?"

"Mainly the art during the times of war," Abigail said, looking up. She was just as quick as her father.

"Amazing. After dinner let me show you two something. I'm sure it will help your research. Better in person than out of some book," Mr. Li'Ved said, taking another bite of his steak. He really didn't seem like a bad guy to me. For some reason Abigail had led him on to be something of a strict man.

I dove back into my meal. The meat was so tender it melted in my mouth before I could even chew it. The potatoes and vegetables were seasoned so perfectly. I had never had a meal this entrancing. I looked up at Abigail and smiled. She seemed to be playing with her food. She caught my smile and smiled back.

Mr. Li'Ved took a sip from his goblet. "Come, let us go have a look. I'm sure you're going to love it." He cleaned his mouth, threw the silk napkin on his plate, and stood to lead us. We followed, though leaving the table was a sad task. All the food was so unimaginably good I didn't want to ever stop. Though I'm glad we did—my stomach was beginning to rip at the seams.

Standing up, Abigail seemed to not want to look my direction. Her eyes were on the floor and she was twiddling her fingers nervously. What was he going to show us?

Abigail opened up. "Daddy, I haven't seen you this interested in something other than work in…well, ever."

"Come on, baby, you know I love history. Look at all we have!" He threw his hands in the air, boasting his collection.

This was true. Everything that decorated this estate was some kind of artifact, art piece, or trophy from what looked like a very, very long time ago.

Leaving the dining room, he led us through the adjacent hallway and through the marble home. We approached large, arched doors. "Here we go," he said as he grabbed the two round, iron rod handles of the chamber's guarded wooden doors. The room opened into one with ceilings so high they looked like they didn't end. Paintings and glass cases were everywhere—it was a museum. Everything was organized so nicely. Glass cases housed single artifacts, and walls were lined with paintings ranging in size from as small as a quarter to as large as a barn door. Each case and piece of art was individually lit to exemplify its unique beauty.

"Wow, this is incredible." My senses filled to the max. I spun around trying to take it all in.

"Thank you, Dean. I have been collecting for quite some time. There are still some pieces that have eluded me. But I will have them. Yes, indeed," Mr. Li'Ved said, placing his hand on my shoulder. His hand was warm—oddly, I could feel its heat through my shirt.

The pieces took my mind on a rollercoaster of curiosity and yearning to know more. Something about it all felt so familiar. A painting caught my eye. I moved closer, breaking away from his grip. It was more than familiar—I'd seen it just today. "This painting—I have seen it before." I pointed and moved closer.

He approached the art, taking it in. "You must be mistaken; this original is the only of its kind."

"No, no, I've seen it in a book." I said.

"What book?" His voice quivered as he spun me around to face him. He was on me like a shark that smelled blood, leaning in close to my face.

"I don't know, just a book?" I responded.

"What did the book look like?" He grabbed my arm tightly. "You must remember that."

"Mr. Li'Ved…my arm."

His eyes gripped harder than his hands. I could *feel* his stare. His blue eyes darkened and dilated as if searching the confines of my own blackened pupils.

"Daddy, stop it. You're embarrassing me," Abigail said, worried.

He released his grip and slicked back his thick blond hair. Taking a breath and standing upright, he calmed down. "My apologies, Dean. I have been searching for a book of such nature for a very long time."

A bead of sweat trickled down my head. The room was so hot—that or the pressure of meeting Abigail's father was getting to me.

"You're sweating, son. Here, let me take your coat."

There it was again. Quit calling me your son. I turned to give him my coat as he gently took it off my shoulders, walked back to the entrance of the room, and placed it on a rack near the door.

"Thank you. It is getting warm," I said, trying to ease the tension.

"Daddy, what is this?" Abigail had found a glass case that drew her curiosity. She leaned in so close to the glass that her breath became visible on the surface of the smooth, clear enclosure.

"That, baby, is the whip that was used at a very bad man's time of judgment back in the time of the crucifixions."

"Which man?" I asked.

He stared at me hard once again. "I don't remember, Dean. I won it at an auction a few years back in northern Egypt."

Shrugging it off, I moved through the museum he had built. So many interesting things, so much history in one room, it was overwhelming. The smell of old leather books filled the air. "What is this here?" A glass case that encompassed a triangular-shaped stone had caught my eye.

"That is said to be the fabled stone that David used to kill the Goliath in the stories from the Bible. Is it true? I don't know, but I wanted it anyway," he said.

"What is this mark on it?" I pointed through the glass.

Mr. Li'Ved moved closer and took a look. "That's nothing, I'm sure. Just a crack from when it hit the monster in the head. All right, that's enough adventure for one night." Mr. Li'Ved quickly moved us out of the room. We made our way to the front door. "I'll find some pieces from the specific era you're studying and pull them for your next visit."

The hallway had an awkward silence to it with the only sounds echoing from our footsteps.

"Ahh, I forgot my jacket! I'll be right back!" I turned quickly and ran back to grab my jacket from Mr. Li'Ved's mini museum.

"Dean!" I could hear Mr. Li'Ved yelling as I neared the two large wooden doors. Pulling them open was like pulling a train, the doors were so heavy. As I grabbed my jacket, I saw something in the back that I hadn't seen while we were in there. A large object covered by a massive black sheet. It must have been at least twenty-five feet tall. The black cloak glistened a bit in the light as air swirled through the room. I couldn't unlock my gaze. Creeping forward, I made sure not to knock anything over.

As I got closer to the towering black sheet, I could feel it. An energy, a familiar energy. Like I knew it…

"Dean," Mr. Li'Ved said, startling me. "You find your jacket?" He was looming just a foot away.

"Yes, sir, right here," I said, taking one last look at the covered object.

"Good. Let's get going," he said.

We moved through the room in line, Mr. Li'Ved following close behind. Exiting the room and once again in the hallway, I said, "Thank you for dinner, sir. It was great."

"You're very welcome, Dean. Come back soon." Mr. Li'Ved reached out his hand, as did I. This time with a bit of caution hoping not to receive the same lapse in consciousness as before. Gripping his hand, I felt nothing. He smiled.

Releasing his hand, I then reached out for Abigail's. "Thank you, Abigail."

"No need, see you in class," she lied as she shook my hand. She wouldn't see me in class.

Turning to leave, I found myself longing to stay.

I am the curious cat.

CHAPTER 8

A PAST LIFE

A COUPLE WEEKS had passed since that night I had gone to dinner with Abigail and her father. Things had been seemingly normal. I haven't seen a creature or felt "off" in any way since that night. I was beginning to think all that I had seen or felt was just caused by anxiety or fear since Abigail had entered my life. Maybe I was scared of letting someone in—she was the only person who had intrigued me to do so in all the years I had been on this earth. Every family I had ever been a part of or fostered into had been repulsive to me. The thought of letting any of them in had been incomprehensible. Then Abigail came along, and it was like I had no other choice but to let her in.

Now that I had, I was glad.

It was a calm and sunny afternoon, and everyone was in school. The town was quiet as the parents went to work and the kids all sat half asleep in class. I couldn't help but wonder what it was that Mr. Li'Ved was protecting under that sheet in his museum. My curiosity would be the end of me one day. I couldn't sit in the church and do nothing; my mind was racing with questions and my body was jittery with energy. Just as I stood up to make my way out of my house—

"Dean!" Bryon came bursting in. "What is up, brother man?"

"Hey, Bryon, what's going on?" I said, putting on my coat.

"Dude, Jade wants to see you. She said she may have found something that is going to interest you," Bryon said. It must have been freezing out—Bryon was covered in a full fur parka, gloves, snow boots, and a backpack. His small demeanor made it look like the clothes were swallowing him alive.

"What is it?" I asked.

"She wouldn't say. She just said to come get you as soon as possible." Bryon hopped a couple steps back, motioning to follow.

"Don't you have class right now?" I asked.

"Oh nah, it's just Home Ec. Mr. Wright falls asleep every class. You ready?" he said.

I nodded yes, grabbed my journal, and followed Bryon out of the front doors. I actually had a lot to show Jade as well. All the stuff in Mr. Li'Ved's house was too much not to tell anyone, especially Jade. The snow had begun to melt across town, making muddy puddles all over the place like land mines.

"The snow melted early this year," I said just as the breeze blew by, instantly freezing my nose. "How is it still freezing if everything is melted?"

"Yeah, I don't know. It must be all the global warming that people joked about. Poor Mother Earth is spazzing out," Bryon said, putting a new pair of headphones on and skipping down the road. I wonder what he was listening to.

The sun shone brightly in the sky, burning off the clouds that remained and warming the town to a nice spring temperature. The trees seemed to open their arms and accept the sun like a wonderful gift from their Mother Nature. This weather was very bipolar. I had never seen it like this before.

Making it to Jade's was becoming something fun to do. Like going to a friend's house to hang out, something I had never really done before.

Bryon entered the secret opening and we made our way down the tree's inner staircase and into the giant underground labyrinth. Something about Jade's hideaway felt safe. The floors made of dirt seemed warm; the tall support beams holding the place together were strong. The bookcases lining the underground walls were old and dusty, containing so much knowledge. The energy of the room was amazing.

"AH! Dean, Bryon! You made it," Jade said with open arms and a dusty face. She made her way over to us, her hair a mess and covered in dirt. Her green eyes barely visible through her smeared goggles.

"All right, Jade, I got him here. Now tell us what it is that you found," Bryon said, pretending to hold up a gun he made with his hand.

"Ah yes! Follow me." She scurried off through the cavern and through a door I had not seen the first time. The door was carved into to wall of dirt, and just past it a narrow hall lined with mining lamps for a hundred yards lit the way to a room at the end of the tunnel. The room it led to was small and dark and had just enough light to see two feet in front. There in the middle of the room was a desk with a large, leather-bound book on it. It was clasped shut with iron locks.

"What is this, Jade?" I asked. It must have been special—it was the only thing in the room, unlike the main room.

"Whoa," Bryon said as he slid his hand down the side of the iron clasps. "This is awesome."

"This, Dean…is you," Jade said as she pointed to the oddly shaped opening. It was just like my birthmark.

"Where did you find this?" I reached to grab the book. Jade and Bryon stood tableside.

"This book came to me two years ago when I first traveled the desert lands of southern Jordan. I was on a dig site on the inner chambers of the Al-Khazneh…"

My hands wrapped around the book, and I felt home. My mind was full, the memories pounding at the gates of my brain and begging to come in.

"The what?" Bryon asked.

"The Al-Khazneh—it is also known as the Treasury at Petra. Part of the Rose City from Ma'an Governorate, Jordan. This is a holy city to the Jews. A place of great spiritual activity," Jade explained, reaching into her back pocket and pulled out a small book full of images of temples carved from rock. "It is said that this is the location that Aaron the high priest, brother of Moses, died. Aaron was said to have been one of the first great prophets of God, appointed by God himself through Moses at Mount Sinai when Moses had received the law." She pointed to a picture of a man holding two large stone tablets and another man standing next to him.

"WHOAAA," Bryon gaped. He reached in his pocket, pulling out a handful of trail mix and stuffing it into his mouth.

"Dude, really? How do you not get fat? Jade, go on." I placed the book back on the desk and traced its every detail. Jade handed me her small picture book, allowing me to flip through the pages. My eyes were as wide as could be, taking in as much as I could. My mind was searching its deepest corners for connections. For answers.

"As I was saying, Aaron was a great prophet, yet very little of his work was ever recorded. I was at the dig site to examine the art of the people to see if there were any more clues as to what Aaron had seen or said." Jade reached for the small book, and continued to flip through the pages. "He had died before the Jews could cross the Jordan River and was not able to give his work to anyone. Anyway, as I was excavating the area, I had remembered a local folktale that I had heard about the Nabateans, the local Arab peoples. It was said that they had found his works and hidden them away inside the temple within the walls to keep others from discovering what he had prophesied."

Her hands stopped on one of the small pages. Bryon took another bite of his trail mix, chewing quietly. I looked at Jade, her glance of approval moved my eyes to the small book. There it was, an image of the very book that lay on the desk in front of us. The design, my mark, the metal clasps. It was the exact one. I looked back up to Jade's amazed green eyes.

"Everyone else had dug and dug and found nothing. By the time I had got there, the place had become a 'world gem' and nothing could be accessed." Jade took a breath. She was now pacing the room. "I'm rambling, I'm sorry. Anyway, there was this itching feeling I had to examine the walls themselves. Within the walls didn't mean it was inside the structure, but inside the walls themselves. The art led me straight to it. Your symbol was thought to have been one of the uncoded words from the Dead Sea, but it wasn't. It was a map! It was the one symbol out of place—it lay there on the wall, so obvious. I cracked into that wall and there it was."

"Wow. You couldn't have just said that?" Bryon said.

"Shut up, Bryon," I said sternly. "Jade, can you open it?" His hands went up in the air.

"Well, that's the thing," Jade mumbled. "No."

"No. What do you mean no?" I spurted out. "All of that, and you can't even open it? How do you know it even has anything to do with me then?"

"I only have one of the keys," she said as she pointed toward an oddly shaped indention in the book. "I can't locate the other. I have been trying to find it ever since I found the book. It just…doesn't seem to exist."

"So then, why did you bring me here?" I demanded.

"Because I thought *you* may know where to find it, seeing as this book has your exact same markings on it. Your birthmark, the book cover. It's not just coincidence, and everything that is happening to you now and finding me..."

"Nothing is happening. I haven't seen one of those *things* in weeks," I yelled. Jade and Bryon both took a step back. I must have startled them. My mind was reeling with shattered hope. "I haven't done anything special in weeks! It *was* just a coincidence. A scientific anomaly." Frustration became me. The two stood there frozen and silent. I stormed out of the room in a fit of annoyance and anger. Jade had brought me here for nothing. That was the exact reason I never got my hopes up for anything.

"Dean, come back here, bro!" I could hear Bryon calling from down the cavern. It was too late; I couldn't do this anymore. I couldn't keep getting my hopes up for an explanation of my life, for something that would never come. I want to just move forward and be happy.

Abigail makes me happy.

Just as I was making my way up the spiral staircase and through the tree trunk, I stopped. Something was pulling at me, pulling at my innermost being to stop. Standing there, I remembered. Through the red rage, I remembered the gift I had, the gift that was given to me at birth. My book. Reaching into my pocket, my fingers traced the outermost markings of the leather-bound journal. The emblem on the front was raised and made of stone. Like it was braille for the blind, my mind read the symbol with great accuracy. I could see it as if it were in front of my eyes at the very moment.

"Dean...you okay?" Bryon saw me standing in the middle of the staircase, frozen. "What's wrong?"

Turning, I quickly ran down the stairs and past Bryon. A trail of dust followed as I sprinted into the small chamber that Jade was still frozen in.

"Dean, I didn't mean to—" Jade said.

"It's fine, move over," I said grabbing the book from the desk. Gazing upon that lock and recognizing the symbol, I knew this was not a coincidence.

"What are you doing?" Jade asked.

Bryon came rushing into the room. "Dude, you're really freaking me out." Jade gave him a pointed look. "*Us,* freaking *us* out."

"I have had this my entire life," I said, pulling out the leather-bound journal from my pocket. "I never knew what it meant. It is filled with stories and drawings that I could never understand. You're right, Jade, this isn't coincidence," I said as I peeled off the stone engraving from the surface of the journal. "I think this is what you have been looking for."

Bryon and Jade took a couple steps forward, leaning in. They watched in silence. Returning the stone key to its rightful resting place, I watched as it clicked into position.

We looked at each other in complete awe.

Slowly I turned the coupling clockwise.

Click…

Click…

Click…

CLACK.

The book's iron-cast guards popped open, dust erupted from the side, top, and bottom. Our hands flew up to guard our eyes from the dust, and Bryon and Jade stood dumbfounded. My mind didn't know what to believe. Have hope, don't have hope. It was all too much to take in.

"Well, go on then…Open it," Jade muttered. I had just been standing there staring. I didn't know what to feel. The excitement led me to feel hope, though my experience told me not to.

I held the book closed. "Whatever we find in this book, it doesn't change anything, right? You'll both still be my friends?" I looked at them for approval.

The two of them nodded in acceptance.

"Yes! Come on already!" Bryon threw up his arms, fists balled as if it was paining him to wait.

I began to slowly pry open the cover. Opening the book was like opening a window to my soul. I felt a sudden rush of life swoop through me as my body was filled with energy. The adrenaline pumped through my veins like a wild fire hose. I was finally going to know who I was—who my family was. Laying my eyes on the first pages, I was flooded with images and words that I could not understand, yet they felt so very familiar.

"What is it! What does it say?" Jade said as she came shoving her way in closer to see.

"What does all of this mean?" Bryon said, leaning over my shoulder.

"Be careful with that! It is very old!" Jade yelled as she swatted away Bryon's curious hands. "So what is it, Dean?"

"I don't know," I said. My eyes were like sponges absorbing as much information as they could. Even with all the visual information, my mind could not seem to piece any of it together.

I stared, hopefully numb at the newfound information.

Jade looked up at me. "What do you mean, you don't know? You had the key to this. You must know what it means." Bryon again leaned over my shoulder to get a closer look.

"I mean, I don't know. I have never seen any of this before. I don't know how to read any of this." I flipped from page to page and then pointed the finger at Jade. "How do you not know what language this is? Aren't you some kind of all-knowing scholar?" Bryon looked at Jade along with me.

"This is different," Jade answered. "I have never seen a language like this in all my years and all my studies. This is...not human. The typography doesn't fit any known language." She gently grabbed the book, first looking at me for approval. "There seems to be no commonality to any of the words either. It is almost erratic and impulsive."

I am the unending disappointment.

"Hmmm," Bryon mumbled, placing his hand on his mouth.

"There are over seven thousand languages in the world today," Jade spoke quickly. "Of which only about twenty-three are actually spoken. Of the seven thousand, I have researched over two-thirds that number and not one looks like this."

"So that means you have one third to go then, doesn't it?" I said madly. My wrist beginning to flicker a lowly red. Jade and Bryon took a step back, just before Jade moved back toward me.

"Dean, that could take years to complete." Jade's voice was soft. She placed her small hand on the top of my shoulder. I couldn't move. My mind continued to be tricked into hoping for something that would never be. She must have felt my sadness, my rejected happiness. Her other arm hand grabbed mine.

"Well, then you better get on it," I snarled, pulling my hand away from hers.

Jade pulled her hands close to her body. "That could take years even if I—"

"Look at this." Bryon had been flipping through the pages. "He looks just like you."

I broke my red gaze from Jade. We both turned to look.

Right there underneath Bryon's bony finger was a man. A man covered in shining golden armor from head to toe. My emblem imprinted on his chest. He stood there, wielding a golden sword covered in flames by his side. There he was staring back into our eyes on the steps of what looked like the gates to a massive towering structure with a blinding light being emitted from its innermost.

"Dude, that is totally you!" Bryon got louder as his excitement rose.

"That's not me. That is obviously someone else." Despite my protest, I wondered. Was that me? My eyes focused. "I mean, look at the way he stands. I don't stand like that. And look at his eyes—they are completely different." I tried to find flaws. Lies.

But he looked exactly like me.

"Dean," Jade said in a stern tone as if to say shut up.

Okay, so I knew it—I just couldn't bring myself to believe it. That was me, but when and how?

"How…" I stuttered.

"I don't know," Jade said, moving in front of my eye line. "But there is a lot of research to be done. I think it would be smart if you two stayed here for a while. I have a couple extra rooms just next to the main chamber and plenty of food and water," Jade said, offering her hospitality. "With everything going on, I'm sure we are not the only ones looking into this. It might not be safe out there."

"Dang, girl, how big is this place?" Bryon questioned. "You've been holding out on me," he said as he made his way back into the main chamber. "I get the bigger one!"

"Jade, you really believe that could be me?" I asked, still in the small room holding the book.

"I don't know," she said as she also made her way down the corridor and into the main cavern.

The walls all seemed so alive now. My mind was racing.

There were so many questions and thoughts rattling around in my brain, I couldn't make sense of any of them. I don't ever remember being like that or looking like that. There was no residual memory left in my mind that could tell me anything or give me anything to hold on to. The one resounding thought that kept repeating itself was that of my parents. If that was me...then who were they?

"Dean..." Jade called from the big cavern. "Come on, let me show you where you will be staying."

With that, I left the book open on the table, hoping that the answers would leap off the page in the night and creep down the hall and into my mind's eye so I could see clearly and understand all that was happening. Jade led me down the hall into the main chamber, which was still nicely lit by candles all around. From there she took me across the room, through an archway supported by stone beams, and into a medium-sized room made entirely of dirt and stone. There in the middle was a twin-sized bed with a hand-stitched quilt and feather pillow. A small dresser stood by its side.

"This is you," she said. "Dean, we are going to figure this out," Jade added, grabbing my hands. Her green eyes stared deeply into mine. "I promise."

"Thank you," I said. She let go of my hands and turned to leave. "Jade."

She stopped in the doorway. "Yes?"

"I'm sorry if I scared you earlier."

"It's fine. Sleep well," she said and left the room.

The smoke danced in the air as I blew out the candles and sat on the bed. The adrenaline had filled my body so quickly that I now became weak as it slowly dissipated from my being.

Being in the underground was an odd feeling as there was no sense of time. No sun, no moon. No light, no dark. As I lay down on the cozy twin bed, I stared up at the ceiling. Nothing but dirt. All around me, nothing but dirt wall. No pictures, mirrors, decorations...just dirt.

This must be what it feels like to be buried alive.

I pulled the quilted sheets over my body and slowly allowed my eyes to close. Abigail's face popped into my head like a familiar ghost. Comforted by her eyes, my mind slipped into its restful abyss.

CHAPTER 9

NILE

THE SMELL OF fresh roasted coffee beans filled my nostrils, awakening my senses. I hadn't slept that good in as long as I could remember. A proper bed, blankets, and a warm place—I felt like royalty in this dirt hole in the ground. Reluctant to leave my warm nesting place, I reached my toes out from under the covers.

The cold, hard ground met my feet, awakening the rest of my senses. Stretching my limbs, I made my drowsy way into the main chamber and followed the smell of caffeine.

"Ah, Dean! You're awake!" Jade said, already busy at a table.

"Is that coffee I smell?" I stretched my arms over my head one more time, taking in a deep breath.

"I went out and got us some breakfast. I figured bagels and coffee is a common good?" Jade said.

"You figured right!" Bryon said, sprinting in from the other bedroom and diving straight into the bag of bagels and slurping his coffee. "Mmmm . . ." Still in his pajamas, headphones around his neck, and hair a mess, his eyes lit up.

I moseyed on over at a good early-morning pace.

"Dean, come look at this." Jade pointed to the book. "I found a few things this morning while you were still sleeping." She placed it on a large tree stump in the main chamber, away from its resting place.

"How long have you been up?" I asked, making my way first to the coffee.

"I couldn't sleep much after everything. There was just too much on my mind, so I went back to the book. There was something that I had to see. Come look at this," she urged. Her dark black hair was up in a messy bun, and now that she mentioned it, it was obvious she hadn't slept. Her hands were shaky from all the coffee and Red Bull she must have used to fuel her all-nighter.

As I sipped my coffee, the warm liquid flowed throughout my body, bringing to life the sleeping cells in a caffeine tidal wave of energy. "What is that?" I asked, standing next to her and peering over the book as I tried to make sense of what she was showing me.

"Maybe we can't understand the language just yet, but the pictures…we can understand those. I think this book is all about you, similar to a biography. Your symbol is all over it from cover to cover." Jade quickly flipped through the pages like a flip-book.

"DUDE," Bryon gurgled, spilling crumbs out of his mouth and onto the book.

"Ugh, Bryon, chew with your mouth closed," I said.

"Sorry." More crumbs.

"Ah!" Jade said as she brushed them off, giving Bryon a death stare. He seemed to say sorry with his eyes, and she looked back to the book. "Look, here you are with your sword, the same one we had seen earlier with your mark engraved. And here you are again in the armor, but look how these people are looking at you, like some kind of god."

This was insane. I looked like some type of warrior. I wished I could remember this. The people in the images had their hands raised and their heads bowed. Some were interlocking arms and dancing with joyous smiles on their faces.

"Here is one of you in battle fighting some weird creature. The same creatures you have been describing to us, the demons," Jade said zealously, looking from me to the book and back to me, pointing to the photo.

"Okay, so what does all that mean? That I am immortal and don't remember it? How is that possible?" I said, stepping back.

"I don't know. All I know is there is actually a lot of Hebrew and Aramaic written in here. Those parts I *can* understand." She flipped to another page. "Look here. It says something about a *being*—you—coming down from the heavens in a cloud of flames to save the people from the Anubis." Jade was tracing her fingers along the lines as she translated.

"*The* Anubis?" I asked.

I was being sarcastic—I had no clue who Anubis was.

"YES! THE ANUBIS!" Jade was wide-eyed. She was clearly too excited to catch my sarcasm.

"I know you are all excited, but what is an Anubis?" Bryon asked, stuffing his already-full mouth with more and more bagels. We looked over to him, and he shrugged, cheeks bulging.

"Jade. Please inform this uneducated hermit who Anubis is." I crossed my arms. I really wanted to know too. This was just getting good.

"Anubis was believed to be the Egyptian god of the dead," Jade explained. "A demon some even said that would bring to life an army of the dead to enslave the world." She turned the page, revealing a closer, more-detailed image of Anubis. A large muscular creature, with a wolflike face covered in gold jewelry and wielding a large spear.

"So I came down in a...cloud of flames and fought this god of the dead?" I asked, crossing my arms.

"YES! And you would win!" Her arms went flying in the air in victory.

"So then why don't I remember any of this?" I asked. I couldn't match her enthusiasm quite yet. "I feel like something so extreme and awesome, I'd definitely remember. Especially fighting a god."

"It could be some form of amnesia. Here is my theory." She began pacing back and forth. Bryon and I stepped back to allow her room to think and explain. The main chamber was quiet in its anticipation of what she would say next. We stood by the desk as she paced her way to the bookshelf along one of the walls and then back and forth. "You came down here on a mission any number of years ago, and someone *trapped* you here."

Her arms went flying again. Bryon and I gave quick glances to each other. I wished I could see what she was seeing in her head right now. It must be an adventure in there. This small Latina had a lot of fire.

"They stopped you from returning to wherever it is you came from and suppressed your memories. Someone who doesn't want you interfering with their plans. Someone like a god of the dead, someone trying to take over the world once and for all," Jade said, making her way over to a small leather chair next to the desk Bryon and I were at and dropping down into it, developing the story.

"Jade, let's think logically for one second here," I said, spinning her chair around to face the book on the desk. "*If* someone had done all that, then why in the past sixteen years have they not taken over the world yet with an army of zombies or demons or whatever it is you say they are?" I asked.

"Yeah, Jade, how do you explain that?" Bryon mumbled as pieces of bagel fell out of his overstuffed mouth. Disgusting.

I'm gonna teach this guy to close his mouth while he eats someday.

"Well…I hadn't got that far yet," Jade said, looking up at me. "It is just a theory, and I believe that if someone is trying to do so, then they are working very hard at it as we speak, and we must begin work as well." She slammed her hands on the table.

I was lost. "What do you mean we must begin work?"

"I mean, you need to remember. We need to start your training; we need to find your armor and sword. Maybe that will spark your memory and bring back what you lost. Let me see that book of yours again." She reached out with a demanding hand for the journal in my back pocket.

"This is crazy," I said, pulling out my book and handing it over. "I can't believe that I actually believe you."

"Dude, what if you are like some god? How freaking cool would that be?" Bryon said before slurping down some hot coffee.

This guy could not avoid food when it was in front of him.

A new feeling had overtaken me, the feeling of excitement and hope. What if this really was the truth? Maybe I could finally find out who I am and what I was put here to do. I just never would have imagined that it would have been anything like this. What about Abigail—what would she think to find out that I was a god?

Come to think of it, she has a similar mark.

What does that make her?

"Dean, your book is filled with notes," Jade muttered softly.

"Yeah, I know. Why are you whispering?" I asked.

"Notes of the end times. Revelations," she said.

"No," Bryon said, leaning closer to us to look at the journal.

"So? A lot of books do too. I never could understand what it said. It's all written in some other language," I said.

"Most of it is Hebrew *and* the same language as in the book. I don't know which one that is, but what I *can* understand is…bad. It talks about a great deceiver and a woman. There are a lot of biblical references in here, a lot to the Messiah and His second coming." She looked through the pages.

"So this one is what, Christian? Isn't the other one written about Egyptian gods though?" I asked.

"Yes, it is," she said.

"So then what does that mean?"

"I'm not sure. It seems as if the two are from different time periods completely. Yet are telling a very similar story. Are there any other things you have from when you were born? Anything at all that could give us a clue?" She handed back my journal.

"No. Nothing. I…Wait." I gripped the journal harder, remembering something.

"What is it?" Jade stood up.

"My basket. I came in a basket at the hospital. I think I remember seeing it in the attic of my first foster family's home. They kept it—maybe that has something?" I looked from Bryon to Jade.

She smiled. "It's worth a try. Do you remember where they live?"

"Yeah, it's next to the hospital." I pocketed my journal.

"All right, then. Let's go," Jade said, moving toward the staircase.

"What? Right now?" I asked, still standing at the desk.

"Yes, we have no time to waste. We need you remembering—and remembering quick." Jade moved to a small shelving unit next to the staircase and pulled down a medium-sized brown leather duffel bag. She began packing it with random items off of the shelves.

"Hey, Jade, can I bring the rest of the bagels? It's kind of a far walk."

Byron was already filling his pockets. This guy.

With that we made our way up the stairs and out of the tree and began our journey back into town. The day was young, and the sun was rising over the mountains. The brisk air was calm and quiet. The birds flew overhead, landing in nearby trees as we passed, singing to the sky in their own beautiful language. Nature was alive and well. A brown bear greeted us as it crossed our path, making its way into his forest home, so gentle in nature. Bryon offered it a piece of bagel, tossing it near its feet. A bit foolish if you ask me, though the bear seemed to enjoy it and continued on its way. Nearing town, we could see a flock of deer grazing in the high grass on the side of the dirt path.

Hope was a beautiful thing. It opens the goodness of the world to the eyes of the beholder.

Everything felt…new.

"ALL RIGHT, IT's just around the corner," I said as we neared our destination. As I turned the corner, an eerie feeling swept over me. Before I could stop us…

"Hello, Dean," a figure said just feet away from where we had stopped. He hadn't even looked up. How did he know who I was? "Good to finally meet you," he added in a raspy voice, standing there with his ashy gray hair hanging down in front of his face. His red eyes darted up from the ground and locked with mine. "I've heard a lot about you," he said as he slid off his gray pinstripe coat jacket, hanging it on a nearby fence post. This guy was dressed to the tee in a purple silk button-up and gray tie.

"I think you have the wrong guy," I said, taking a step forward.

Jade and Bryon stayed frozen in place, not knowing what to do. The town was oddly quiet. No trucks moving about the dirt roads. The small cabins all silent and unwavering. The only thing that could be heard was the broken streetlamp hanging low above the street. Clicking with each flash of the round, yellow light.

"Oh no, I believe I have just the guy I'm looking for. You've been talking to my little cousin, Abigail," he said, rolling up his sleeves to reveal burn marks and strange tattoos all up his pale, white arms.

"Hey, man, we are just friends, okay? I don't want any trouble," I said, trying to remain calm.

My wrist began to warm up. I took my stance.

"Well, who says I don't?" he said, taking a step toward me. My wrist was now glowing red and hot. His eyes, they were like the others I had seen.

"I don't think you do..." I said, glaring back into his dead eyes. "Bryon, Jade, get behind me."

This guy couldn't be related to Abigail. No way.

The two stepped back.

"You seem to know a lot about me. Who are you?" I said, holding my ground.

"Ah, Dean!" He gripped his chest. "That hurts. I would think with the *history* we've shared, you would have at least remembered me." The veins in his arms began to pulse, and his muscles bulged, tightening his skin. His once-scrawny stature was growing.

This time I wouldn't wait for something to happen. I lunged as fast as I could, faster than one could blink, throwing a meteor of a punch. It was as fast and as hard as I had ever punched before I was scared it was going to kill the guy. I closed my eyes as my fist connected. The air shook.

Something was off.

I opened my eyes. My fist hadn't connected at all…He…he had caught it. It was like stopping a speeding bullet, no ricochet, no vibration, just pure stop. I stood there, staring. Dumbfounded.

Bryon and Jade, wide-eyed and slack-jawed, stood in awe.

"Seems the stories were wrong." He looked up with a smirk, tossing his long gray hair backward, still gripping my fist. He lifted me up off the ground like a whiffle bat, like I weighed nothing.

"What are you?" I asked just before being tossed like a bag of sand through the wooden fence and across the open field behind us.

I went tumbling amid the rocky, ungroomed ground. My face bloody and body bruised and bleeding, I felt as if King Kong had punched me square in the chest and then beat me into the ground.

"Dean!" Bryon yelled from the other side of the fence.

Jade was flipping through a book, searching frantically for something. Surprise, surprise. I hoped she'd find something and quick.

I raised my hand with the little strength I had left and motioned for Bryon to stay where he was.

"Pathetic. I was expecting so much more from you, Dean," the guy said as he ducked through the hole in the fence, making his approach to my crippled body. "There was so much fun I wanted to have with you, so many battles that the people would talk about for eternities. Just like old times!" His red eyes locked on mine. "I guess I will have to settle for a quick victory over the great Dean Mi—"

He was cut off as a huge explosion of lightning blasted between us.

BOOM!

A blinding light sent him flying almost fifty yards away.

My ears were ringing as if a concussion grenade had gone
off right next to me. Crawling and flipping on the ground, I
gripped my ears and shouted for Bryon. Opening my eyes, my
vision was blurry, though I could see Bryon and Jade running
toward me. My brain was shocked, dizziness set in as I tried to
stand.

"Dean…Dean…are you okay?" I couldn't make out who it
was.

Their voices sounded mumbled as the ringing persisted.
Jade came sliding in to where I was lying. "We got you. Come
on. Stand up." Bryon was running close behind. She picked me
up off the ground under her arm as Bryon came and took the
other side.

"We need to get out of here," Bryon yelled, though to me it
seemed like a low whisper.

Looking up, I could see Abigail's cousin wrestling with
something. Something bright. Something fast. Both were
moving fast—so fast they seemed to be jumping from one
place to another.

"What's going on?" I could feel the blood dripping from
my mouth. My eyes fluttered.

The two seemed frantic and were moving as fast as they
could with my dead weight underneath their arms. I don't remember even being picked up. My feet dragged and bounced
off the ground, hitting one large rock after the other. We headed for the fence opening.

I could hear pounding in the distance from where the other
two were fighting. Then, just as suddenly as it had begun, it
was quiet. I tried looking around for the man in gray suit, but
I couldn't find him. Or the other thing I couldn't see either.
They were both gone. As we neared the hole in the fence to
make our exit, Bryon and Jade stopped.

"What are you doing? Let's get out of here." I shoved my
weight in their arms.

"Dean," a soft voice said from behind us.

"What are you two doing? Let's go," I said again as they began turning me around.

A middle-aged blond man in shining silver and gold armor faced us. He was the tallest man I had ever seen. He stood solid and strong like a grown oak tree. His blond hair reached down past his shoulders and chest, glowing in the breeze. His blue eyes, aged and wise, had a familiar feel to them.

He was glorious.

He took us in with a deep gaze. As did we.

"Dean. You must come with me. There isn't much time," he said, turning to leave to an awestruck crowd. His accent, it was foreign. I couldn't place it though.

"Who are you?" Bryon asked first.

The man hastily turned back to us and paused. "I am Nile. A friend," he said as he revealed a necklace with a similar marking on it—my marking.

Jade and Bryon looked at each other and then to me. I stood, using my own strength, and gazed at the stone. Reaching for it, he interrupted, "I'll explain more soon. First we must get out of this place."

Agreed. All of the commotion would have drawn some attention, especially a hole in the fence and fire in the field. Local authorities would be here in no time. Nile reached out for me, motioning to Bryon and Jade that it was okay. He gently lifted me into his arms like an injured child.

We took a familiar route. It was the way to my place, the church. How did Nile know where I lived? How did he know my name? How did either of them know my name? I was in and out of consciousness.

My life is an endless list of unanswered questions.

I am the riddle.

We approached my safehold. She stood as elegant as ever, wood chips and all, welcoming us into the safety of her bosom.

Finally, we made ourselves comfortable inside my old glorious home. "Okay, guy—Nile—what's your deal?!" Bryon yelled pointing his finger.

At that moment, Uncle Homer came running out from the master quarters, yelling. "Boy, I told you not to come back with anymore of those bruises. Haven't I taught you anything!" Uncle pointed his old bony finger in my face. Nile gently laid me down on the red carpet in front of the pulpit.

I had never seen Uncle move so fast or be so angry.

"And you!" He was pointing at Nile. "What happened? You were supposed to be watching him! How did you let this happen?"

Wait, what? Did Uncle know this guy?

"Yes, sir, I take full responsibility," Nile said, bowing his head. "Legion, he was cloaking his power. I didn't know this would happen." Bryon sat on the front pew, lacing his fingers together, while Jade paced back and forth, biting her nails.

"He isn't ready. I told you. He is just starting to remember. We need more time." Uncle Homer was wringing out a warm cloth from the altar. He shuffled over to me, muttering something under his breath. He placed the wet, warm cloth on my forehead. My body felt warm instantly. Alive.

I managed to cough. "What is going on? Uncle, how do you know this guy?"

"Dean. My boy. There is so much you don't yet know. I was waiting for the right time, for you to remember on your own." Uncle Homer had his hand on my head.

"I am a friend," the big, blond man said. "Your uncle here was assigned to look after you on this earth. He was the only one strong enough to hide you without being noticed."

"What is he talking about, Uncle?" I asked.

But Uncle ignored me, instead talking to Nile. "We need more time—talk to *Him*."

"*He* will not listen to me. We cannot wait any longer," Nile said.

"Talk to who? Wait for what? Who was that guy in the field and how did he know who I am?" I stood to my feet, stumbling under the weight of my own body. I was becoming impatient.

Uncle looked up at Nile, distress in his old, wise eyes.

"His name is Legion," Nile said. "Though here he goes by the name of Kip. A very powerful demon. He and I have been battling for the past four generations, ever since you went missing."

Bryon and Jade stared silently at Nile, as did I. Waiting to hear more, my mind reeling from what this stranger was telling us.

"We begged Him to reveal to you your past, to heal you. He would say that 'in the right time you would return,'" Nile said, looking up at my roommate, J.C. "Those times were some of the hardest any of us had ever known. Try as we might, we just could not handle them without you. The humans even came up with a name for it—"

"The Dark Ages," Jade interrupted.

"Very good, Jade," Nile continued. "The balance had been lost and the scales tipped. Darkness ruled."

"All this because…I was…missing? Why?" I asked.

"You were hidden in Homer's custody for generations. Still to this day, we maintained to hide you from the Dark ones." Nile moved up the aisles of the church, observing the art. "They had taken your memory, your power. How, we still do not know. You were the only one He entrusted with His name. You were His chosen one, do you not remember?" Nile stopped and looked at me.

"Who is He?" I asked.

"Your father was so proud the day you were chosen." Nile moved closer. "The day He took you in to begin the training. You were such a young boy, yet so strong. Stronger than us all."

"I DON'T KNOW WHAT YOU'RE TALKING ABOUT!" I yelled at the top of my lungs as my wrist burst into flames. The heat waves emanated off my being like ripples on a summer asphalt road. My breathing came fast and deep, blood flowing like a raging river through my body. Jade, Bryon, and Uncle covered their eyes as a wind-like force erupted from my core. The cuts and bruises disappeared from all around my body. I stood in fire.

I am fire.

Nile slowly moved through the heat and flames. "My friend." His calming voice pierced my anger and confusion. His eyes were soft, filled with compassion. Like he could feel my hurt. Like he could feel my confusion. His large but gentle hand touched my shoulder. I began to cool down, it was as if he were taking away the pain. The energy from within returned to normal as I dropped to my knees.

Tears streamed from my face. I could feel Uncle's hand on my other shoulder.

"Who am I?" I said through the knot in my throat.

"You really do not remember, do you?" Nile asked. "You…are the son of the great Michael."

That statement meant nothing to me. Michael. Michael who?

"Michael…*the* Archangel Michael?" Jade exclaimed, leaping from where she was standing.

I stayed there on my knees, head hanging low as tears hit the ground like bombs from above, trying to absorb what was just spoken.

"Yes, Jade." Nile looked at Jade and back down to me. I looked up into his safe blue eyes. "*You* are the strongest of us all, even more so than your father. That is why He chose you."

"Who chose me?" I whispered as the last tear dropped from my eyes. It was so much to take in. I had not processed what was happening.

I looked over to Uncle and then back to Nile. They said nothing, slowly shifting their gaze behind them.

"Him," Nile said solemnly as he admired my cement-formed roommate. "The Son of God, The King of Kings, The Light...You must remember."

"I...can't..." I said, staring up at good, ol' J.C. Sadness and defeat swept over me.

"You must," Nile said softly as he slowly reached out his open palm, touching my sweaty forehead. "You must remember. We need you to."

The second his warm hand made contact with my clammy skin, a shock-like feeling electrocuted my mind. As if electric paddles had been placed directly onto my brain. Light flooded the room. My head whipped backward. Images flashed through my mind like passing buildings on a runaway train. I caught one for a brief second: it was bright, an arena-like setting such as the old Roman Colosseum, yet made of marble and gold.

A man approached me with an outstretched arm. "Get up, son. It's time to come back..." the deep voice said just as the image was wiped away and a thousand more whooshed by.

Another image caught my mind's eye, something so bright and warm. I couldn't make out what it was. The light it was emanating was brighter than anything I had ever witnessed; I could feel its warmth as the shining silhouetted figure drew closer to me. I reached out, and a feeling of comfort and security came sweeping in.

Just as I neared its embrace, I came to.

I gasped, as if being dropped in a lake of frozen water, searching for oxygen.

"Dean." Bryon leapt from where he was sitting to help stabilize me.

"I'm okay," I said, reassuring everyone. "I heard him."

"Heard who?" Jade asked.

"My father," I said looking up to Jade. "I heard him!" I turned to Nile.

He was gone.

"Nile?" I said as we all turned, looking for him. "Nile!"

He had vanished, and none of us had noticed.

"NILE!" I stood, yelling, anger replaced my joy. "No!" I yelled again, throwing over a flower setting from the pulpit. I wanted answers. I wanted to know more. My body became weak and my sight began to fade as my eyes grew heavy. With one last breath, I exhaled, "Father..." before falling back down to earth, eyes struggling to stay open.

"What should we do?" I could hear Jade's muffled voice.

Uncle Homer's raspy voice barely audible was the last thing I heard. "Let him sleep. He has been through a lot."

My eyes fluttered shut.

I am the lost wonderer.

ƆHAPTER 10

RESURGENCE

A BLINDING LIGHT was all I could see, soon fading to that of a beautiful summer day.

I was in a garden.

Surrounded by lush green bushes decorated with colorful fruits of all kinds and trees taller and wider than anything I could ever imagine. The soft grass was like walking on a cloud, bowing under the weight of my feet.

Not too far off, a gentle flowing river could be heard just behind an alien-like wall of magnificent crystals. Crystals so tall they shot up through the ground like skyscrapers reaching for the sun. Like diamonds, they sparkled bright, rainbows being born of their geometric prisms left and right with the changing rays of light.

"Hello!" I shouted. "Is anybody out there?"

"Son, I'm over here," a deep voice responded from the river.

Curious, I began to make my way through the thick brush. My heart started to race as I drew nearer and nearer to the origin of the voice. Everything was so gloriously shining with white light and beams of energy. I reached for the massive crystals, tremendous in size, placing my small hand on their hard, smooth surface, I could feel their energy, their life. This garden seemed to be made of music, light, and love.

It was as if everything were alive, breathing.

Admiring the stones, I continued to make my way around their guardian-like structures. Rainbows of light bounced in all directions. Green vegetation and trees alike surrounded their base. I could hear the gentle flow of a river beginning to near.

There, in the beams of light, a man knelt in the shining silver and gold armor I had seen before. The same that was in the book.

"Come over here, son," he said without getting up as he gathered water into a skin-like container. The light reflecting off his armor was almost too bright to handle, like staring into the sun itself. I shielded my eyes.

"Hello," I said sheepishly.

"Hello," he said, turning from the river.

My mind processed the moment so slowly it was as if I could see every second passing like an extension in time. His bright eyes were pure white, no drop of color at all, and seemed to glow from their enclosure. He stood tall and strong like a king, with an aura of gold light surrounding his entire being.

"My son."

I stared up at him in awe. His presence, glorious.

"Father," I said, staring, "Father!" I leapt, running into his strong embrace. "I remember." Tears streaked my cheeks.

"My boy, I don't have much time," he said urgently, grabbing me by the shoulders.

"What's happening? Where are we?" I asked.

I had so many questions. Like a child with an eager mind. I am the curious cat.

"I'll explain all soon," he said. "Ever since you were captured, Earth has been growing dark. They have grown stronger than we anticipated."

"I don't understand. Where have you been, and why did you abandon me?"

"I didn't abandon you, my son. I would never. He chose you for a reason. You are stronger than I ever was and ever could be," he said. "Your mission was to protect the humans from all the evils, to maintain the balance. And you did so for generations among generations, thousands of years." He held me at arm's length with a proud smile. "Though it seems the abominations had been training all those years as well, learning. You were taken and placed in the darkest corner of Hell by Santhanus, one of 'the most unclean's' strongest demons. The fallen ambushed you after they found they could not defeat you on their own."

Visions flashed into my mind. I was surrounded, a hundred—no, a thousand—demons with gnashing teeth and clawing appendages ripping at my skin. I could see my father; he was flying down toward me from within a cloud of fire. Reaching out his hand. Santhanus. He stopped him. Pain. All I could feel was pain. His claws were under my ribs, gripping my soul.

"Son."

I snapped out of it.

"I tried to save you, but I was weak. I could not enter that realm. I begged Him to save you day after day for years on end...I thought you were lost to me. It took every ounce of my being to not defy His rule and try to go back for you. He gave you an ability that none other like us possessed." My father's eyes were filled with compassion.

"Who is us?" I asked.

"The Archangels." He looked up. I followed his gaze. Flying like beautiful eagles above us, they soared. Their wings glorious and wide. The purest-white feathers I had ever seen lifted them through the clouds. Rays of golden light danced among them.

"Angels…what did He give me? What ability? Who is he?" I asked, looking back to my father.

"Son, I have to go…I'm sorry I couldn't tell you more," he said as he rushed to tie the water sack to his belt.

"Wait, Father, I have so many questions! How did I escape? Why don't I remember any of this?" I shouted.

"I love you, my son. Remember, He is always with you. Have faith—your strength is returning, I can feel it. Humanity needs you now more than ever, my boy. Two weeks." His voice faded as he vanished into a strobe of blinding light.

"Father!" I yelled as I once again became weak, and my eyes grew heavy as if being pulled down by bags of cement.

In an instant I was out. Dark.

—§—

"Dean…Dean." Bryon's voice broke the silence in my ears.

As I opened my eyes, the candlelight brought him into sight.

"Phew! We thought you died! Hey, Jade, he is okay! He's alive!" Bryon yelled. Jade was sitting on a pew sifting through the pages of a large leather book. I was back in the church. The old wooden church. Warmly lit by the remaining candles Uncle Homer must have brought out.

"What happened?" I asked.

"Dude, you just passed out and hit the floor." Bryon's arms flailed about in what I assumed was a lame impression of me. "Your head bounced like a basketball. We thought you accidentally died. You were out for like three days!"

"Three days!" I yelled.

Bryon laughed. "Ha ha, nah. It was more like a few hours."

"You idiot," I said, sitting up and punching him in the arm. "I spoke to him."

"Spoke to who?" Bryon asked.

"My father."

"You spoke to the Archangel Michael!" Bryon's eyes widened. "Man, that is so freakin' cool! What did he say? Was he all, 'son, come hither. I must tell you of my battle stories'...or, or what! Tell us!"

"Jade, what are you reading?" I asked, avoiding Bryon's mindless questions. He continued acting out what he perceived to have happened in silence.

"The book from my library. I'm trying to make sense of this all," she said, flipping through pages. Jade always seemed to be in her own world when she was in a book. Or she simply chose not to pay attention to us until she needed to. Good choice.

I stood, making my way over to Jade. "Let me see that," I said, grabbing the book from her. "My father said that humanity needs me more than ever. I think your theory was partly right."

"What do you mean partly?" Jade asked, intrigued.

"I am not a god by any means, but I think you were right about an army of the dead," I said, now flipping through pages myself.

"Oh shit." Bryon stood wide-eyed between the pews.

"Look here, it says, 'The army of the Lord will be led by the chosen one, the son of the highest general.' The general must be my father, against the army of darkness."

"So *you* are going to lead an army? An army of what?" Bryon asked.

"Angels," I said matter-of-factly.

"Angels? How the heck are you going to lead an army of angels when you couldn't even fight off that rich kid in the suit earlier? And is that what you are, an angel?" Bryon jumped off the pews and came closer to Jade and I.

He had a good point. "Yes…no. An Archangel."

"Archangels are the first in command of the third choir, the protectors and messengers…I thought there were only three though," Jade said, running her fingers through her hair with a concerned look on her face.

"How do you know all this?" I asked.

"There are three orders of angels according to Pseudo-Dionysius the Areopagite…" Jade continued. We stood in a circle around the altar with J.C. at the head.

"Who?" Bryon was utterly lost…as was I, but I'll let him ask the questions.

"He was a Christian theologian and philosopher in the late fifth century." Jade grabbed the book back from me and pointed to a page with drawings on it. "Look."

The drawings were of these seemingly floating bodies with three pairs of wings, and another of a being with four faces and two sets of wings. The next was similar to what looked like a wheel covered in eyes. The next two looked more human-like but with pretty wings.

"The first choir is made for those holy beings serving closest to God and the Son. They are called Seraphim." She flipped the page and pointed to an image. "The ones who literally are on fire with their burning love for God, covering their bodies with six wings. The next is a Cherubim. This being has four faces, one of a man, an ox, a lion, and an eagle. These beings guard God's throne and the way to the Tree of Life." These were creatures I had never seen before, massive in size like something that could take on the likes of Godzilla. And beautiful, their faces so perfect and bodies muscular and strong. "Next are the Wheels, they literally look like wheels covered in many eyes to see all and hear all, presenting man's needs to God." The images in the book were incredible, I began to feel a sense of remembrance. The colors were all so bright and vivid, the creatures themselves looking like kings and queens of alien races, all bowing to a mysteriously bright light in the middle of the pages. Surrounded by white marble and pure gold accents, the locations felt so real. So close.

"The second choir is held by the Dominions. They are described as looking like beautiful humans with wings of an eagle and wielding staffs with balls of light fastened to the heads of their scepters. They are the ones keeping charge of the lower angels and are said to rarely make appearances to humans... I could go on and on. The Virtues are next, then the Powers of Authorities maintaining the cosmic balance, and finally the Archangels and angels."

Jade flipped the page and there he was. My father. The page itself was engrained with gold and light.

"That's him," I said, pointing to the image of the man in shining armor. "That's my father."

"Whoa..." Bryon gawked.

"Wait, look here. There is a fourth image outside the ring of the three choirs. What is that?" Jade said as she saw a scribble on the page. She ran again to her bag and pulled out a magnifying glass. "Dean, that's your symbol."

I grabbed the magnifying glass.

She was right.

"Look here, it is hidden in all three of the choirs. Look." Jade pointed out that there it was, in each of the descriptions and images, the small symbol hiding away.

"Whoa..." Bryon was like a broken record player. Though I was thinking the exact same things.

"There is probably another clue in here somewhere..." Jade began flipping through the pages again, brushing her long brown hair away from her eyes. As she searched, all I could think of was my father. I had finally met him after all these years.

He didn't abandon me, he did love me.

It just occurred to me, I didn't ask him about my mother.

"Dean. Look." Jade stopped on a page and pointed to a small drawing. It was an image of a newborn baby still wrapped and in a basket. There on the basket was my symbol, the same one that marked my body. "Look how all the symbols of each choir are there in line with yours. Incredible."

"Okay, guys, slow down," Bryon said, placing his hand on the pages covering the images. "I'm still wondering how you are supposed to lead some army to fight some other army. I mean we are barely scratching the surface of all this. A few hours ago you thought you were human with some kind of superpower, of which you can't even control." Bryon was adding some good insight. The wind creaked at the rickety windows.

"You're right. I don't know how to control this…gift," I said, looking Bryon and Jade in the eyes, speaking honest truth. "All I know is my father needs me to remember—*humanity* needs me to remember. I don't know how any of this is possible or why I was the one 'He' chose to give this gift to, but I've got to try. This is the first time in my entire life that I have a purpose, that I am meant for more. I can't let my dad down. I can't let you guys down," I said with hope in my heart and a fire in my soul. I guess hoping wasn't such a bad thing after all.

"Great speech, Dean. Still not too sure. And who is 'He'?" Bryon said.

Bryon was stepping on my hope. I knew it was for the best. I know he is trying to pull the answers out of me. I looked over to Bryon and then to Jade.

"He…is Him…" Jade said, pointing to the large statue of my roommate, good old J.C.

We all looked, it was something so surreal none of us knew how to truly react.

Uncle Homer came walking in through the back room. "Bit of a rollercoaster, these last twenty-four hours, eh, boy?" His hands shook as he carried a tray of drinks to us. "Hot cocoa. Good for the soul, trust me," he said with a wink.

"Uncle, who are you?" I warmed my hands with the hot mug.

"No time for that. Seems you are at a bit of a disadvantage. None of this was supposed to happen for at least another generation. I guess that's what you can expect from Lucifer though, huh? Always impatient and power-hungry." Uncle made his rounds, handing out the cocoa and came back to me. He placed the tray on the tabletop and grabbed my hands palm face up.

"Lucifer?" Bryon choked. "I'm sorry, did I just hear you say *Lucifer*, as in the devil?"

"That is correct. The snake himself," Uncle said, still observing my palms. The wrinkled skin on his hands felt like leather infused with life and wisdom.

"Well...I'm out." Bryon turned, placing his hot cocoa on the table, and began walking to the front door.

"Bryon, come on, man," I said. "We can't do this without you." He stopped just before the door and turned back to face us. I really couldn't do this without Bryon. Although he brought out some annoyance in me, he always had good intentions. He is my best friend.

Wow. I never thought I would have one of those.

"Oh, yes, yes you can. You don't need me at all. What do I bring to the table, huh? You're a super angel, Jade is a historical genius, and I'm what? The good-looking, handsome, wise one? What good does that do you?" Bryon stated with his hands on his hips. And there is the good, old Bryon I know and love.

"Oh, wise one, we need your knowledge and guidance. Please don't leave," Jade said, jokingly monotonous.

"Funny, I'm out." Bryon turned again.

"Bryon, wait, we do need you. You are the glue," I said.

"The what?" Bryon and Jade said.

"The glue, man. You hold us together. You help keep us grounded. We need that. Please, for me?" I asked.

"The glue, huh? You need me, huh? Fine. Fine. But I'm not happy about it," Bryon said slumping into one of the far pews. I saw a small smirk quickly appear and disappear from his face.

"Ah-ha. There she is," Uncle Homer chimed in, pointing to a line on my hand.

"What is it?" I pulled my hands closer to my face.

"Your partner. You're going to need her if you intend on winning against Lucifer." Uncle Homer made his way to the altar, got on all fours, and began knocking on the wooden floor beams.

"Uncle, what are you doing?" I asked, walking over.

"Remember all the stories I would tell you about my time in the desert? About my time overseas?" He found what he was looking for as he hit a hollow spot.

Lifting the wooden plank, he pulled out a tattered cloth.

"What's that?" Jade ran over and leaned down next to Uncle.

"This is what is going to keep you all hidden. Can't be traveling the world all willy-nilly then, can you?" he said, standing up and unraveling the cloth. Inside was what looked like a necklace of sorts.

"Traveling the world?" Byron said from afar. "I'm sorry. Did I hear that correctly?"

"When you were taken from us, Nile fought for your sword. The Sword of Light. Its power is unprecedented, and Lucifer knows that. We hid it from him and all others. Even those on our side know that with it in their hands, the tides could be shifted."

"Where did you hide it?" I asked. The wind from outside rose, causing the walls to shiver and the windows and doors to shake.

"The only place we knew it would be safe: its original resting place—"

"Eden," Bryon said, standing up and walking over to where we were. We all quickly looked at him, eyebrows raised. "What? I read the Bible once before!" Our looks persisted. "Okay, I read the cool parts. Sue me." Uncle grabbed the book from Jade and flipped to another page. The image was of a flaming sword at the gates of The Garden.

"Where in the world are we going to even start looking for that?" Bryon said, pulling out a bagel from his pocket and stuffing it into his face. "No one has known the actual location of The Garden since…ever."

"'After He drove the man out, He placed on the east side of the Garden of Eden Cherubim and a flaming sword flashing back and forth to guard the way to the tree of life.' Genesis 3:24." Uncle Homer pointed to the photo. "This is the only place Lucifer knows he is not allowed, and the only place no angel dares threaten the Cherubim."

"But how do we get there?" Bryon asked again.

"You will head to the Middle East. To the place where the four-headed snake meets…Baghdad."

"DAMN IT!" KIP yelled angrily as steam billowed off his shoulders. "Every time I'm close…he messes it up!"

The room was a hot, dark, wet dungeon decorated with black candles. The bed in the middle of the room was lined with red silk linen and a tall wooden bed frame boasting a red-and-golden canopy attached to the intricately carved posts. A large firepit surrounded by a round wall of stone lit the room from nearby. The pungent smell of mold and charcoal lingered in the stale air.

"Be calm, brother. You're going to overheat again," said the slithering voice of a young girl lying in the bed.

"He probably told the boy everything by now! His strength is returning, I can feel it." Kip paced back and forth, furious.

"Not to worry, I have smelled the child up close. He is not who he once was. His powers have diminished," she said again as she ran her fingers through her long black hair. "You will defeat him with ease."

Kip stopped his pacing in front of the pit of fire. His pale, scarred face illuminated by the yellow and red flames. "That is the last time that pest Nile interferes with my business. I need the stone!"

"You know Uncle will not give you the stone—he is saving it for you-know-who," she said with a stern face and monotonous temper.

"I will take it then if that's what it takes. I will not fall again to that lackey Nile. Let alone the brat," Kip said, placing his hand in the fire playing with the flames.

"Come to bed, Legion. Come keep me warm," she said with an enticing tone, softly patting the bed.

Kip made his way over to the bed and sat at the edge. She crawled over to him and began to unbutton his shirt from behind, placing her hand on his chest. "Come, brother, now is not the time to get worked up." Beth's face came into the candlelight as she placed her head on his shoulder and whispered something in his ear with her forked tongue.

"I will get him if it's the last thing I do. I don't need Uncle's help. I will prove to him I am the one who deserves the stone," Kip said, paying little attention to Beth's advances.

"Yes, we will show him your strength…The kingdom will be yours," she said, turning his head toward hers and placing her lips onto his. The fire raged as it grew and danced around the room. The two intertwined their decrepit bodies and rolled in the flames.

SOME TIME HAD passed, and the day grew dark as the sun receded behind the mountains. The birds and all the animals had settled in for the night, and the woods were quiet. All the lights in the town were slowly put to rest one by one as the people headed home. Over at the Li'ved castle, a light shone through one of the windows. Mr. Li'Ved was in his office, sitting at his desk. Always in a suit and tie; this time it was blue. He sat hunched over as he scribbled signatures on paper after paper. It was business as usual.

"Yes, Flint. What can I do for you?" he said, without skipping a beat as he signed away at the documents.

With that, a puff of smoke materialized into a large, dark creature. It stood there on its backward legs, burnt skin, its eyes piercing red, with a snout-like face and tusks like a boar's.

"Sir. I have news," it said in a raspy, deep voice.

"Have you found it?" Mr. Li'Ved said monotonously, with his eyes glued to his papers as he continued to sign.

"No, sir," the creature said.

"Well, then what is it you are bothering me for at this hour?"

"I apologize, sir, but I believe I have located the boy."

Mr. Li'Ved stopped his signing and placed the pen on the table, slowly turning to look at the abomination.

"Where is he?" Mr. Li'Ved said, staring into Flint's deep red eyes.

The ugly demon took a slight step backward. "Here, Your Grace. In AngelFire."

Mr. Li'Ved shrugged it off and turned back to his desk. "Impossible. I would have sensed his energy."

"Legion himself fought the boy earlier," Flint said, taking a small step forward.

"Good, so then he has been dealt with." Mr. Li'ved said, beginning to sign his papers again.

The creature said nothing.

"He *has* been dealt with…" Mr. Li'Ved reiterated, stopping the signatures and gripping the pen tightly.

"No, sir, a war angel interfered. Nile."

"Nile!" Mr. Li'Ved jumped out of his seat. "He has been a pain in my ass for millenniums. Where is the boy now?" His eyes enraged with red fire. His body literally steaming through his suit.

"We don't know, sir. He disappeared after the encounter. Legion was forced to retreat."

"You are certain of the boy?"

"Yes," the beast continued. "I first took notice of him when I was on mission. He was at a party. He had the mark, sir. His power is growing. I have tracked him for the past month to make certain before coming to you. It is him."

"Show me." Mr. Li'Ved approached the creature, reaching out his hand.

The creature closed its fiery red eyes just as Mr. Li'Ved's hand touched its forehead. Visions of Dean went flashing by first at the party, then in the junkyard, running up to the house and speaking with Abigail, and finally with Bryon and Jade as Legion approached.

"Ah!" Mr. Li'Ved exclaimed as he pulled his hand from the beast. "I let that boy in my house! I fed him and let him leave! I knew I had sensed something in him, as did Beth. I thought he was a half-breed!" Mr. Li'Ved quickly turned and gripped his desk, crushing the edges in his bare hands. "I showed him the room of antiquities. His power, it is diminished. It is so low I couldn't tell." He flipped his chair over his desk. "AH!"

"Sir, he was here?"

"Abigail." Mr. Li'Ved said deeply. Burn holes began to appear through his suit jacket.

"What would you like me to—"

The door to the office swung open.

"Hey, Daddy! I…" Abigail said as she came bursting in.

Faster than the blink of an eye, the creature was gone without a trace.

Abigail looked around. "Were you talking to someone in here?"

"No, baby," Mr. Li'Ved said as he reslicked his hair back on his head and straightened his suit.

"Oh, I thought I heard you talking," she said, still holding onto the door handle. "What happened to your chair—"

"Yes, I'm sorry, I was. It was a conference call. I know how much you hate when I bring work home. I didn't want you to know. I'm sorry," he said as he walked up to Abigail, placing both hands on her shoulders and staring her in her eyes. "And the chair. You know how I get when I receive bad news. It was just something I wasn't expecting to hear, that's all. It will be dealt with."

"It's okay, Daddy," she said, looking him deep in the eyes and pulling him in for a hug.

"Did you need something, baby?" he said, pushing back a bit, still in her embrace.

"Oh yeah, I just wanted to tell you that I am going over to Cherry's for a little while. We are going to have a girls' night, is that okay?"

"Of course, baby. Just be careful and make sure to call me when you get there."

"Thanks, Daddy," she said, giving him another big hug.

Just as she was turning to leave, he asked, "Hey, baby…Where has Dean been lately? You haven't had him over."

"I don't know, I haven't talked to him in a while. Why? You never care about any of my friends, weirdo," she said, looking back at him.

"He seemed like a nice young man. Be sure to invite him over for dinner again soon, okay?"

"Ohhhkayy...bye, Daddy," she said with a confused look on her face as she made her way out the office door.

"This time he won't be leaving so easily..." Mr. Li'Ved whispered to himself under his breath. He sat back at his desk, readjusting his suit and wiping it from where Abigail had hugged him.

Leaving his office, he made his way through the marble-laden hallways and into his room of antiquities. Dimly lit, the room was cold and eerie. As he made his way to the large object being covered by a black linen, his hands dragged on each piece of art, seemingly drawing memories from each. Growing near, the black sheet began to shake violently.

"Soon...your time will come soon," he said, placing his hand on the object.

THE NIGHT WAS brisk as Abigail made her way over to Cherry's house. A full moon lit the town with its soft blue light as the stars hid in its wake. A car would pass on occasion on the empty dirt roads, lights blinding as they passed Abigail. The cold air stung her nostrils and awakened her senses. The thought of Dean had tormented her. Though she tried to think little of him and the way he had felt, it was like wishing for rain in the middle of a drought, impossible to not think of. *Where had he gone? Did I do something to upset him?* The thoughts swirled around like snow in the breeze. As she walked the lonesome roads, he was all she could think of. *Why had her father taken a liking to him so much?* The confusion danced around her mind like a ballerina performing "The Nutcracker." About halfway to Cherry's house, Abigail stopped.

The thoughts were too overwhelming. She turned, changing directions to head to Dean's place.

Cherry could wait.

Hidden in the woods, watching as she altered routes, Kip stood in the shadows.

Abigail could feel the eyes burning a hole in the back of her head. She whipped around in a circle, seeking the energy.

"Hello? Daddy?" Abigail shouted.

Nothing.

She continued forward, back on the path to Dean's.

The eyes appeared once again, finding their target, following her every move. As she passed under each lamppost, her golden-blonde hair shone brightly as if lit for the stage by spotlight. Not far behind was the dark shadow creeping around the beams of light.

The church in sight, Abigail drew near and could see a light on inside the wooden enclosure.

Buzz. Buzz.

Her phone vibrated in her pocket. She stopped under the lamppost just outside the church to check it. The message from Cherry read: *Where are you?*

She started responding: *Be right there I had to stop for—*

Before she could finish the text message, she saw it. The reflection in her phone showed a man standing behind her.

Abigail screamed. "Ah! Get back!"

"DID YOU HEAR that?" I asked. A scream had come from outside the doors. "That sounded like Abigail."

The three us looked at each other and ran for the door, me outpacing the others in only a few strides.

—§—

"Abigail, don't be afraid. It's me, Uncle Flint," the tall man said.

The man came into her view under the lamppost from out of the shadows. He was a tall, gangly man and pale as could be. "Don't you remember me? I've known you since you were a little girl."

Abigail shook her head no and trembled as she stood frozen in fear. She must have heard the door of the church slam open. She turned to look and then back to the man.

He took a step closer. The man continued as he approached Abigail. His black-and-white suit began to stretch at the seams. His arms and legs seemed to grow in length. His six-foot stature increasing in height. "You need to stop what you are doing. Your father cannot have you interfering with his work."

"I don't know who you are—please just stay away from me," she said, taking a slow step backward and tripping on a crack in the road. She stumbled onto her butt.

—§—

"Abigail!" I shouted from the doorstep, spotting her red jacket under the lamp and a man quickly approaching.

"Dean, you aren't ready." Uncle Homer came from behind me, grabbing at my arm. "I will call for help. Stay here." I couldn't wait. I couldn't stand by, idly watching the girl my heart beat for tremble in fear. I looked at Uncle, still holding my arm, and gently pulled my hand from his grip. "Dean," he whispered faintly, eyes closing.

I turned to Abigail and ran. Uncle's eyes had looked so scared. I had never seen his eyes like that before, full of fear.

"Please just stay away," Abigail said fearfully, crawling backward while keeping the man in sight. As she did, her birthmark began to flicker a white glow.

"You must not interfere. You don't know who you are dealing with. I am here to protect you." The man stepped forward again, now reaching out his long, ghoulish arm.

"Dean!" Abigail shouted, not turning away from the pale man.

His eyes began to glow the bright red.

"She said stay away!" I yelled as I came running in between her and the man, putting Abigail behind me. Jade and Bryon must have followed me out, as they slid on the snow right next to me. The man pulled his long, skinny arm back to his side. Jade and Bryon grabbed Abigail and began pulling her back to the church, dragging her feet through the snowy ground.

"Don't worry. Dean's got this. He's kind of...special," Bryon said through heavy breaths.

"You don't know who I am, do you, boy?" the man asked me as I stood at the ready. Both of us stood under the streetlamp, our bodies prepared. The roads were empty and frigid as an icy breeze blew past. The smell of burning charcoal was becoming all too familiar. Sweat drops began to form on my forehead. I could feel them freeze as they fell.

My wrist began to glow a deep blue.

The man turned his head ever so slightly, looking at my wrist.

I remembered. "Those eyes..." I had seen those eyes before. The familiarity was hitting me like a belly flop in still waters.

"Dean, get back!" Abigail shouted just before Bryon and Jade pulled her farther away, nearing the doorstep of the church for safety.

The man looked deep within my soul. "Yes...these eyes."

His body began to grow and morph, shredding his clothes as he grew bigger and bigger. His arms stretched down to the ground, his knees broke and bent backward, his jaw dropped eight inches as it broke open and reformed into a snout. The sound of breaking bones echoed in the quiet streets, causing chills to run up and down my own. The tusks came next as they grew out of his mouth, shaking his head. His ghostly pale skin darkened from one shade to the next instantaneously, now blackened and burnt.

The creature stood there nearly the same height as the lamppost overhead.

I stood my ground, as the memory of Chase's party flashed through my head. "I remember you," I said. "I'm not afraid of you." I felt my body begin to give off a great heat. My long, black peacoat blew in the wind as burn holes formed all through it.

"Asorath," Abigail quietly mumbled.

"Huh?" Bryon asked.

"Nothing," Abigail said. Her body language shifted from fear to confusion as she released tension.

Jade and Bryon gawked in amazement as neither had ever seen anything like the creature before. *He is going to kill him. Asorath is different, stronger*, she thought to herself. Abigail's eyes widened as she fought to get past the human blockade Bryon and Jade had made. With all her might, she broke free and pushed between the two to get a better look at the looming monster.

"Abigail…" Bryon murmured, reaching for her shoulder to stop her.

"He's going to get killed!" Abigail yelled as she made a move to run toward Dean.

"Abigail, stop!" Bryon ran and tackled her to the snowy floor. "He's got this. Trust us," Bryon said, looking her in the eyes and then up to Dean. Her facial expression was filled with anger. Knowing who Flint was pulled at her heart as she desperately tried to wriggle free from Bryon's clutch.

MY BODY BEGAN to grow so hot that my favorite coat was now disintegrating. My bare skin held against the icy wind. Scars tattooed my body. My mark was glowing brighter than I'd ever seen before.

"I see your strength is returning," Flint said, looking down on my ant-sized body, oozing goo dripping from its mouth with each slimy word. "No matter, I will make quick work of you yet."

He lunged forward in a fiery ball of smoke.

We clasped hands as he reached for me, our strength even. Face-to-face, we stared the other in the eye menacingly and unwavering. The heat emitted from the two of us began to melt the very ground beneath our feet. His body literally on fire.

"You are stronger than I thought you would be—it is coming quicker than we anticipated," the creature struggled to say as it pushed back against my shaking fists.

"Just like riding a bike," I forced out as I tried not to show that I was giving it my all. Veins pumping jet fuel through my body, throbbing above the skin.

The creature was becoming too much to handle. I dug my feet into the ground as the creature pressed harder. "AH!" I pushed back harder, my muscles grew and bulged. The ground below me began to break and depress as I was forced down into it. The heat became unbearable. I turned my head, breaking eye contact with the creature to protect my eyes from the smoldering waves of the flames. My bones felt like sticks of bamboo bending under the pressure, about to snap.

The lamppost was red-hot and bending from the melted metal.

"Dean!" Jade yelled from the church. "Dean…" The rest was inaudible.

I pressed with all my might. The creature grew bigger, its hands the size of stove tops set to high heat.

"AHHHH!" I let out a loud yell as I was brought to my knees, still pressing against the creature.

"I'm going to enjoy this," Asorath said as my strength gave way.

My hands dropped by my sides, and head hung in defeat. On my knees, I sat in the asphalt crater. The bright glow from my wrist faded.

"Father…" I whispered as I looked up at the creature's gaping, snarling mouth, which was fast approaching.

"Dean, no!" Abigail shouted. I turned to see her breaking free from Bryon and Jade's protection.

She ran as fast as a beam of light, grabbing hold of me.

I remember her holding me. It was warm. A different kind of warm.

Her wrist flared up a pure white light, brighter than the sun, blinding the creature.

"Ahh!" Asorath let out a loud roar, covering its eyes from the piercing white light.

Another flash of light exploded onto the scene.

Nile. Uncle. Both of them were standing above us.

"Dean, Abigail, get out of here," Nile said in a strong, calm voice, then turned to the creature. "Asorath, you are not to interfere with the balance! Be gone!" he yelled at the blinded creature. Uncle stood by his side, chest puffed and muscles enlarged. He looked young and strong.

"Nile. Homer. How nice of you to join us. These two cannot protect you forever, boy," Asorath snarled. "Your father will hear about this," the monster said in a raspy voice, pointing at Abigail. Once again, it was gone in a puff of smoke.

The night was calm.

The cool night air returned abruptly as the heat subsided. Nile and Uncle stood by our side as Abigail sat there with my weakened body in her arms, surrounded by the asphalt in the meteor-sized crater. Abigail was looking down at me with tears in her eyes. She was saying something, but I couldn't make it out. This was all so surreal. It was an out-of-body experience. I could see her mouth moving, yet I couldn't make the words. I couldn't move. My body was drained. I couldn't speak. I am the observer.

Their heavy breathing could be seen in the frozen air as Bryon and Jade ran over where Nile, Abigail, Uncle, and I were under the melted streetlamp. "Dean, are you okay?" Jade asked, standing over top. All of them were looking down on me from above. The light from the lamp glowed around their heads like halos. How ironic. I could feel my body losing what little strength it had left. With the four of them around, I felt safe. I let my eyes shut. Still conscious, I rested, aware of my surroundings through sound, I could hear them speaking.

"He is out. Get him inside," Uncle commanded.

"Is he going to be okay?" Bryon sounded scared.

I had never realized how much Bryon really cared until now. He truly was my best friend. I tried to open my eyes. Though they weren't fully open, I could make out images through the small slits.

Nile looked over at Bryon, placing a hand on Abigail's shoulder. "He is going to be okay," he said as he placed his arms underneath my body, lifting me from Abigail's clutch. Abigail's arms dropped by her side, along with her eyes.

"Come on, Abigail. Let's get inside. It's too cold out here," Bryon said, helping her up as she stared at the ground. A tear fell from her wide-open eyes. "Come on," he said again, lifting her to her feet. The five made their way into the church. The warm interior enveloped the icy bodies that entered. Lit by a small fire, the light danced around the room. "What just happened? What was that thing?" Bryon asked.

"That was Asorath, otherwise known as Flint," Nile said.

"What did he want with us?" Jade asked. Their shadows flickered in the candlelight. The statue of J.C. glowed above the flames.

"He is a very strong demon, one of three considered to be a hierarchy of Hell. He came for him," Nile said as he looked over at me lying by the fire. Uncle had shuffled off to another room in some hurry.

"Dean was not prepared to fight him. Maybe generations ago he would have succeeded. His memories have not fully returned yet, thus neither has his power—he is not ready. I should have sensed that Asorath was near; the stronger demons seem to have learned a cloaking technique," Nile said, reaching into his coat.

I am the wallflower.

"Take this." He handed a medallion to Bryon—it was shaped like a triquetra. "Next time you're in trouble, press this to your heart as hard as you can, but only if it is life and death."

Bryon reached out his hands in acceptance. Jade stood next to him, trying to see what Nile was handing him. Abigail stood close by the fire. Kneeling down, she gently grabbed my hand. I could feel energy and life slowly flow from her body to mine. I am the blossoming wallflower.

"I cannot continue to interfere. He has already taken notice," Nile said, moving closer to the statue of Jesus.

Bryon took the necklace and placed the gold chain around his neck, tucking it under his shirt with a big smile on his face. "Did you get a magic necklace, Jade? Oh, no?"

"Must mean you're the weakest one. I obviously don't need one," Jade said and walked off to the side of the podium a few feet from the small fire.

"Yeah, well…Agh," Bryon mumbled.

Nile turned from the statue, making his way to Abigail, who was sitting next to me still holding my hand. "You were very brave doing what you did."

She looked up at his bright blue eyes.

"But very stupid. Why did you do that?" he asked, sitting next to her.

Abigail turned back to staring at the ground, gripping her knees.

"You are a very special girl. Here, let me see." Nile reached for her hand, examining her mark. "You are very special indeed. There will be a time where you will need to make a choice. You are not only your father, Abigail. You are your mother too. Remember that. Remember…when the day comes, He believes in you." Nile motioned to the statue of Jesus. Abigail's eyes followed and quickly turned away.

Nile stood. Without saying anymore, he closed his eyes and tilted his head to the ceiling. There was a blinding flash of light.

"Wait!" Jade yelled after him.

It was too late—Nile was gone.

"So what are we supposed to do now?" Bryon looked over to Jade.

"Abigail, are you okay?" Jade walked over to her sitting by the fire, no longer holding my hand. "Did that thing hurt you?" She reached out her hand and placed it on her shoulder.

"I'm fine." She rolled her shoulder away. "How is Dean?"

"He is going to be okay," Jade said, looking over at me. "Whatever you did out there...saved his life. How did you know you could do that?"

"I didn't," Abigail whispered.

"Well, it was incredible. I thought Dean was the only one. May I see your mark?" Jade stretched out one hand, requesting hers.

She slowly untucked it from her folded arm and put her hand in Jade's.

Jade turned Abigail's hand over to examine her wrists marking. "Incredible, I have been through all of my books ever since we discovered what Dean was, and I have never seen this one. Yours is not mentioned at all."

Abigail pulled her arm back. "What do you mean you discovered what Dean is?" She turned to look at me with tear-filled eyes and a small smile that just cracked the corner of her lips.

"Ahh..." I meant to say her name but *ah* was all I could get. I wanted to tell her myself. I was in and out, still seeing and hearing what was going on. Abigail grabbed my hand once again, as if to tell me to stop trying to move.

"He is quite incredible," Jade said, looking over at my resting body lying by the fire. I could hear the wind licking the sides of the church.

"Dean's an angel," Bryon said as he sat in a pew and kicked his legs up on the headrest, pulling out his necklace to stare at it in the light.

"Bryon!" Jade threw her hands in the air.

"What? She asked what you meant, we gotta tell her. I mean, she did just save him from a massive demon."

"Yeah, well..." Jade stuttered dropping her hands.

"No," Abigail mumbled.

"What?" Jade asked.

"An angel? How is that possible?" she said, releasing my hand and looking at me and then Jade.

"Well, technically he is an Archangel, the son of the Archangel Michael to be exact. There is an order of angels and they are all different. Dean is a warrior. Maybe you are some type of a warrior angel too!" Bryon jumped out of his chair, standing to face us.

"Dean is an angel," she said, almost with a laugh. "Of course he is."

"Archangel," Jade said. "Apparently this choir or tier of angelic beings look very similar to us." Jade walked over to her with her large leather book, opening it to the page describing the angels. "I know it's a lot to take in and it can sound a little crazy, but it's true."

Abigail took the book and began closely examining it. She was like a doctor performing heart surgery, her eyes glued to the pages as her fingers brushed over the art. Gently gliding over my symbol, her eyes seemed to light up. Her breath was heavy and slow. The fire crackled and danced, beautifully lighting her face. The breeze from the outside world gently swimming through the treetops whistled in harmony with the crackling fire.

"What did that thing mean, 'Your father will hear about this'?" Bryon asked, breaking the silence.

"I don't know," Abigail said without looking up from the book, still tracing the images.

"Abigail, if you know something, we need to know," Jade said gently, pulling the book from her. "Who is your father?"

Abigail quickly looked up to meet Jade's eyes. "He is just a businessman. I don't know how he could have anything to do with this, or that…thing," Abigail said, moving away from Jade, turning her back to her.

"What kind of business?" Bryon asked, standing next to Jade.

"I don't know, actually," she said, speaking quickly. "I have never thought of asking him. I know he owns a lot of businesses and gives most of what he makes to charity, though. He isn't a bad guy. He would never be involved with someone or something like that monster."

"What is your father's name?" Jade asked.

"Lucien. Lucien Li'ved," Abigail responded, turning back to Jade and Bryon.

"I've never heard of him," Bryon said, crossing his arms. "Maybe your father made a deal with this demon, Asorath, and that is why he is so successful?"

"Not with that one…" Abigail said quietly, and I could almost see the wheels in her head begin to turn.

"Huh?" Bryon asked, dropping his arms. Jade's eyebrow jumped; she seemed to have noticed as well.

"Nothing. That's crazy talk," Abigail said, moving back down to where I was resting. She placed her hand on my side.

"Anybody could have made that deal," Jade said as gently as she could. "I think we better find out what it is your father is really involved with. Maybe he can tell us what your mark means too. I mean, he is your father."

Abigail nodded, staring down at me. Her hand was warm on my side. I could see compassion in her eyes. "Yeah. Okay," she said, standing and making her way back to the table that the book was resting on.

Bryon moved away from where he and Jade were standing and sat down on the front-row pew. He pulled up an old piece of paper he found on the ground and covered his face as he leaned into the wooden bench for rest.

Jade knelt next to me, checking my wrist for a pulse and placing her ear to my chest listening for the still-beating heart. She sat there next to me, making herself comfortable. I wanted to thank her; all I could do was think it. Alas, I digress. She then covered me with an old, wool blanket that had been next to the fire. I enjoyed the notion.

Abigail sunk her teeth into the book, starting from the very beginning, reading each and every word with extreme focus. Her eyes flashed with intrigue and excitement, turning each page slowly and with gentle hands like an archeologist discovering an ancient, lost link to existence.

Ever so faintly, I could hear Uncle's voice in the other room. It was too quiet to make out though.

The three settled in for the night as the fire crackled and danced with great energy. The cold mountain breeze continued its wood and wind orchestra, whistling through the frozen branches. Nothing else stirred. The wind was the only one awake to govern the night. Darkness laid its frosty black bosom on the small town.

CHAPTER 11

FROM DARKNESS WITH LOVE

A S DARKNESS GAVE way to the new day, rays of sunshine passed through the glass mosaics of the church. The light danced around the room in a beautiful assortment of colors, gently warming the interior. The light in the room brightened, and eyelids began to crack open ever so slowly. Jade rose to her feet, stretching her hands as far above her head as she could possibly reach, not realizing I was no longer lying there next to her. She rubbed her green eyes in rough circles just before placing her glasses on her nose and ears.

Bryon rolled over on the floor, violently pulling his jacket over his head to block the rays of light. "Ugh, it's too early," he muttered.

Abigail was next to wake, slowly rising and elegantly sitting up with crisscrossed legs, stretching her hands onto her head and giving it a good morning scratch. Her golden blonde hair glistened, reflecting the sun.

"Good morning," she yawned.

"Good morning," Jade responded.

"Mmm," Bryon mumbled.

"Where is Dean!" Jade exclaimed, finally noticing I was gone.

Bryon jumped up from his grave. "Oh no! That thing probably waited for us to fall asleep so they could take him!" He grabbed for his shoes and stumbled to put them on in his haste.

"Dean!" Abigail exclaimed. "Dean!"

The three of them began to search every nook and cranny of the church, tossing chairs, yanking open doors. The hysteria began to rise.

"What are you guys doing?" I said, having watched the entire scene unfold standing in yawn of the front door, holding a white paper bag and a brown carton of coffees.

"Dean!" Abigail yelled, relief coloring every feature as she ran over and wrapped her arms around my waist, nearly causing me to drop all that I was holding.

"Geez, you guys act like I died. I just went to get us all some breakfast, figured you'd be hungry," I explained.

"You scared the crap out of us," Bryon said as he also ran over and wrapped his arms around me.

"What, no hug?" I joked, looking over to Jade, who took a seat and grabbed her book, looking at us with distaste. Abigail and Bryon held tight.

Bryon released his grip, punching me on the shoulder, and made his way to sit next to Jade with a smile on his face. Abigail also released her grip, though taking a second, she stopped and glanced up into my eyes. Looking down into hers, I could feel a warmth that the sun could not provide.

"All right, lovebirds, come on. I'm starving over here," Bryon said, as he couldn't wait any longer to eat.

Breaking eye contact, I walked over to the other two. "So what's going on? What happened last night?" Abigail lingered.

"You don't remember?" Jade asked, grabbing the cup of coffee I offered.

"Of course I remember. Well, up to a certain point. I remember holding off that demon as long as I could and seeing a bright flash of light, but I don't remember much of anything after that. What was that?"

"That…was her," Jade said as she nodded to Abigail.

I looked over. "How did… ?" I stumbled on my words.

"I don't know," Abigail said shyly.

"She ran over and grabbed you just as Flint was going to eat you, or something. And then this super bright light came out of her and blinded it. AND THENNN Nile showed up and told Flint who's boss," Bryon said, gasping for air as he finished the explanation and crushing his breakfast in his hands.

"Wait, so lemme get this straight. You, Abigail, somehow scared off a massive demon and saved *my* life?" I asked, looking over from Bryon to Abigail.

Abigail shrugged and smiled.

"And who is Flint?" I asked, rotating back to Bryon.

"That's his name. The demon. His name is Flint…Well, actually it's Asorath, but he goes by Flint here on earth," Bryon said as if it was common knowledge, taking a sip of his coffee.

I looked over at Jade. Confused to say the least.

"Nile explained everything," Jade said, following up. "Everything except who she really is." Jade now turned her attention over to Abigail, my eyes followed.

"What do you mean?" Apparently, I was full of questions.

"She has a mark like yours, only different. And it's not mentioned in any of the books," Jade answered "How she did what she did makes no sense. I can't explain it. Though the demon did say something interesting just as it was retreating."

"What did he say?" I asked.

Jade, still looking at Abigail, answered, "He said that her *father* would hear about this."

"Mr. Li'Ved, I've met him. He seems like a great guy. What does that mean, Abigail?" I asked.

Abigail glared just the slightest bit at Jade. It wasn't much—maybe the light had played a trick on me—but I could swear I had seen a small reaction to what Jade had said. "I don't know. I really don't. I didn't know about any of this until you told me that night," Abigail said.

"Wait, what?" Bryon said, stopping midsip. "You knew about this before last night?"

I spoke for Abigail. "Something happened a while ago where we found out we were similar. But we didn't know what it was or how any of it was even possible. We've both even seen that demon before. At a party. Only he was much smaller."

"So, you knew about Dean?" Bryon asked.

Jade's arms were crossed, "Ha!" she let out, uncrossing her arms and placing her hand on her head, moving a few steps away.

Abigail moved in front of Jade and tried explaining. "No, I only knew what you knew. I was at the party when Dean did…what he did. And only one other time, he came to me—he was hurt…and I helped."

"You've seen Flint before?" Bryon asked me, confused.

"Yeah, once before, but he didn't do anything then. He just stared at me." *Ha, he should have killed me then,* I thought to myself.

"He must have been tracking you ever since you two saw each other," Jade interjected. "That means he may know about my place *and* the sword. We need to find that sword, and we need to find it now." Jade slammed the book down.

"Jade's right. We need to go now," Bryon said, reaching under one of the pews and grabbing the bags they had put together last night.

"Where are you going?" Abigail asked quickly.

"There is no time to explain. Jade and Bryon are right. If we are going to get ahead of this, we need to go now. Lucifer is not waiting for any of us. He is moving up plans fast. We have less than two weeks according to my dad," I said, grabbing a few things from my room and stuffing them into my bag.

Jade slung a pack over her shoulder. "Lucifer must be close. There is no way all this is going down in AngelFire without him keeping an eye on things. Especially you, Dean. We need to find him—the more we know, the better."

"No!" Abigail shouted.

"What?" Jade asked.

"Abigail, what is it?" I asked.

"You can't." Abigail ran over to me, placing her hand on my chest.

Jade placed the bag on the ground. "Why not?"

Bryon looked at Abigail curious.

"You just can't. Dean, it's too dangerous."

"It's going to be okay," I reassured her, placing my hands on her shoulders.

"I don't want to lose you…You're the only one who gets me. You're the only one who is like me." Abigail grabbed my hands, placing our wrists together.

"I'm going to be fine. We'll be back in no time," I said, holding her hands.

Abigail's eyes started to well, begging me not to go. What did she know that she wasn't telling us? She looked at Jade and Bryon quietly, raised my hands, kissed them, and turned to leave.

"We don't have time for this, Dean," Jade said.

"Give me a second, okay?" I said, already following after Abigail.

What was it about this girl that continued to draw me in? Abandoning my sense of urgency to calm a girl. To make her feel okay, comfortable, at peace. The wind blew and the shards of ice cut at my face like frozen razor blades. The weather was becoming even more unpredictable. Calm snow one moment, melting spring air another, and now a punishing blizzard.

"Abigail!" I tried over the howling storm. "Abigail!" I shouted again. Fighting the blizzard, I forced my way through the powerful winds, walking nearly horizontal. "Abigail!"

There, her red coat. I spotted it through the white haze.

"Abigail, what are you thinking? It's freezing out here. You're going to get sick." I placed my hand on her shoulder. She turned with a face full of tears. "Abigail, what is going on?"

"You can't leave. He is going to know. He will know, and he will find you and kill you!" Abigail shouted, barely audible above the storm.

"Who is? Who is going to kill me?" I shouted back.

"I can't lose you, Dean," she shouted as the winds began to die down. I could hear again.

"Abigail you are not going to lose me. I can do this, I promise." I pulled her into my arms.

"You don't get it. You are the only one who has never placed expectations and judgments on me. My dad expects me to run his business someday. Everyone at school expects me to be little Miss Perfect. Everyone judges me as a spoiled rich girl. I get teased for not having my mother," she said as the tears began to swell in her eyes once again.

"Abigail. No one thinks those things," I said, holding her a little tighter.

"Yes, they do," she said.

"Everyone loves you. I'm sure your dad thinks very highly of you if he is trusting you with all his life's work. And Cherry—what about Cherry? She loves you, she admires you, and she tries to copy everything you do, right? And a lot of people don't have moms. I mean, look at me. I don't know my mom and I turned out okay, right? Wait, don't answer that," I said making her giggle.

"Dean…I like you," Abigail said, pulling away.

"I like you too, Abigail," I said. "I really like you. You're the only one who gets me too. Abigail, I…"

"No, don't. Don't do that. Don't say what you're going to say." Abigail pulled away. She started backstepping into the storm.

The winds began to pick up once again as snow swirled all around us.

"What are you doing?" I shouted.

"I can't do this. I'm sorry." I could barely hear her as she continued backstepping. "Just don't go! Don't leave! He will find you and he will kill you!" she shouted, becoming less and less visible.

"Who will? Who is? Abigail, you're not making any sense!" The wind was roaring again. The snow was blinding. She mouthed something just before the snow hid her from my sight. I couldn't quite make it out.

I turned and ran back inside the church.

"Finally. Geez, what did you two talk about, the dictionary?" Bryon said, sliding out of his chair.

I slumped off the pounds of snow that padded my shoulders. The warmth of the fire was immediate. The air was welcoming and warm.

"She was talking about someone knowing. And trying to kill me," I said, stretching my hands in front of the flames.

"Knowing what? Who is going to kill you?" Jade asked.

"I don't know, she didn't say. Or I didn't hear her; the wind was too loud. She said someone would know that we were leaving, and they would come after us. To kill me." I looked at Jade and Bryon.

"She knows something. I don't trust her." Jade grabbed the book off the table, twisted its lock, and placed it in her bag, "We need to find out how her father is involved. I bet he has something to do with it."

Bryon punched his hand. "Let's do this!"

—§—

"*She did what?!*" Mr. Li'Ved slammed his fists onto his desk, splintering it into a thousand pieces. Flint and Lucien were in Mr. Li'Ved's home office once again. The familiar smell of rich leather and Cuban cigars filled the air. A couple small lamps lit the room, a warm yellow reflecting off the brown leather chairs and wooden fixtures.

"Lucien...what are you not telling us about her?" Flint asked, standing in his natural form, tall, ugly, and dead. "Should we know something that—"

"No. There is nothing. I will get her under control." Mr. Li'Ved said as he composed himself and slicked his nice blond hair back. "What of the boy?" Mr. Li'Ved grabbed a small glass from his dry bar and placed a cube in it. Grabbing a rather large clear bottle, he uncapped it and poured the brown contents into the glass.

"I haven't had eyes on him since Nile returned," Flint said through his disgusting snout. "He has been enforcing the order diligently, deporting our soldiers left and right...And, sir...Homer is back."

"How! I thought he was taken care of at the Red Sea. What is going on!" Spit came flying out of his mouth. Heat waves emitted from his head. Flint winced.

"We will be ready for them next time they show their faces—we have watchers keeping their eyes on all known rifts." Flint took a step forward.

"Homer." Mr. Li'Ved took a drink of his single malt scotch from his crystal glass. "Are we still on track?"

"Yes, sir," Flint said, reaching for a remote to flip on the television in the room.

News channel after news channel flashed on the screen. Genocide, war, pollution, nuclear testing, child trafficking. They all passed through the television one after the other.

Horror and sadness made up the faces of the victims across the world.

"Good. Now get out of here." Mr. Li'Ved said as he took his seat in the soft diamond-stitched brown leather chair. "And find the boy! I can't afford any more slipups, least of all from the likes of him."

Flint bowed his head. "Your Grace."

"And find me those—" Mr. Li'Ved yelled just at the moment Flint disappeared. "Worthless demon, can't do anything right."

THE BLIZZARD HAD finally passed with the morning sun making its glorious appearance. "That's him, just there," Jade said. She had made a call earlier that morning to someone she said would help us out. A man in a cowboy hat pulled up in an old 1967 Dodge pickup truck. He didn't say anything as he stopped in front of us, just gave a friendly tilt of the hat. Jade, Bryon, and I loaded our gear into the back of the old truck. As much as we had wanted to leave sooner, the storm would not allow it.

"You sure you guys want to do this?" I looked over at them.

Bryon winked at me with a glance of approval and hopped into the bed of the truck. "Come on, these demons aren't waiting for us!" He reached out a hand, I took hold and pulled myself into the truck bed as well.

Jade followed suit.

I am we. And we are I.

As the truck sped down the old dirt road, we bounced in the back with each bump and hole in the path. The wind rushed by, our ears blurring out almost all noise. "So how do you know this airplane guy again?" I shouted out to Bryon.

"He subscribes to me on YouTube! He watches all my videos!" Bryon smiled as he yelled back over the noise of the wind and truck. "When I told him who I was traveling with, he said he would be more than happy!"

"Who did you say you were traveling with?!" I shouted.

"You! The superhuman! He loved how you put that guy through the wall. Big fan!" Bryon smiled and nodded.

I smirked, not quite of approval but a smirk nonetheless.

Jade must have been tired—she was passed out cold within ten minutes. I can't imagine how she was sleeping through the combination of cold and bumps.

I stared out of the bed, watching the pine and aspen trees go whooshing by. The thought of all that these majestic and silent green giants had seen over their life was mind-blowing. Growing from what once was seemingly useless, small, and defenseless into something so strong and elegant. Something so wise and useful, the trees had seen it all. What secrets they held, none of us would ever know...

About thirty minutes had passed when the truck came to a slow halt.

"Okay, we're here," the driver said with a Southern twang, leaning one arm out of the window. We had stopped just outside an old run-down airstrip. It was surrounded by a tall chain-link fence with barbed wire wrapped all around the top. There was a sign that read "DO NOT ENTER. PRIVATE HANGER." The rest was rusted and blown off by what looked like shotgun blasts from all the scatter shots.

"Thank you!" I saluted the cowboy taxi man as we jumped down out of the truck.

Bryon gave the truck a good one-two, letting the driver know we were all out. "All right, team, let's go meet Scott," Bryon said.

"Wait, you haven't met the guy yet?" Jade asked.

"No, he just subscribes to my channel. He said he knows how to fly though, showed me pictures of his plane too." Bryon pulled out his phone and showed Jade and me pictures of the plane. It was a nice plane, a white jet made for the elite class, one would say.

"All right, seems okay to me," I said, shrugging my bag up onto my shoulder.

"All right." Jade exhaled with disapproval.

The three of us made our way through a large hole in the fence and onto the airstrip. The tiny airport had a few small hangers that looked to be made out of scrap sheet metal and the air strip itself was all dirt with a grassy median covered in snow. Old planes from the '60s and '70s filled the hangers with a few broken-down aircrafts rusting out in front, icicles formed on the propellers.

"You sure we came to the right spot?" Jade asked.

"Hey! Bryon!" a young man yelled, waving both his hands in the air as he came running out of the hanger on the right.

"Scott!" Bryon yelled back as he made his way to meet the young pilot.

"That's Scott?" I asked Jade. She gave me a side eye glance with a deep breath.

Scott couldn't have been older than sixteen, waving his arms in the air in oversized overalls and boots too big for his feet. He had engine grease all over his face and a big smile to accompany. Bryon and Scott were shaking hands when Jade and I walked up to join. Scott's attention shifted toward yours truly. "Wow! You're actually here! Man, I'm a huge fan! I loved how you tossed those guys around like rag dolls!" Scott exclaimed, shaking my hand violently without letting go. "Man, me and my friends try to act out that fight together, but we just can't figure out how you did it!"

"Pshh." Jade mumbled.

"Oh, I'm sorry, it's a pleasure to meet you as well, friend. Any friend of Bryon's is a friend of mine!" Scott smiled, shaking Jade's hand. "Wow, you're real pretty, ma'am."

Jade blushed. That was the first time I had seen her act like a girl. Weird.

"Scott...Scott." I attempted to calm Scott. "Where's the plane?" I said, placing my hand on his shoulder and edging him away from gawking at Jade. We had to get moving. No time for flirting.

"Oh, right! Let's get to it! Bryon said y'all were in a rush. Follow me!" Scott said, waving us to follow him back to the hanger he had just come out of.

The airfield was quiet, like a ghost town full of broken-down birds. It seemed we were the only ones there that day. Probably the only ones there in years.

The skies were clear and blue, like the vast oceans with no ending, only adventure. What a beautiful contrast to the white, snowy ground.

"There she is!" Scott said, pointing.

At the end of his fingertip lay a rusted brown-and-white propeller plane with duct tape holding together one of the wings. The cockpit was housed by a semi-cracked, clear bubble windshield. Without saying a word, Jade turned and started walking the other way.

"Jade." I turned and ran after her. She was quick, almost fifteen yards away by the time I caught up. "Hey, Jade. Where are you going?"

Jade whipped around. "There is no way I am flying all the way to the Middle East in that death trap."

"How else are we going to get there then? We have to find that sword, you even said it yourself." I gave a fake smile back to Bryon and Scott waving my reassurance.

"We can't find the sword if we *die*!" Jade yelled the last word, making certain that Scott could hear. Scott looked over to Bryon, who simply shrugged his shoulders.

Scott patted the plane. "Miss Jade, is it? I assure you, ma'am, this here plane is plenty safe. She may not look it, but she sure can move," he yelled over the distance to us.

Jade pointed to the left wing, yelling back, "There is duct tape holding that wing."

"Like I said, she ain't pretty, but she makes up for it in reliability."

"Reliability," Jade said mockingly. I put my hand on her shoulder, which she quickly shook it off. We walked the end zone back to where Bryon and Scott had been waiting.

"Jade, come on. It's the only way." Bryon leaned in. Jade stood there with her arms crossed. "Jade..."

"I'm *thinking*," Jade responded.

"Exploration. Discovery. Cool ancient stuff no one has ever found..." Bryon tempted her.

"Fine," she said, her eyes twinkling a bit at that last one.

"Woo! Let's go flying!" Bryon said, running to the plane and jumping in the back seat of the open cockpit.

"All right then, let's get wheels up! This is going to be the longest one old girl has done yet!" Scott said as we all closed in on the aircraft.

"What?!" Jade exclaimed as Scott handed her a helmet from the back of the plane.

"Don't look so scared!" I said to Jade. "You got me!"

"Oh yeah that makes me feel so much better," Jade said.

We—now four—loaded into the plane.

"All right, gentlemen and lady, this is your captain speaking," Scott said just before he flicked the on switch. "Please keep your hands and legs inside the aircraft at all times. Should you feel airsick at any point, please try to miss the wings when you stick your head out the side."

Ruh. Ruh. Ruh.

The plane's engine sputtered, trying to turn over. "One second," Scott said, biting his lip as he turned the key one more time.

Vrooooom. Bum Bum Bum Bum Bum.

The old plane actually turned on. The engine was loud and strong, the propeller was spinning so fast that it quickly became invisible.

"All right! Here we go!" Scott shouted from the cockpit. The plane began to inch forward. Jade tightened her seatbelt as she performed the sign of the Father, Son, and Holy Spirit above her heart. The old broken-down plane made its way out of the hanger doors and onto the airstrip. Snow swirled all around as the wind from the propeller spun the air. We were all lined up for takeoff. Scott checked a few of the gauges, and when all looked good, he slowly pushed the throttle forward.

The plane began to roll. The noise from the single engine grew louder and louder as the plane increased its speed. Halfway down the runway, we began to get lift. The tires began to bounce on and off the ground, just as they neared the end.

Liftoff.

The plane now floated among the beautiful New Mexico skies. Jade was already reaching desperately for a vomit bag. Bryon had thrown his hands up behind his head and tilted his hat down for the long ride. There was a serious look on my old, ugly mug face. Now that the journey had actually begun, I knew everything was going to be weighing in. No more irresponsible teen. I must become what this world needs. Popping the collar on my spare black peacoat, I sat in for the long flight.

The beautiful blue sky generously opened her arms, allowing passage. Soft, pillowy clouds filled the heavens. Their prestige shone through at its most magnificent as rays of light lined their edges. The golden lining shone brightly and warmly. The cool fresh air passed under the wings of the plane, lifting it higher and higher.

What a familiar feeling.

ABIGAIL WAS ON the move.

Horrid thoughts filled her head, thoughts of Dean, thoughts of Asorath, thoughts of her father. Contemplating her next move and the words she would use to sway her father from killing Dean. Something bigger was going on than what her father was telling her.

She had been kept in the dark far too long—it was time she knew what was really going on. She practiced the questions she would ask as she walked down the side of the ditch bank with great fervor. Pine trees surrounded the narrow dirt road for as far as the eye could see. The forest engulfed her small figure. As the sun began to set, the shadowed treetops darkened the forest floor. Dust flew into the air with each step as she dragged her feet along the ground.

"Daddy, I need you to tell me the truth…"

"The truth. I don't think you can handle the truth, little cousin." An airy voice wafted through the air.

Abigail stopped in her tracks. The sweet smell of pine needles slowly began to fade, just to be overtaken by the smell of rot and death.

"Beth?" Abigail asked, just before turning around. "Is that you?"

"Poor little Abigail, you are feeling left out, aren't you? I told your father to tell you truth ever since you were a little girl. Who knew Uncle even had a soft side?" Beth said through her long black hair dangling down in front of her pale, white face. Her black lace dress flowed in the wind.

"What are you talking about? We are the same age. How would you..." Abigail took one step forward.

A dark voice came from behind her. "Oh, my Abigail. So naive, so young." Kip, wearing his purple suit, walked into the moonlight from out of the shadowed woods.

"Kip? What are you two doing here?" Abigail looked around. The open field darkened to its final point as the last ray of light disappeared beyond the horizon. A slow fog rolled in from within the trees, circled by the forest.

Kip approached Beth, running his bony finger along her shoulders. "What are we doing here? What are you doing here...all alone?"

The two drew in closer. The white moon seemed to glisten on their skin.

"Does your father know where you are right now?" Beth hissed.

The trees crackled in the wind as if aching to move. Aching to help.

"No, I was on my way to see him." Abigail's breath froze.

"Where are your friends? Why aren't they with you?" Kip asked, grabbing Beth's shoulders and smelling her neck. The moon now fully lit the ground in a soft blue light. The stage was set.

"Huh?" Abigail crossed her arms over her red jacket.

"Dean and the other two—you *are* friends with them, aren't you?" Kip moved past Beth and closer to Abigail, only about six yards away now.

"How do you know about Dean?" Abigail dropped her hands to her side.

"Oh, dear cousin, we know all about Dean," Beth said, approaching Abigail next to Kip. The two split up and began to circle her.

Abigail tried her hardest not to flinch. *What do they know?*

"He is very special to us." Beth's long black hair danced in the wind. Her pale skin shone brightly in the steady light.

"What are you talking about? You guys are starting to scare me." Abigail tried to keep her eyes on both of them as they circled her, but it was getting harder.

"Don't play dumb, Abby. We know you are in love with Dean. We are just trying to protect you. You are family after all." Beth moved in closer and played with Abigail's hair.

A sigh of relief came. *Maybe they don't know everything,* she thought.

"We also know he is trying to ruin all of Uncle's hard work. *Your father's* hard work. You wouldn't want that, now would you?"

Abigail quickly glanced up. "What are you talking about?" This could be a clue into what she was looking for. "What work is my father doing?"

"Uncle has been working very hard for a very, very long time to move this family forward. Into our rightful place. We can't have someone like Dean coming in and ruining it all now, can we?" Beth continued as she played with Abigail's flowing blonde hair.

"What do you mean, our rightful place? And what does Dean have to do with any of this?" Abigail said with a fake laugh.

"This earth belongs to us. To your father and you and us!" Kip said, raising his voice in excitement. "Your little boyfriend is a worthless piece of trash and has no business even being called an angel!"

Her eyes widened and darted to the floor. They know.

"Let alone an Arch!" Kip was getting angry as he yelled, pacing back and forth in front of Abigail and Beth. His eyes began to burn a deep red as he glared up from the ground and into Abigail's eyes. His mouth dripped with saliva like a dog exposing his sharpened teeth.

Abigail jumped in fear. Slow, welling tears began to leak from her stony face and wide eyes. Kip moved just inches behind her.

"Oh no, no, don't cry. Don't be scared, little Abby. We are not going to hurt you…just your pesky boyfriend." His breath on her neck evoked goose bumps up and down her body. Kip turned to Beth. "I told Uncle she was not ready. She can't even handle seeing a true form. Just like her mother."

"My mother? You knew my mother?" Abigail asked.

"Oh, we more than knew her," Kip said. "But that's for another time. We have more pressing matters to address."

"I don't know what you're talking about," Abigail said, fighting the fear, trying her hardest to maintain her poker face.

"Abby, you don't have to lie to us. We know all about Dean. We know he is an Arch. We know you've met your crazy Uncle Flint. You just don't get it yet, do you? You don't know who you really are. Why Lucifer has never shown you our true forms. Purebreds," Beth said, wrapping her hands around Abigail's chest from behind. "It would never work between you and Dean either way. Your father would just not allow it. The balance would not allow it," Beth said with a soft, comforting tone.

Tears continued to fall from Abigail's unwavering face.

"We really have no other choice but to…well, to kill him," Beth said bluntly.

"No!" Abigail leapt forward, away from her two sickly tormentors.

"Abby don't make this harder than it has to be. Come with us, little cousin, and we will explain everything. Even tell you all about your mother…and your brother," Beth said as Kip paced back and forth, fuming.

The trees reached out their branches in a failed effort to help.

"Get away from me! Get away! I don't believe anything you are saying!" Abigail shouted. Her wrist began to flicker. The winds began to rise. The whistling noise screamed through the branches like a raging choir.

"That's new…" Kip said as he looked over at Abigail's wrist. Beth stopped where she was and stared as well, obviously dumbfounded.

"Uncle failed to mention that little bit, didn't he, brother?" Beth said to Kip.

"Yes, sister. He did," Kip responded. "Calm down now, Abby. We are not going to hurt you." Kip slowly inched forward with outstretched arms. His hands were like claws, his eyes red as fire.

"I said, get away!" Abigail screamed.

The winds grew to biblical proportions as they formed around her body. She was the eye of her hurricane. The leaves and snow on the ground were lifted into a tornado-like storm that twirled around her. Her wrist began to glow blindingly bright. Kip and Beth both lifted their arms, shielding their eyes. Their skin began to bubble in the blistering light.

"Stop her!" Beth yelled to Kip over the roaring wind before turning back to Abigail. "Abigail, you need to come with us. We can tell you who you really are. We can keep you safe! Everything is going to be okay!"

"STAY…AWAY!" Abigail screamed. The winds grew stronger, knocking Beth to her knees and forcing her to dig her feet and hands into the ground to keep from being blown away.

Beth's eyes darkened, all color stripped away, leaving nothing but the blackest of blacks. Her body quickly transformed into that of a ghastly, dark, formless cloud. Allowing the wind to take her, she enveloped the tornado surrounding Abigail. "You can't escape the darkness within. It is who you are. Sooner or later, it will consume you," Beth whispered as she circled Abigail in the whipping wind.

"Shut up!" Abigail shouted.

The darkness that had lain upon the forest floor was illuminated as if a thousand suns had come up to shine.

"Your father's blood is strong in you. You are meant for the throne. A woman, not your brother..." Beth was saying as Kip came bursting through the dark tornado, tackling Abigail to the ground and hitting her as hard as he could over the head with a large boulder. His body in his natural form: half flesh, half bone. Completely blackened and burnt, dripping with bubbling oil.

"You girls talk too much," he said in a raspy voice to Beth as she regained her human-like form.

The winds died down and the darkness swept the forest floor once again. Abigail lay there in her grassy bed, unconscious.

"It seems Uncle has some explaining to do," Kip said, looking down at Abigail, picking up her wrist and examining it.

"Indeed, it does," Beth mirrored.

The chill of night returned. The silence was loud.

KNOCK. KNOCK.

Kip stood next to Beth with an unconscious Abigail draped over his shoulder like a prize-winning kill. Footsteps could be heard as someone approached the door.

Mr. Li'Ved opened the entrance. "What have you done?" he asked in a tempestuous tone, grabbing at Abigail's limp body.

"Don't worry. She isn't dead...yet." Beth took a step into the house, Kip following.

"Abigail, baby, can you hear me?" Mr. Li'Ved gently asked, supporting her neck and holding her like he once did when she was a child. He rushed her through the castle into his illustrious suit.

"She's out cold. Kip gave her a good one-two. We had no choice really," Beth continued,

Kip quickly looked away and down to the ground with his hands clasped together.

Mr. Li'Ved placed Abigail down gently on a side sofa near his king-sized bed. His body began to steam and grow. His ears sharpened, and his skin began to darken. Two nodules began to form just above his eyebrows.

"Wait! Wait! Uncle, please!" Beth said, running over to Abigail and grabbing at her wrist. "This almost got us killed. We really had no choice—she was about to go supernova."

"Ah!" Mr. Li'Ved screamed, releasing an explosion of thick flames. Beth and Kip flew backward into the wall, and the entire room was condensed into ash and soot.

Kip coughed, standing up. "I'm sorry, Uncle. I had no choice, really."

"When did this happen?" Mr. Li'Ved asked.

"Just moments ago, in the forest about a mile out," Kip said.

"What was she doing there? Was she with him?" Mr. Li'Ved asked.

"No, sir, she was alone. We were out there keeping an eye on her. We wanted to make sure she was protected. The balance has been disturbed," Kip said like a little kid making up lies.

"She was running through the woods crying. We stopped her to see if she was all right," Beth lied too.

"She said that she was on the way home to see you. To tell you that…well, to tell you that the boy had hit her. He tried to kill her, she said. She said that he had found out who you were. Who she was. And he tried to…" Kip lied. "When she told us the story, she grew enraged. She was so powerful, like nothing we had ever seen before. Almost more powerful than us. She is overflowing with power…a power unlike the rest of us."

"Almost as if she was…" Beth trailed off, realizing what she was about to say. Her eyes dropped.

"Hold your tongue!" Mr. Li'Ved turned and shouted at Beth, pointing his large finger in her face. His face transformed to a giant mouth with a thousand teeth and six eyes, and back to human in the blink of an eye.

Beth and Kip cowered, backing up and grouping together.

Spit flew from his mouth as he angered. "There is nothing different with her. She is purebred from my very blood! You are not to question that!" Calming himself and reestablishing his controlled demeanor, he said, "You are not to speak of this to anyone. Is that understood?"

"Uncle…" Kip muttered.

"I asked you a question," Mr. Li'Ved reiterated.

"Understood," the two answered together in unison as they dropped to their knees.

"Was anyone else with you?" Mr. Li'Ved asked.

"No, Lucifer, it was only us," Beth answered. "Has Flint brought you what you are looking for?"

"He is to return in three days. We shall see at that time," Mr. Li'Ved said.

"And of the stone?" Kip asked.

Mr. Li'Ved glared at Kip with a menacing look. "Get out of my house."

The two bowed and turned to exit. Mr. Li'Ved grabbed Kip by the arm just as he was walking out. "Lay another finger on my daughter, and it will be you who is sent to the ninth this time."

Kip's eyes glared at Mr. Li'Ved with anger and then to the ground in obedience. Like a cowering dog.

Mr. Li'Ved shut the door behind them and tended to Abigail. He reached over and examined her wrist. The mark had changed. It had grown larger, beginning to wrap around her hand.

"Why are you doing this to me?" he asked aloud.

CHAPTER 12

FRIEND OR FOE

"MAYDAY! MAYDAY! MAYDAY! This is Bravo-Niner-Three-Four! Hold your fire, hold your fire!" Scott yelled as the bullets whizzed by our heads. "Switching transponder to 7700."

"Scott! You said you knew these people!" Jade yelled from the back seat, her voice getting caught in the wind and gunfire.

"We are friendlies! Mayday! Mayday! Hold your fire! Again this is Bravo-Niner-Three-Four requesting to land! My name is Scott Hildman, son of Captain Norman Hildman! Please!" Scott begged with the radio. The other side was just a slew of enraged voices yelling at us in another language. "Dean! What do we do!" Scott turned to face me.

"How am I supposed to know? You're the pilot! I thought you knew these guys!" I yelled back.

"I do! I did! They must have got new people!" Scott yelled.

DING! DING! DING!

"We're hit! We're hit! Brace yourselves! We are going down!" Scott yelled.

This was it. This is how we die. I can't believe that after everything, this is how we go. I looked at Bryon—his eyes were wide. He was scared. I could feel his fear as he held the sides of the plane and closed his eyes. Jade's eyes were closed, and her head was bowed, her hands clasped together.

"Please, Father...help us," I whispered.

"Hang on!" Scott yelled as we approached the ground.

The sky passed by so fast the landscape was a blur. Scott pulled back on the controls. The nose lifted.

"Ah!" We were like the choir.

Ringing. That is all I could hear. Everything was a blur. Nothing was moving anymore. I could feel the hot ground beneath my back and sand between my fingers.

My father's face flashed in front of my eyes. "Get up."

I felt myself slowly coming to. "Bryon! Jade! Scott!" I stood, wobbling with each movement. The golden sands stretched as far as the eye could see. The crash site was a flat semi-straight line in the dirt surrounded by rolling hills of hot sand a few miles out of town. The plane was a wreck, to say the least. The wing that had been taped was somewhere off in the distance. The propellers were bent and crooked. The wheels had broken off and rolled about fifty yards away.

I am the undying prayer.

"Anyone?"

"I'm over here," Bryon yelled from behind the plane about ten feet away.

I moved as fast as I could in his direction. He was lying in the sand.

"Bryon. Are you okay?" I asked, leaning down next to him and lifting him to his feet.

"I'm fine. Just a little rattled. Where is Jade?" He rubbed his head and then his eyes.

"Oh, thank God! Solid ground!" Jade said, spilling out of the aircraft and onto the crash site. Her lips pressed to the dirty floor as she knelt on all fours, praising the earth and its unchanging form.

"Come on, Miss Jade. It wasn't that bad!" Scott said as he dismounted from the cockpit. His voice was trembling—so was his body. I gotta give it to him—he held his own in that near-death situation. The kid got us here. Given it wasn't the preferred method of landing, we did land, and we are alive.

"You!" Jade said. "You." She ran toward Scott and tackled him to the ground. "You almost killed us!" Jade clearly didn't see things the way I did.

"Jade! Quit it! Stop!" I ran over and pulled her off him. "We are alive. We are fine."

"He lied! He said he knew these people! He could have killed us and then everything would have been for nothing!" Jade tried lunging at Scott again, but I held her back.

Scott slowly got up off the ground. "I'm sorry. They must have switched controllers."

Bryon grabbed his leather duffel bag from the half-wrecked plane. "I don't know, I gotta agree with Jade on this one. We did almost die about three times, and that was before being shot down. If Dean hadn't caught the wing and retaped it back over whatever ocean that was, I don't know... I just don't know. But, man, it is *hot* out here! Hot as Hell, in fact! Ha! Get it? Hot as Hell... because we are about to fight the de—never mind."

Jade and I looked at Bryon unapologetically dead-eyed, though I did smirk on the inside. Good one.

The weather was about fifty degrees Celsius, a scorcher of a day. The fiery embrace of the hot wind was as if the very plasma from the sun itself had reached out for a hug. The sun shone bright throughout the clear blue sky. Jade swung her arms and escaped my clutch, storming off down the dirt strip some ways.

"Wow," I said, staring at the "plane." "How did we even make it?"

That poor airship looked like it had seen World War III up in those skies, barely making it down alive. Bullet holes peppered the wings and body.

"Thank you," I whispered, looking to the sky.

"So where are we exactly?" Bryon asked, seemingly unbothered.

"Welcome to Baghdad," Scott said, raising his arms in the air.

The heat smashed against our faces in a blistering wind accompanied by the smell of burning trash, smoke, and raw sewage. The smell alone could melt a hole in a person's skin. The sound of car horns, traffic sirens, and the occasional bomb populated the noise spectrum of whispers that filled our buzzing ears.

"How in the world did you even get us to this close to Baghdad?" Bryon asked, dumbfounded.

"My dad is—was—friends with one of the air traffic control guys here," Scott said. "Apparently he helped fly his wife and him out of a war zone years back? Our plane should have been tagged so that any time he wants to come this way or has to stop to fill up, he can just come right in. We were able to make it through all the other fly zones. Apparently, someone on this end didn't get the message."

"Mmmhmm…" Jade said from her solitary position.

"Okay, so now what?" Bryon asked.

"Now we walk," I said, grabbing my pack from off the hot ground and shifting the sunglasses from my forehead to my eyes. I began making my way away from the plane.

"Walk where?" Jade asked, returning to the group. "You don't even know where we are going."

"Sure, I do. We are going here." I pulled out a map I had tucked away in my jacket pocket and pointed to a red mark front and center.

"And where is that exactly?" Bryon asked.

"That is the Tigris River, right where it splits," I answered.

"How do you know that's where we are supposed to go?" Bryon asked.

"Uncle thought I never listened to his old war stories and blabbering," I said. "This is where he has been talking about for years. He had mentioned it again before we left—I just put two and two together. The four-headed snake."

"Genius," Jade muttered. "That is exactly where we need to go. Once we get there, I am sure there will be some locals that will be able to direct us even farther from there. Just like it says in the Bible, it is not Eden itself that the Garden was, but east-ward. Meaning just at the split of the Tigris would be…here." Jade pointed on the map to a river split. "The Diyala River, just below Baghdad. That should only be about fifty miles from where we are at now."

Scott nudged his way into the huddle, looking over the small map. "What are you gents talking about over here?"

I grabbed Bryon and Jade around the necks, bumping Scott back a bit. "Give us one second, Scott." I turned back to the private meeting. "We can't take Scott."

"Why not?" Bryon asked.

"We can't risk losing the one guy who can get us back home, if something should go wrong…" I whispered.

The two looked at the accident-prone teen scratching his butt and head at the same time. Scott turned and waved from outside the huddle.

"You're right, it's best he stays here," Bryon agreed. The two and I stood up and turned to Scott.

"Scott, buddy. We need you to stay with the plane," I said.

"What? I thought I was going to get to go with y'all. I mean, I—"

I jumped in. "Scott, this is a very dangerous mission, and we need someone as skilled and sharp as you to be prepared to get us out of here if something should go wrong."

"So I am, like, the getaway man?" Scott asked.

"Exactly." I wrapped my arm around his shoulder. "You are the getaway man. Every good mission needs a getaway man, and you are him. You are the only one who can get us back home."

"Yeah, man, think of it like a secret undercover mission," Bryon added, "and you're the man to get us away from the bad guys when they come chasing us."

"Ah man, that's awesome! All right, I'll do it!" Scott agreed.

"Great! Hang with the plane. We shouldn't be more than a few days," I said, patting Scott on the back.

"See you soon, bud," Jade said, also patting Scott on the back.

Scott was beaming with a smile that reached as far as the west is from the east. His new position as getaway man was his glory. I could practically see the movies playing out in his head with explosions and gunshots—and he was a hero.

"Don't go dying on us!" Bryon added as we walked away. Why? Why would he say something like that? I gave Bryon a darting glare.

"I'll be right here! Don't you worry! I'll just be working on the old girl!" Scott yelled.

Scott became a speck in the distance as we dragged ourselves through the hot sand and across the tan hills. The far-off noises became louder and louder with each step, as did the stench. The sand- and rock-covered city was tan and brown, highlighted by the virulent sun. The only green that could be seen was the occasional tree on the side of the dirt roads. War-torn buildings were missing entire sides; rubble of brick and steel filled the yards. Entire structures and neighborhoods were blocked off by tall reinforced steel walls. Cars were bumper to bumper, trying to make their way to gas stations that read, "No gas." Everything being suffocated by the yellow dirt.

Curious sign for a city known for their oil.

"Balango! Balango!" A boy was selling some soda on the side of the road to the waiting cars.

"I'll take one of those!" Bryon said, running up to the boy.

"Bryon, you don't even know what that is. What are you doing?" Jade grabbed Bryon as he pulled out some spare change.

"Dude, it is burning out here. I need something to refresh me," Bryon said, handing over some American coins to the boy. "Here you go. Thank you!"

The dirt-covered boy handed over the drink and popped the top for Bryon. Bryon kicked back the drink, holding it straight up in the air. That soda disappeared quicker than a drop of water on summer pavement. "*Mmm…*Wow, that was refreshing!" Bryon said with a big smile on his face.

"No more crazy stunts like that," I said, looking Bryon dead in the eyes. "We don't know their culture here. We need to lie low. You know we don't even have passports. If we get caught, I don't know what will happen."

Bryon gulped and nodded in compliance.

We three amigos continued to walk down the dirt path as the entire scenery began to change. From going through the trenches and war-struck town of traffic jams and no green to paved roads lined with palm trees, tall beautiful buildings filled with businesses, and orderly traffic.

"Did we just go through the twilight zone or what?" Bryon said, looking around at the near-instant change in cityscape.

"Look." Jade pointed. Men in uniform were stationed in corners of the streets. Wielding AK-47s, pants tucked into their black leather boots, and looks that said *stay out.*

"We need to get around them. They will stop us for sure if we try to walk past," Jade said.

Looking around, it seemed there was no other way around—we would have to walk right past them. Like rats in a maze with no secret passage to the cheese. The sound of low-flying helicopters rumbled the ground.

"What are we *doing* here?" Bryon said.

Great. The last thing we needed now was for Bryon to start to second-guess the mission.

"Come on, this way." I spotted an alley between two of the buildings. The alley was dark and wet. The smell of dry blood was all too familiar. Bryon and Jade didn't seem as comfortable as I did. The last alley I was in seemed like ages ago. Knowing what I know now, maybe I would have been more scared then. Maybe not.

"*Psst.*" A noise was heard from the corner just before the alley. "*Pssst.*"

Jade stopped where she was. "Did you guys hear that?"

"Over here." A young man's voice came from the shadow of a stairwell just next to the entrance of the alley.

Cautiously, we walked over. "You are looking for The Garden, yes?" the voice asked.

"How did you know?" I leaned in, intrigued.

"Follow me." A hand waved us in from behind the shadow. I began to take a step into the stairwell.

"Dude. We can't just go in there. We don't know who that is—what if it's a trap?" Bryon asked, placing a hand on my shoulder to stop my mindless movement.

"I agree with Bryon," Jade said. Her green eyes had a touch of worry to them.

"How would he know what we were looking for, huh?" I whispered. "He is obviously involved in the other balance. Yeah, maybe it's a trap, but maybe it's not. What if this is the only way we are going to find it? We have to try."

"If he were on our side, why is he waiting in the dark?" Bryon argued. "That is super creepy, and you know it. I feel like that is not something that some angelic being would do—but maybe something else."

"Weirdly, I still agree with Bryon," Jade said. "Again, this is too coincidental. They must have been watching us."

"I get it. It is really creepy, but this is our only lead at the moment and we don't have a whole lot of time. Who knows what Abigail is finding out as we speak," I rebutted.

After a moment of consideration, I broke eye contact and made my way down the dark staircase. Jade stared at Bryon with worried eyes, contemplating what they were about to get themselves into. After another moment, Jade let out a deep breath and stepped down into the staircase.

"Ah, hell," Bryon said, shaking his head and hustling down the stairs to catch up with us. "Wait for me!"

The staircase was not lit at all. It was as dark as the night sky, only this sky had no moon or stars. Blackness surrounded.

"I have a bad feeling about this," Bryon whispered into the dark air, reaching for the nonexistent handrail. "Dude, I'm going to fall. I can't even see my hand in front of my face."

"Ah!" Not even two steps later and Bryon came stumbling down, smashing us together on the ground floor. "Sorry." I couldn't really be mad—he did warn us. Jade and I helped him to his feet.

Bryon continued to talk. "Sir? Hello? Are you still here? I told you guys this was a bad idea."

A brief second passed, and a large metal door began to creak open. Light spilled out from the underground basement. The young man, wrapped in a black headscarf and robe, pushed the door open. He held the door open to the candlelit room. "Come, quickly."

We quickly moved into the mysterious chamber and out of the dark, eerie stairs, the boy quickly closed the door behind us, locking it in three different places. The loud sliding locks echoed throughout the room.

"Whoa! Hey, man, we aren't looking for any trouble! Why are you locking us in here?!" Bryon looked left and right, attempting to pull open the door. His feet were both on the door as he pulled with his hands.

"Bryon. Bryon. Calm down," I said, placing my hand on his shoulder. Bryon came down off the door, a bead of sweat dribbling down his forehead. The room was like a large cavern filled with what looked like old military equipment. Weapons, computers, papers, everything atop a natural dirt floor.

"My name is Abd al Alim. You can call me 'Al,'" the voice from under the cloak said, calmly pulling back the headscarf to reveal a soft-faced young man. His green eyes shone in the candlelight, his left eye cuffed by a large scar from his eyebrow to the bottom of his cheek. His tan complexion was smooth and sun-kissed. "I'm sorry for the theatrics. I had to be discreet so that they did not follow," he said, ruffling his short black hair and relieving it of his hat head. "Everyone on both sides has been watching the rifts with hawk eyes ever since the balance has been tested. You, sir, have been at the topic of conversation for quite some time. You must be stirring up trouble back where you're from."

"How do you know who I am?" I asked.

"Everyone knows who you are. On both sides. It was said that you had been killed many generations ago. No one knew where you had gone. The great protector just…disappeared. Now that you have returned, they are scared. The balance is beginning to shift back to the light," the boy continued as he wrestled through some wooden crates, looking for something.

His voice was soft and a bit eerie. "I knew that you had not been killed. I could sense your energy, though faint. I knew you were still with us. I knew that you would be coming this way to find the Garden. To find your weapon. You will need it to if you plan to defeat him."

"If I had been killed, would I not have simply returned? And what do you know of my weapon?" I asked, moving closer to where the boy was ransacking. The entire basement was trashed. Papers and boxes were thrown everywhere, with objects of all kinds lying on the ground and wooden shelves covered in spider webs.

"You really don't remember. We spiritual creatures do not simply die and return to Heaven or Hell. When we die, we are sent to an endless void of nothingness. Oblivion. Never to return," he said, stopping and staring me in the eyes. "With you believed to be dead, the light began to fade and darkness grew. They became confident and strong. Your men of the light did not know what to do without you. But now that you are back, I must take you to find your sword. Without it, I am not sure you can defeat him again. He has grown stronger in your absence. Sin and death have flourished like a virus, filling the wretched dragon's blood." Al struggled through the containers again.

"Lucifer," I whispered. Al stopped his scavenging and grabbed me by the arm, once again looking into the windows of my soul.

"Lucifer," Al said in such a tone that was condemning and stern.

"Yeah, yeah. We know." Bryon dug his hands in his pocket, pulling out a bagel.

Jade inched forward closer to Al, eyes like an eagle locked and focused.

"Have I ever killed him before?" I asked.

"Did you not listen to a single word I just said?" Al released my arm. "If you had killed him, he would be in Oblivion, and we wouldn't be having this conversation. Though you are the only one who can. Your father has been the only Arch to ever defeat Lucifer. Though in his victory he had only the power to trap the demon in his cage in Hell. He did not have the power to kill the creature."

"My father has fought with the devil?" I asked.

"Your father defeated him," Jade said, placing a hand on my shoulder. She could tell there were thoughts firing off like supernovas in the vastness of my mind.

"Your father was wounded in the battle, so the Almighty reassigned him to other works. Though in exchange for his valiant fight, he awarded your father a son—you. No spiritual being had ever been given this gift, this honor of a child. With your birth, The King of Kings endowed you with a gift. Something none other possess. It is said that a small portion of the very matter that He used to create all that is, the original purity, runs through your veins," Al said, never breaking eye contact. Staring back, I saw that the green eyes Al had were not green at all but a mixture of moving colors. Galaxies among galaxies. Tens of thousands of stars and universes all housed in the eyes of this young man. Finally breaking his stare, Al said, "That is why we must find you your weapon. Here." Al found what he was looking for.

He held up a compass that looked as old as time itself. It was the size of a fist, beautifully crafted out of pure gold. Al opened it up. Instead of it having a needle pointing north, south, east, and west, it looked like the night sky. Stars, moons, purples, and greens all flowed within the glass casing within the gold as if it were alive.

"Whoa." Bryon reached to touch it.

Al swatted away his hand. "I have been saving this for your return. It will only work for the chosen one. This compass will lead you directly to where you are looking for."

"How does it work?" Jade asked.

"Only the endowed knows." Al gently handed it over.

"I don't know what to do," I said, taking hold of the artifact.

"Feel the energy. Let it flow through your soul." Al said in a softer tone, "Pray for the sight."

I closed my eyes. Al stood back. Jade and Bryon noticed and did the same, taking a few steps back. My breathing began to slow. My wrist began to glow a bright blue, lighting the entirety of the room.

"I can feel it," I said. "I can feel it!"

In an instant, an orb of energy exploded from the compass into a three-dimensional spherical map encompassing the entire room. Visions of desert and trees flew past our eyes with lightning speed, whooshing by. It was like being inside a video game; it was like memories. Stopping randomly and then continuing to speed past locations, it was as if our heads were on a swivel turning left and right to catch the sights. Finally, the vision stopped on what looked like a massive rock in the middle of the desert, surrounded by nothing other than sand and heat. Just as quick as the map had appeared, it all came rewinding back into the compass. It was gone. I opened my eyes.

"That…was…AWESOME!" Bryon shouted, spinning in the air.

"What does it mean?" I asked Al.

"It means we must begin our journey," Al said, looking at me. "I know where we are to go. It is not an easy journey, and we may run into some trouble. But I can get us there. Are you ready?"

"What, like right now?" Bryon asked.

Al nodded yes.

Jade leaned over to me and whispered in my ear, "We? You think it is a good idea to bring this guy with us?" I looked at Bryon and Al and smiled. Putting my arm around Jade, I turned her around to speak in private.

"We wouldn't have got to this point without him. We have no one else," I whispered.

"I don't trust him—something feels off," Jade whispered.

"We don't really have a choice. It will be okay, trust me." I grabbed Jade by the hands and looked her in the eyes.

After a moment of consideration, she said, "Okay. I trust you." We turned back to the group.

Bryon looked to Jade, Jade nodded yes, and it was agreed.

"All right, then. Let's do this," Bryon said, taking a bite of his bagel.

Al went scavenging through one more crate. "You will need this." He handed over an old leather necklace with an opal-like stone on the end of it.

"What is this?" I asked.

"This will protect you from the dark one's sight," Al explained. "Your power is growing, making it easier for them to track you. This will cloak your energy."

"What about us? Don't we need to cloak our energy too?" Bryon asked, throwing his hands in the air.

Laughing at Bryon's sincere concern, I put on the necklace.

"I think you'll be okay, Bryon," Jade said. "Plus you still have that one Nile gave you."

"Oh, right." Byron pulled out his amulet. "Phew."

"All right, then. Let's go," Al said, throwing his headscarf and cloak back on covering every inch of skin.

I am the seeker in the night.

CHAPTER 13

THE BIRTH OF DEATH

A DARK VOICE came rumbling out of an arched black, rock hallway. "What news do you bring, soldier, that you have called us together?"

Asorath stood in the middle of the stone cavern hundreds of miles underground. Carved from the hands of demons themselves, the catacombs joined as a cavern, dark and wet. Red-hot magma flowed from six surrounding archways like waterfalls of lava into a river of fire that led to the middle of the room becoming one, forming into a moat that surrounded the perfectly round stone floor. The river of fiery death bubbled and sizzled. Hidden away, their eyes focused on the demon, center stage.

Asorath bowed his head. "Elders, I wish I came bearing good news. Such is not the case. He is losing touch. She has blurred his vision."

"How sssso?" a snake-like voice said, coming from the third tunnel clockwise.

"The balance is shifting quickly. Our kind is falling by the thousands. Yet, he focuses on her and the stone," Asorath announced, his voice echoing throughout the cave.

Another voice came from the sixth tunnel behind Asorath. "Why do you not simply kill the girl?" The voice was so cold and deep, it froze the lava coming from its tunnel.

"We cannot," Asorath said a bit quieter.

The slithering voice came again. "Why notttt?"

"We have tried. She is…protected." Asorath bowed his head once again.

A slow, raspy voice came from the first tunnel on the left. "Who has tried?"

"Myself—Legion—and his sister, Beth. The girl is not like us." The room was silent, waiting for his next words.

"She is his kin. She is just like us," another voice said, coming from the fourth.

"I believe there is something Lucifer is not telling us," Asorath said. He paused before saying the next words. "I believe she is a half-breed." The entire room exploded into accusations being crossed left and right from tunnel to tunnel, all aimed at Asorath.

The deepest voice of all came from the fifth tunnel on the right. "Silence!"

The cave fell silent in obedience. The drip of falling water droplets could be heard hitting the hard, stone floors.

"What makes you say such things? Lucifer knows best of all the rules," the deep voice continued.

Asorath turned to face the tunnel. "Her mother. The woman Lucifer laid with, she was a soul tossed out of the church and condemned to Hell. She attempted to end herself. Lucifer made a deal we were not aware of. He spared the woman from death in exchange for a child," Asorath said. "Lucifer in his lustful haste for child did not know who the woman was—"

"And who might that be, demon?" the deepest rumbling voice asked.

"She, elders, was of direct lineage of *her*—the virgin," Asorath said with his head standing tall.

The deep voice shook the room in quickened anger as it grew louder. "Impossible. We tracked her lineage for generations. They have all been wiped out. I made sure of it myself."

The others echoed.

"Impossible."

"Lies."

"Lies!"

"This is the truth, I swear by it, friends. I do not come to deceive. Her bloodline is that of the woman. The child's mother did not have the strength to survive the birth, her sacrifice…it cleansed the child."

"How did we not know of this until now?" the cold voice spoke.

"The child had not shown signs outside the realm until recently," Asorath continued. "She has been accessing both sides. We had never seen anything like it—the mixture was undetectable. We cannot touch her. Her strength is unmeasurable. Weak at the time, but growing…quickly."

"We must guide her into the right directionnnn," the slithering voice hissed from the darkness of its tunnel. "We must bring her into the darknessss."

"Who has He sent to protect the girl demon?" a raspy voice trembled.

"The boy. Michael's son," Asorath said.

"Had he not been taken care of by your hand a thousand years ago?" the deepest voice rumbled.

Asorath bowed his head in shame. "He was."

"You're certain the boy is the son of Michael?" the cold voice said, freezing the air.

"Yes, I have fought him myself," Asorath continued. "His power is returning at an incalculable rate. We must take action before it is too late. Together, the boy and girl would be unstoppable. Our plans are in effect and soldiers are awaiting orders."

"What do you proposssse?" the snake-like voice asked.

"Lucifer is not fit. He is torn. Enable me. I will get the job done. I will move our kind into the kingdom. I will not fail you. Strengthen me, brothers. I am ready."

"What news of his other—the boy?" said one of the demons who had been silent.

Asorath turned in anger to face the tunnel from which the voice had spoken.

"The child is too young. He does not know yet how to control his power. He will destroy everything. His power is too strong. If we released him now, there would be nothing for us to conquer. Lucifer keeps him locked away. We could not access him if we wanted to." Asorath spoke quickly. "I will get the job done. What say you?"

The room began to buzz with mumbled conversation. Back and forth, the demons in the hidden tunnels argued. Asorath stood on the round stone floor surrounded by the melting hot lava, looking from tunnel to tunnel as each spoke. Water steamed as it dropped from the cave top, hitting the red-hot magma below. After a few moments, the room slowly grew quiet.

The deepest voice came, shaking the cavern. "Do not fail us."

With its words came forth six glowing red eyes the shape of almond-like rubies, stacked three on one side, three on the other. The creature's clawlike hand emerged from the darkness in a slow track toward Asorath. The dinosaur hand pointed its finger as it neared Asorath, slowly it touched the demon's forehead. In an instant, a red explosion of light brightened the room from the point of contact.

Like ants attacking their food, demons of all shapes and sizes crawled out from under the ground and through the lava. Screaming and yelling in anger and agony, they ravaged and swarmed the room. As fast as a tornado, they circled and spun around Asorath, crawling and ripping their way into his body and mouth, his eyes and ears, his skin and bone. Absorbing them into his being, his eyes opened wide. The red glow was like beams of light reaching the top of the cavern.

Darkness filled the room, the screams and cries of the damned echoed and pierced the cavern walls as they became one in the shell of Asorath's burnt and damned soul. Just as quickly as they had come, they were absorbed into his being.

The demon hit his knees, his head fell forward, and his eyes closed.

"How do you feel, brotherrrrrr?" the snake asked.

Asorath took a deep breath and slowly let it out. Heat left his body in waves, steam bellowed from his shoulders. As he leaned his head back, he opened his once-red eyes. His eyes now blacker than black, pure darkness, nothingness, no shine, no glow. Black. Standing from his knees, his once-bony, skeleton-like body was now that of an ox. Strong and muscular, no skin, no hair, his exposed muscles the color of the night sky. Standing thirty feet tall, his clawlike hands reached to the ground, his chest barreled with strength and size. His snout-like face had grown wide, his tusks elongated. From his back, dinosaur-like spikes lined his spine.

Taking in a deep breath, he exhaled. "I. Am. Death."

CHAPTER 14

SILVER TONGUE

T HE LAND SURROUNDING the mansion was quiet. The cool mountain air stood as still as a statue against the clear glass windows. An eerie feeling—no wind blowing, no animals wandering, no trees dancing or creaking. Complete silence.

Like a hot knife through butter, the sound of soft breathing could be heard inside a room in the castle. Abigail's sleeping breath moved the air inside her room as she rested her bones, recovering from the excitement earlier that day. In the other room, about fifty yards away, mumbling could be heard ever so slightly through the closed doors of Mr. Li'Ved's office.

"Good work, Barbas. With this, you have made your kind proud," Mr. Li'Ved said to a small gremlin-like creature. His modest stature that of a koala bear, he stood on his hind legs with his pointy ears perked straight up. His big brown eyes stared at Mr. Li'Ved with pride as his large gaping mouth smiled, revealing hundreds of razor-like teeth.

"Thank you, master. What will you do with it now?" Barbas asked, staring at the object he had just handed to Mr. Li'Ved.

"Don't worry about that, my loyal servant," Lucifer said, ogling his new prize. "Just know that we will be advancing our plans. Time is becoming short; we must take action. Ready the spirits. Await my orders."

"Yes, master," Barbas gurgled up. He bowed his head and vanished into a cloud of smoke.

"Very good job, my little demon," Mr. Li'Ved said to himself as he stared at the small object wrapped in a tattered cloth. After a few moments of adoration, he made his way to his artifact room. The door's hinges creaked as it gave way to his most prized possessions, all held in one glorious room.

With the artifact in hand, his eyes locked onto the large object hidden under the black cloth.

Click. Clack. Click. Clack.

His wood-bottomed shoes tapped the ground with each step, marking his approach. Passing the glass-encased antiquities, each seemingly more valuable than the other, he arrived at the large, odd-shaped object.

The towering covered item began to shake as Mr. Li'Ved approached. Standing there, Mr. Li'Ved reached out his right hand, grabbing hold of the black sheet, with his newest trophy in his left. With one strong downward pull, Mr. Li'Ved exposed the tall, rocklike Goliath.

Standing eight feet tall, the stone loomed over Lucifer like a giant looking down. The top of which was sharp and pointed like the peak of a mountain with two smaller ridges to the right and left of the taller center peak. The sides and back were rough and unsymmetrical, round and sharp rocky edges texturing the stone. While the front was smooth as glass and black as night, its matte finish reflected not one atom of light. The shaking stopped the instant the rock face was revealed.

—§—

THE CREAKING OF the door must have been enough to wake Abigail in the silence of the house. She had made her way downstairs and followed the clacking of her father's wood-bottomed shoes.

"Daddy?" Her soft voice yawned as she approached the open door to the artifact room, stretching both arms above her head. Her blonde hair a mess from the deep slumber. Though his focus was so intense that the quiet noise of her freshly awakened voice was not heard.

"Come forward, boy. I have something to show you," he said to the stone.

Abigail stopped at the entrance of the room just after spotting her father speaking to the stone. She knelt down and hid behind the opening of the door, just peeking her head in enough to see and hear what was going on. Her senses awakened in an instant, and adrenaline pumped through her veins, her eyes dilating like that of a hawk and ears perked like a rabbit listening for danger.

"You make all that fuss and then don't want to show me your beautiful face?" her father said, trying to coax the stone.

The matte black rock face began to reveal the outline of a shape.

"That's it," Mr. Li'Ved said.

The shape began to form. Becoming larger and more distinct, it began to look almost human. The blackness of the stone evaporated away, making visible an abomination.

"There he is," Mr. Li'Ved said.

The creature's face was as the shape of any average man, though missing both eyes and a nose. Also lacking hair and ears. A smooth head and seamless face. His mouth gaping wide open at the bottom of the face, positioned as normal just above the jaw. Every anatomical muscle fiber in plain sight, yet black as tar. No masculine or feminine appendages were apparent, although exposed. Its muscular neck led down to a well-maintained body. The muscle mass was that of a conditioned athlete, strong and solid. Out of its chiseled chest jutted four S-shaped horns, one on top of the other two on each chest. The arms and shoulders were exposed muscle with razor-sharp, ridgelike bones slicing through every three inches of surface lining the sides of its arms. The rocklike abdomen was as one solid piece of meat.

"My son," her father said.

"Hello, Father," the deep, alien-like voice said. His mouth dripping tar like blood.

"Son? Father?" Abigail whispered to herself, hiding in the back of the room just a stone's throw away, having moved in from curiosity.

"What is taking so long?" the faceless creature asked.

"Patience, my son, we are almost there. Today we have made a tremendous leap forward with this find," Mr. Li'Ved said as he pulled out the cloth, unraveling it to expose a railroad-like spike of a nail. Rusted and chipped, the pointed end was darker than the rest.

"I don't care about your silly toys! I have been patient! Release me!" the boy snarled. The rock enclosure shook as the creature slammed his fists on the glasslike stone.

"You remember who you are speaking to! These 'toys' are what is needed to release you!" her father yelled back at the image of the creature held within the flat stone surface. "It is not as easy as you may believe, and you are not ready. You do not know how to control your strength."

The boy paced back and forth. "You let that worthless halfbreed you call a daughter run the grounds of earth like it is her playground, and yet you will not release *me*?! I hate you! I hate her!"

"Half-breed?" Abigail muttered from her hiding place.

"You will respect her!" Mr. Li'Ved said. "She is our still our blood. Half-breed or not."

"You play by every rule of His, except that one. You knew what you were doing with the woman. You knew who she was. Release me, Father. I am ready to claim my throne."

Mr. Li'Ved moved closer to the stone. "You must learn to control your strength or there will be no throne for you to claim."

Just as Mr. Li'Ved had finished his sentence, Abigail lost her footing from where she had been leaning in closer to listen, and she stumbled forward.

"Ah," she said, catching herself on all fours.

The creature turned its head to face Abigail. "Hello, little sister."

"Abigail?" Mr. Li'Ved slapped the smooth surface of the rock, causing the image of the creature to vanish instantaneously. A look of fear and shock painted his face.

Abigail slowly stood up. "Father, who was that? Who were you talking to?"

"Abigail, you don't know what you are talking about. You are still delirious from earlier. You hit your head very hard, baby," Mr. Li'Ved said, calmly approaching Abigail.

"Who was that? I know what I saw. Why were you calling him son? What were you talking about?" Abigail asked, taking small steps backward without breaking eye contact with her father.

"Abigail, come here. Let me take you back up to bed," Mr. Li'Ved said, reaching out his hand to take hold of hers.

Abigail took a few more steps backward. "Don't treat me like a little kid," Abigail said with anger in her voice. "Stop lying to me." Her wrist began to flicker and glow a bright red. Her blue eyes faded to black.

"Abigail, baby. It's time to calm down now! Come here, come to daddy." Mr. Li'Ved said, reaching closer to grab Abigail by the hand.

"You're a liar!" she yelled, releasing a pulse of energy and sending Mr. Li'Ved flying backward. All the artifacts in the room shook and fell from their posts. Her kind voice…changed. No longer sweet and innocent, but dark and malevolent.

"Abigail. You. Will. Obey me!" her father yelled as he rose from the ground. His body fuming, his eyes red and black. He ran as fast as a lion after its prey, with her in his sight. A black aura surrounded her.

"You told me he was dead. You told me I was going to inherit the kingdom," she vociferated. "You are going to re-lease him, aren't you?" Mr. Li'Ved grabbed her by the arm. She fought back, taking hold of his wrist, bringing him to his knees, nearly crippling him. "Aren't you!" Her voice deep and echoing.

"Yes." Mr. Li'Ved looked her in her dark eyes.

There seemed to be a sense of pride he felt looking into her rage-filled heart. Evil personified brought to his knees by a small blonde girl. Her hair danced in the dark air as the en-ergy emitted from the two tossed and turned the room. Ar-tifacts, paintings, placeholders alike flew through the air and crashed to the ground in a whirlwind of art. Mr. Li'Ved still on his knees in the grip of his daughter. "I've never seen this from you, my daughter." Her grip tightened. "I—am…so proud of you. But you need to let Daddy go. I need you to calm down, and I will explain everything," he struggled to say through the agony she so easily inflicted.

Abigail took a second, still staring into her father's now-blue eyes. A moment passed as she released a deep breath along with his wrist. The items swirling around crashed to the floor, the room stood in shambles. Quiet and broken. Her hair returned to her side, and blue filled her eyes like drops in the dark ocean. Though this time, something seemed to have changed. The blue was not quite as blue. Mr. Li'Ved exhaled and grabbed his wrist, rubbing it in pain.

"Good girl," he said, standing to his feet as she dropped to her knees with tear-filled eyes. Like waterfalls, her tears fell forming a pond beneath her disheartened face.

"Who was she?" she sobbed.

"You mustn't worry about that, Abigail." Mr. Li'Ved reached down, placing his hand under her chin.

"No…" she said, breaking eye contact and looking back to the ground. The puddle of water grew. "I am not your daughter. I am a half-breed, and you know who my mother was. Tell me."

"Darling, you are my daughter and more like me than you know, very powerful too from what I can now see. You will make a perfect queen." Mr. Li'Ved placed his hand on her shoulder.

Abigail jerked it away from his grasp. "Do not touch me. You may never touch me. I am nothing like you. How did that, that *thing* know who my mother is? Why won't you tell me?"

She jumped up and began to run as fast as she could, out of the room and down the hall.

"Abigail," her father yelled from the room, his voice echoing in all the halls, "don't run from Daddy." His annoyance was returning.

The *click, clack* of his shoes could be heard following her trail. Her panicking breath came heavy with each gasp of air as she sprinted.

Her father appeared right in front of her. "Where do you think you are going?" He grabbed her shoulders. Shocked, she tried to wriggle free. "I think it's time you cooled off."

"Let me go!" Abigail responded.

Dragging her deadweight body down the hall as she kicked and screamed, she could see no remorse in his eyes.

"I hate you! I hate you! You won't get away with any of this! Dean is going to stop you!" Abigail screamed as she wriggled on the ground, trying to release her arm from her father's grip.

"You think I don't know about your little boyfriend and his pals," her father said without looking down, continuing to drag her down the marble-floored halls. "They think they are so high and mighty with their love from Him!" A hint of jealousy in his voice was apparent among the fury. "Well, they aren't! Everything I need is already in motion!" Mr. Li'Ved stopped and leaned down to look her in the eyes. "And I have a little friend of my own taking care of those pesky little twerps as we speak! So quit this fit and act like a queen. Or you will never be one." He was so close, the spit rained on her face. His breath like steam entered her pores.

Mr. Li'Ved turned from her and approached a stairwell at the end of the hall. He dragged her down a spiral stone staircase into their basement. The stairs were cold and hard, giving no mercy as her legs bounced from one to the next. The sound of her bones smacking the floor was unforgiving.

"Where are you taking me?" Abigail asked.

"Someplace I know you'll stay. I knew I had to lock up your brother. I never thought I would have to lock up my daughter too. You kids, so ungrateful." He tossed Abigail into the dark dungeon-like room. "I'll come for you when the time is right and your precious angel is dead." Mr. Li'Ved slammed the heavy wooden door closed. The sound of a large lock echoed through the room from the outside in.

Darkness. Pure Darkness.

"No! You can't!" Abigail cried out, though it was helpless. Her screams could not be heard, nor the pounding of her fists on the solid tree of a door. "Dean, please hurry," she whispered, sliding her back down the stone wall.

—§—

AFTER MAKING HIS way back upstairs, Lucifer picked up the landline. "Where are you?!" Lucifer shouted into his old black telephone.

A Middle Eastern man could be heard on the other line. "I'm going as fast as I can. I continue to run into…distractions." Shouting could be heard in the background.

"Do your job!" Lucifer yelled. "Bring me what I ask for. We are running out of time. He is advancing his armies."

"Yes, master," answered the man on the phone.

"HEY, AL, WHO are you talking to?! Come on, man. Let's go! Stop being so weird!" Bryon said. Jade and I turned to see what Bryon was yelling about. The two were about ten yards behind.

Al ended the phone call on his satellite phone, flipping it closed.

"Who were you talking to?" Bryon asked.

"I was making sure the roads were clear up ahead. The rebels have been setting traps for the government militaries near our route," Al said.

"Oh. Okay. Well, cool, thanks. Come on. Let's go. Dean and Jade are getting ahead of us," Bryon said, waiting for Al to move in front of him. Jade and I waved to him.

Al complied and began walking again, following Jade and I. Bryon looked around in all directions. He seemed to be suspicious of something.

"Mr. Dean." Al ran to catch up with me. "Mr. Dean."

I stopped and turned to speak with Al. "What's up?" I asked.

"How long have you known Bryon?" Al asked.

"I don't know, not too long. Why?" I could feel my curiosity grow.

"I sense something about him that is off," Al whispered. "Dark, one would say."

"Bryon?" I chuckled, looking over at Bryon, who was searching his backpack with great vigor and finally pulling out a candy bar and jumping for joy. "Nah, Bryon is cool. I would have known if he was off."

"Would you? You are just now regaining your powers. Didn't he come into your life right as you began to see the darkness again? And he has been trying tirelessly to help you find this weapon of ultimate power without asking for anything in return. Don't you find that a bit odd?" Al sounded very convincing, yet I was not swayed.

After a moment of thinking, I said, "Nah, Bryon wouldn't do that. He wouldn't hurt a fly. I mean, look at the guy."

Al and I looked over at Bryon, smiling from ear to ear, eyes closed as he enjoyed his candy bar, chocolate smeared on his face, and sitting in the hot sand. Just as he was doing so, a small fly landed on his candy bar. His eyes popped open so large they could be used to see molecules on a microscopic level. His smile turned to a frown and he *smashed* the unlucky bug between his hands, laughing with malice. Returning to smile and enjoy the rest of his chocolate bar.

Al and I looked at each other.

"Okay, well, still," I said. "Bryon wants to help, that's all. I trust him."

Al squinted at me. "Be careful who you trust, Mr. Dean."

"Hey, guys! I think we are getting close," Jade yelled from the very front of the group. Al, Bryon, and I all went running to where Jade was standing at the top of a desert hill comprised of golden sand. Jade pointed out into the horizon. "Look."

At the tip of her finger about ten miles in the distance was a large rock standing all alone. Like a guardian of the desert, it stood its ground, firm and strong. A lone soldier surrounded by the vast emptiness of rolling hills of sand. The bright yellow sun was dropping quick and reflecting off the glassy pebbles. "We had better hurry if we are going to get there before sundown," she said.

Al was typing something into his phone while we were still looking at the rock. Bryon turned and caught a glimpse of Al just as he was putting his phone away. The two locked eyes for a brief second. "All right, let's get going then," Al said, taking the lead. The three of us followed. Bryon looked at me with suspicious eyes. I nodded it off and smiled, taking a step forward. Bryon followed.

Displacing sand with each step, we made our journey through the remaining desert. With no buildings in sight, the only thing to fix our eyes on was the stone. Sand was our solitary company. Desert our grave.

Heat waves rippled off the ground, rising into the air, cooking everything the invisible radiation passed through. A desert microwave. The air was so hot it was tangible, like walking against an invisible wall of fire. The smell of fast-moving electrons burned our nostrils, hot energy draining our own. Though the sun was slowly falling, the temperature remained constant. I could taste the air.

Sweat radiated in our bodies' vile attempts to cool themselves off. All except one. Looking over at Al, Bryon shouted, "Hey, Al, aren't you hot?"

Jade and I turned to look.

"Of course, what kind of question is that?" Al responded.

"Why aren't you sweating like the rest of us then?" Bryon demanded.

"Bryon, come on," I interjected, trying to stop an argument before it arose.

Bryon stepped closer to Al. "No. I want to know. You are completely covered from head to toe in all black, and you aren't sweating one bit."

Al responded without hesitation. "I have been out here for hundreds of years, Bryon. I am accustomed to the heat. My body has grown and adapted."

"See, simple. Let's go," I said, taking a step forward to continue on. Jade followed behind me, but Bryon stayed, staring at Al as Al stared back. His starlike eyes seemed to anger as he turned and followed my steps. Bryon fell in line.

The distant ball of fire continued to descend.

CHAPTER 15

THE FOUR-HEADED SNAKE

O UR DESERT JOURNEY to the monumental rock continued with still nothing in sight but the hills of sand and
the solitary stone in the distance. The sun had nearly reached
the horizon. The walk had been quiet, very quiet.

"Hey, Bryon, you okay? You haven't said a word for like two
hours." I slowed down to get to Bryon.

"I don't trust him," Bryon said.

"Who, Al?" I asked.

"He isn't right, Dean. He is hiding something," Bryon said,
wiping sweat off his brow and placing his hands on his head.

"Funny, he said the same thing about you," I said.

"He is trying to turn you against me because he knows that
I know he is up to something. I mean, can we really trust him?
We don't even know the guy. He came out of nowhere and is
all of a sudden the nicest guy in the world, taking us to a place
that for generations he has be searching for. Yet, it is only ac-
cessible by you. You heard him, that compass thing only works
for you, no one else, and now he knows exactly where to go

for whatever it is he is looking for." Bryon stared in my eyes. I hadn't seen him so serious, ever.

I looked over at Al. "He just wants to help. Yeah, he is pretty weird, but what is normal anymore? He was kind enough to bring us this far. I think he would have done something the second he found out where the location was."

"What if he still needs you for one more thing?" Bryon asked. "Like how the compass didn't work for him. There must be another safeguard, don't you think? Something he can't do on his own."

"I didn't know you or Jade either when we first started all this, and now look." I glanced over at Jade. She seemed to be taking notes in a journal, looking up and down at the rock.

"This isn't the same, and you know it. I mean, how can you not feel it? I get a completely different vibe from this guy than I did from Nile. There was a certain energy about Nile, something warm and good, and Al doesn't have it. Dean, I know how you feel—you want to find this thing and learn more about your family and purpose, but…" Bryon placed his hand on my shoulder.

"You don't know anything about how I feel," I pulled away, "or what it's like to not know who you are or who your family is. And you don't know Al!" I shouted, sure the other two hadn't quite heard the conversation, but they saw the annoyance on my face as I marched forward in front of the group. "Come on! We need to speed it up. The sun is almost down," I yelled.

Jade and Al looked back at Bryon. Jade didn't know what to do with the situation. Al, on the other hand, had a devious smirk of pride on his face. Bryon shook it off and marched on. Al ran to catch up.

"I told you that you cannot trust him. He is trying to turn you against your own kind," Al whispered in my ear.

"Now is not the time, Al. I don't know what to think about anyone," I answered back. "Let's just keep moving. I don't want to hear about either of you anymore."

His eyes seemed to shift in color as I spoke.

"Don't turn your back on him, Mr. Dean. I believe he is working with the darkness. He hides his true form from us. We cannot trust him," Al whispered again. This caused me to turn and look at Bryon, who was following with a look of anger on his face.

"Maybe you're right. Now shut up and keep moving," I said, turning forward again.

The four of us continued to walk. The desert was beginning to cool off. The air was no longer thick with heat but now felt as if a tropical beach was nearby. In fact, the air itself began to feel cool. The sand underneath our feet was no longer searing hot but cold to the touch. The sun fell. The desert sky was a soft yellow and orange mixed with pinks and grays.

"Jade, what's going on?" I asked.

"I don't know. I..." Jade tried to answer.

"We are here," Al said, pointing upward.

Above, about two hundred feet in the air, hovered the mountain of a rock. There it was, levitating of its own free will. Yet, it cast no shadow. In awe we all looked up, admiring the goliath. The bottom of the rock was rounded and jagged like that of an iceberg. It was beautiful.

"Whoa." Jaws dropped simultaneously. "Jade..." I struggled. The ground began to shake violently as if the earth was breaking apart.

"I don't know. I don't know." She tried maintaining her balance.

"What's going on?!" I yelled over the sound of earth cracking and shifting beneath our feet.

"I don't think we are supposed to be here!" Bryon yelled back.

Trying our best to maintain footing on top of the vibrating ground, our arms flailed wildly. In an instant, two bolts of lightning came crashing down from the sky, one almost immediately after the other. Dirt and dust exploded into the air, creating a cloud of brown and gold particles. Our ears were ringing from the sound of the thunderous boom.

Bryon yelled out, "Dean, you okay?"

"Yeah, I'm good," I yelled back, "Jade, Al, you guys okay?"

"We are okay." Their voices came sifting through the zillions of molecules floating around in the air. The dimming light of the descending sun reflected off each particle of dust, creating a golden mask impossible to see through.

As the dust began to settle, two towering beings slowly became visible.

First, their feet the size of boats, their legs taller and thicker than ancient redwoods, their skin made of pure gold accented by beautiful designs of white marble swirling around. Atop their glorious skin floated a thin layer of elegant blue and white flames dancing with a calm grace. The beings were so tall that their waists were belted by the lining of the clouds in the sky. Their upper bodies were hidden beyond the fluffy, white, floating marshmallows in the air.

"What are those?" Bryon asked.

"WHO DARES STEP FOOT ON THE HOLY GARDEN?" their thunderous voices came booming down to earth, shaking the ground once again. The sound was something of antiquity and beauty accompanied by an almost robotic vibrato.

"Not much of a garden, aye?" Bryon leaned over and whispered into Jade's ear.

Jade stared at Bryon and rolled her eyes.

Al said, "Ancient ones! We come seeking an ancient relic. There is—"

"SILENCE!" their voices came in unison.

The quiet air returned like an old friend in the night. Stillness. The sheer power I could feel from the beings was paralyzing. Nerves fluttered their wings. I knew it was I who needed to speak. It was a power unlike any other. *Be strong.* I remembered my father. Strong. *I am strong.*

I spoke with confidence and power behind my voice. "Holy ones, my name is Dean Michael, son of The Great Archangel Michael." I lowered myself to one knee and bowed my head. "I come seeking your aid. There is a great darkness coming to my home, and I cannot overcome it on my own."

The desert was still, the air thin and motionless.

Whoosh.

"What the…" Jade said.

The air began to move, though not side to side like normal but rather…downward. Confused by the phenomenon, we looked to the other for an answer. Just then, out of the sky we saw it, a great, large hand coming from above the clouds. The force of the truck-sized hand pushed the air down with such force, it blew the ground away like that of a powerful helicopter making its approach.

"Close your eyes!" Jade yelled.

The dust flew so fast it was like razor blades against our skin.

"No, duh!" Bryon yelled.

The hand slowed and came to rest atop the desert surface.

"COME," the voices rumbled from the sky as the dust settled. I looked at Bryon and then over to Jade, seeking their approval. With a shrug of disarray from Bryon, I moved forward onto the platform of a hand.

The upward force of the hand as it began to rise into the clouds brought me to my knees with wind pounding against my face. The gravitational force was that of a spaceship launching into the dark void at near breakneck speeds. I am the bug against the windshield.

The hand slowed its ascent as it crossed the line of the clouds. Now, above the weather, the sky was crystal clear. Bluer than any blue I had ever seen before, with the golden rays of light reflecting off the magnificent bodies of the celestial beings. Shielding my eyes from the glow of their skin, the oculus in my head began to adapt, becoming friends with the light. Uncovering my eyes, the sight I saw was magnificent and fantastical. Colors unlike any seen by man, indescribable.

The beings had brought me but inches from their faces. The pure wonder kept me on my knees as I absorbed the beauty.

Not one but four faces on each head of the two beings. One of an ox, one of a man, another of a lion, and one of an eagle, just like the picture in the book. Seeing them in person was mind-bending, images like memories flashed through my mind. Their skin was covered in what looked like the purest-white marbled designed tattoos, swirling and lining their neck and faces.

I was as a speck of dirt next to a boulder compared to their massive size.

I stood to my feet, establishing myself. "Your Holy Ones, I—" I nearly fell from the surprise of their thunderous voice.

"SHOW US," all eight heads said nearly simultaneously, echoing the others. Their heads spun slowly around their massive necks.

Instinctively, I moved forward, revealing the mark on my arm. Each face spun to see, to verify, and their eyes widened as each discovered what they were looking for.

"We have been expecting you," they all said.

—§—

"I WONDER WHAT is going on up there?" Bryon asked. The beings were no longer loud enough for the three on the ground to hear. The silent desert stood patient.

Jade plopped down on the sandy hill, waiting patiently like the earth.

"THEN YOU KNOW what I have come seeking," I said, standing tall and strong.

"What you seek is within your grasp. You need only but the faith of a mustard seed," they spoke softly, robotic and angelic at the same time.

I forced my voice to be calm. "I have the faith, but where might I find my sword? I don't remember. Please help me. I come humbly before you seeking what you guard."

"Seek not with your eyes, but with thine heart. Seek and ye shall find. Ask and it shall be given to you," they replied in riddle, spinning from ox to eagle.

"I don't know what you are saying. We are running out of time. There are dark forces at work and the Evil One is getting stronger. Please, Holy Guardians, I need your help. We all need your help," I said. I didn't know what else to do but beg. The weight of the world was heavy.

"Your vision is clouded by the mind," the beings said, shifting from face to face. "Purify your soul and clear your thoughts, only then will you see. Only then will your heart be set free from whence it last came."

"Where did I come from? What happened to me? I don't remember! Why won't you tell me!" I became enraged in a fit of helplessness, and my wrist began to glow a bright red.

"YOU WILL *NOT* IN THE GARDEN OF GOD!" the beings clapped back with their earthshaking voices. All eyes illuminated a blinding white light, their tattoos lit up just as

quick and of the same bright, glowing white light. "WE ARE
THE GUARDIANS OF THE GARDEN. YOU WILL RE-
SPECT HIS HOME!" Their voices were so powerful that I
was knocked onto my back from the wind, blowing my face
and hair like a powerful typhoon.

"Guardians," I spoke softly as I stood to my feet, "I do not
mean to disrespect. Please accept my apologies. I seek only your wisdom and guidance. Show me what I must do to
see—show me how I can find what I seek and once again defend the people."

A hand from the other being not holding me in the air
slowly rose out of the clouds with an open palm upright and
facing me dead-on. Approaching slowly, the palm began to
glow a small, light blue glow the size of a human hand right in
the center of its large barn-door palm.

"Come and see," the voices said.

I moved forward, slowly stretching out my arm and bringing my own hand in line with the small blue glow. I closed
my eyes just before touching down, but a second later I was
launched backward once again, landing on my back on the soft
surface of the supporting palm. The hand lowered from its position.

"No." My words were heavy and slow, breathing erratic as if
I had been sprinting a marathon. "No. That is not true. What
did you show me?!" I shouted with tears streaking my face.

"You have seen the truth. Take this knowledge, and you
will find what you seek," the voices said calmly.

"No! That isn't the truth! That cannot be! I refuse it! I
refuse what you have shown me!" I continued to shout
through falling tears.

"Leave behind the desires of the flesh," the beings said.
"Leave behind the wants of the world, the lusts of the heart.
Then and only then will you become who you once were.

Should you ignore this...YOU...WILL...FAIL—just as be-fore."

"That is not what I asked for—that is not what I asked to see!" I shouted.

The hand on which I was held in the sky began to lower it-self down below the clouds and back to earth. "No! Wait!"

"Seek and you shall find. Ask and it shall be given unto you. This is the world of the Lord. Go with God. Live by faith, not by sight." The voices could be heard ever so faintly as I was lowered to the ground.

"Where is it?! I don't understand!" I continued to shout.

The hand approached the ground. On my knees, I sat in de-feat. Gently the hand turned, sliding my body off and onto the sand between the three others and once again returning to its resting spot above the clouds.

"Agh!" I shouted and slammed my fists into the sand. Just as quickly as they had appeared, the holy beings disappeared in the strike of two bolts of lightning. The sky had turned to black. The sun had taken its final resting spot and gave own-ership to the moon and stars. Uncountable, the stars were like diamonds tossed into the night sky.

I rose to my feet.

"Finally! I didn't think you were ever coming back. Where is it? Can I hold it?!" Bryon said, making swordlike swinging gestures.

My eyes were red from the tears, my face solid as stone. I turned and walked.

"What's wrong? What did I say?" Bryon stopped.

Jade ran to stop me. "Dean. Hey," she spoke softly, "is everything okay? What happened up there?"

"Nothing. Coming here was a waste of time," I said. Up the spine of the desert hill, I made my way.

"What was that all about?" Bryon asked.

Al ran after, following my path. "Dean. Where is it? Where is the sword?" he asked nervously.

"I don't know." I continued to walk up the crest of the hill.

Al jumped in front of me. "What do you mean? Where is it!" His large eyes widened.

I stopped, throwing my hands up. "I mean, I don't know! For all I know it's gone! It doesn't exist! There is no sword!"

After a moment of silence, I turned and trekked on. Al stood dumbfounded and at a loss for words.

Bryon and Jade had stayed back and watched the commotion unravel. Jade shook her head, disappointed, and turned the other direction, walking away as if seeking a moment of solitude.

"Jade, where are you going?" Bryon asked.

Jade continued walking in silence.

"Well, that's fine. I'm okay here all alone. I'll just wait here," Bryon said with bewildered eyes, scanning the dark desert void, jumping at the smallest noise. His eyes darted from side to side, dilating, trying to see all he could in the darkness of night. "Mannn...DEAN, WAIT UP!" Bryon said, running in my direction.

Alone, I walked in the stillness of night. My path lit by the moon and stars with nothing but a dark void on all horizons. I went through every second of what the Guardians of the Garden had shown me. Against every fiber in my being, I fought it, denying the visions now burned into my mind. No.

The faint sound of running footsteps tickled my ears. "Bryon, I'm not in the mood, man," I said to the sound.

The steps grew louder and quicker, fast approaching.

"Dude! Stop!" I yelled, turning to scold Bryon.

Without having time to even turn and face him completely, I was violently tackled to the ground. The blow had knocked the air out of me, and I struggled to regain my breath. Sand

blinded my eyes as the small stones entered and cut the surfaces of the cornea. "What are you doing! Stop!"

Taking punishment, blow after blow I wiped my eyes,
clearing them of the dirt.

When I could see again, I realized who was hitting me.
"Al?"

Al's eyes were large and yellow like that of a feral cat, his
teeth exposed like a shark attacking its victim. Hundreds of
razor-sharp teeth lined his upper and lower jaw. His skinny,
bony body was exposed from its clothing.

"Where is it?! Where are you hiding it?!" Al shouted
through his hypodermiclike teeth.

I fought him off, holding his jaw open by the teeth, keeping
him from ripping off my face. Blood dripped down my hands
from the sharp teeth gnashing away to get free.

"Ah!" A few of his teeth pierced my hands deeper. Punc-
tured and bleeding, I maintained my grip. "Get off of me!" I
shouted, kicking Al off.

The crazed maniac went soaring through the air. More than
a football field's distance.

"I know they gave it to you! I know they told you not to
give it to me!" Al shouted as he stood up from the body-sized
crater in the sand.

"I don't have it!" I shouted through heavy breaths. Where
was Bryon and Jade? What did he do to them? The thought
was like a carrousel—round and round it went.

"LIES!" Al began sprinting at me once again. Like a lo-
comotive, he came rushing in on the spine of the hill, eyes
locked on mine. His claws exposed and teeth drawn, he barreled toward me. I stood ready this time.

"Come on, come on," I whispered to myself.

My wrist remained human.

"COME ON!"

Nothing.

Al was getting closer and closer.

"Ahhh!!" I shouted, preparing for impact.

"Not on my watch!" I heard someone yell.

Bryon came hurdling in from the hillside, smashing into Al with all his force and knocking them both down the other side of the sandy dune.

"Bryon! No!" I shouted, running after their now-rolling bodies. Careening down the hillside, they flipped head over heels, heels over head, side to side, kicking up dirt in their wake like a wheel of fireworks on the Fourth of July.

Finally, their bodies came to rest at the bottom of the hill, barely visible in the dim night sky.

"Ah," Bryon groaned, placing his hands under his body and trying to lift himself up. Slowly getting to his feet, he looked around for Al. They had rolled the distance of a mountain down the hill. I ran as fast as I could. I could see Bryon stand up. Just behind him the sand began to move and rise, Al's eyes slowly emerged from beneath the ocean waves of sand, glowing in the moonlight. Bryon didn't see him.

"Bryon! Watch out!" I shouted. Bryon turned, but it was too late.

"I'll kill you!" Al shouted, lunging at Bryon from beneath the sand and tackling him to the ground. "I have wanted to do this since you walked through my door, you worthless human!" Al yelled, swinging his sharp claws at Bryon, grazing his side.

"Dean, get out of here!" Bryon fought to take control of Al's swinging arms. Just as he did, Al lunged forward with his shark-like teeth and bit down.

"AHH!!!" Bryon shouted as blood squirted from his neck and shoulder.

"NO!" I froze in shock for a brief second. "GET OFF OF HIM!!" I shouted, sprinting toward Al and Bryon. As I was closing the gap, my wrist lit up a bright blue.

The blue light flooded my icy veins as tears swelled my eyes, the feeling of helplessness was overwhelming. My friend. I am the bleeding heart.

Bryon lay motionless. Filled with rage, my ears began to ring. Dizzy with each step, I couldn't believe what I was seeing. How could I not have listened? Bryon tried to tell me. My heart pounded in my stomach. I came swiftly in, grabbing Al and ripping him off Bryon's weakened body, tossing him like a rag doll some distance away.

"Bryon, Bryon..." I lifted him onto my knees and into my arms.

"Hey, Dean, looks like I was right," Bryon managed to force out, followed by a blood-gurgled laugh. He lay there on his back, blood squirting from his throat and sides.

"Hang in there, buddy. Jade!" I cried out, holding Bryon's weakening head. I looked around, left and right for her. Where was she?

Bryon's eyes began to droop. "Hey, hey, you stay with me, okay? You stay with me. You're going to be all right, I promise." I lied. I didn't know what would happen to him.

His body began to go limp.

"Jade!" I yelled again. "Hang in there, Bryon, okay?"

"Don't make promises you can't keep," Bryon said faintly through a weakening voice.

"Your little friend wanted to be the hero. I just showed him what happens when you try to save another!" Al shouted from the distance, drooling spit and blood from his gaping mouth. Bryon's blood. I'll kill him. I'll kill them all. The blue light quickly morphed to red. Hate.

"Go. I've got him." Jade came running in, taking hold of Bryon and looking over to me. Fear—I saw fear in her eyes.

"Ahh, is poor little Dean going to cry?" Al pressed on. "I've always wanted to know what the tears of an angel taste like."

I faced him—he faced death.

"Go kill that son of bitch," Bryon managed to whisper out of slow, shallow breaths.

"Come on! You're weak! Just like your mother," Al said.

I am vengeance.

I rose to my feet, looking away from Jade and Bryon. My body emitted heat waves as I squared up, eyes locked on my target with a thirst for revenge. Glass formed below my feet with each meltingly hot step. The veins in my body smoldered a red glow like lava flowing through the pipelines of this anatomy. Each step becoming quicker and quicker, I began to run, to sprint toward that which caused me pain.

Al mirrored and dashed head-on in a game of chicken.

Our silhouettes could be seen on the ridgeline of the sandy dunes, illuminated by the backlight of the full moon, two figures sprinting full force at the other. Collision inevitable.

"Ahhh!" we both screamed, nearing each other, preparing for impact.

Just as we were about to collide—

BOOM! Lightning streaked through the sky, injecting the ground between us with pure purple-and-white energy. The two beings stood in their place, blocking the way between Al and me.

"ENOUGH!" their voices came like sonic booms from a fleet of passing jets destroying the sound barrier as they slammed their identical golden scepters into the ground. Everyone covered their ears in agony from the sheer volume. Al and I in a standstill blocked by the enormous Guardians. "YOU WILL RESPECT THE LAND OF GOD!"

Their eyes could be seen lighting the sky with pure white light hundreds of feet in the air. "YOU!" One of them pointed to Al. "YOU HAVE VIOLATED THE FOURTH LAW. FROM WHERE YOU CAME, YOU SHALL RETURN."

"No, no! Please don't send me back! I won't tell him where you are, I promise! Anywhere but there! Please no!" Al begged as the scepter once again hit the ground.

A fissure began to form in the ground beneath his feet. A yellow-red aura came from below, and the sounds of cries and bloodcurdling screams broke the silence of the desert. Blackened and diseased hands reached through, grabbing hold of Al, pulling and ripping at his body. "No! No! I can't go back! No!" His body, wrapped in bony, lesioned arms, was pulled slowly into the flaming fissure. The warm sands returned, covering the fissure into nonexistence.

The night air became cool and slow. I ran back to where Jade was holding Bryon's dying body.

"Guardians, I beg you...help him," I said from my knees, looking up to the sky.

"From where four becomes one, giving life to the land, so too shall life be restored," the Guardians said, lowering one hand to the ground.

Lifting Bryon's now-lifeless body into my arms, I walked over and onto the hand. Jade followed.

Bryon's head and legs hung motionless.

The hand began to rise into the clouds, this time moving closer to the mountain in the sky. As they grew nearer, the mountain became more visible, tangible, covered in greenery, succulents, and trees of all kinds. Golden animals roamed the mountainsides, watching all that was happening. The Guardians lifted us to the top of the mountain where there resided a small pond surrounded by leaves of gold and animals that seemed to glow in the starlight. The reflection of the moon shone brightly in the still waters. From the miniature pond, four openings, one from the north, south, east, and west, poured water down the mountainsides, dropping off the floating rock and into the endless abyss of the vast skyline.

"The four-headed snake," Jade uttered. "We found it. This is where the Garden of Eden stemmed from. This is the water of life, the land of creation. Dean, we made it."

I looked over to Jade, still holding Bryon's decaying body. I couldn't feel any excitement. I couldn't feel anything. Stepping off the hand and onto the grass, I carried Bryon to the pond. A soft, blue glow seemed to originate from the center of the waters. Surrounded by the trees, the animals came to see what was happening. Each glowing through the trees.

One slow step after the other, my feet teased the water. Then my knees, then my hips. I stood there, looking at Bryon's closed eyes and still chest, and gently dipped him in the waters. After a moment of complete submersion, I brought him up, spilling water off his lifeless body back into the pond. Hoping his eyes would open, chest move, for any sign of life...I stared.

Nothing.

"Come on, Bryon. Don't give up on me now, buddy," I said, holding him close. "We need you, pal. You need to be strong. I know you can hear me." A beat passed and still nothing. "Why isn't this working!" I shouted at the Guardians. "You said this would work! Save him!"

"Oh, you of little faith. It is not us who can save the boy," the Guardians echoed in their loud thundering voices. "You must believe."

"You have to do something quick, Dean," Jade said desperately. "His brain will be hypoxemic any second now. He won't be able to recover from that."

I looked back to Bryon hanging in my arms. "Come on, Bryon. I know you're in there."

I lowered him into the waters once more, closing my eyes. My wrist began to glow a soft, white, luminescent glow. Tilting my head up to the sky, eyes closed, I whispered, "Please, God."

The waters began to glow brighter and brighter, the white light competing with that of the moon and stars. The burst of light slowly narrowed into a beam shooting straight to the heavens themselves. Jade shielded her eyes from the sunlike brightness of the wonder and glory of the light. The powerful beam gently receded back into the waters of the small pond. Bryon's body still hung in my helpless arms.

"Come on, come on," I whispered.

Bryon coughed and spit up water, opening his eyes. "What happened?" he said, reaching for my neck and sitting up in my arms. The numbness I had felt was overtaken by a rushing warmth.

"Bryon!" Jade and I shouted with joy. Our eyes brightened and opened wide in excitement. The animals of the Garden seemed to glow even brighter as if in celebration. They cheered and danced around the illuminated pond in a beautiful array of light and love.

"What's going on? Where are we? And why are you looking at me like that?" Bryon said.

Jade and I embraced him in a strong hug.

"Dean, Jade…I can't…breathe." He managed to get out from our tight hold.

"You're so stupid!" I yelled, punching Bryon in the chest. "What were you thinking?!"

"I saw my friend in danger," Bryon shrugged. "Plus, I had been wanting to do that for forever. That guy pissed me off! I coulda taken him, too, if you hadn't intervened."

"I'm sorry I didn't listen to you," I said. "I could have gotten us all killed. I was just so focused on—"

"It's all good, we get it. Just promise you're not going to try to get us killed by some shark-toothed demon again…*and* admit that I could have taken that guy," Bryon said in all seriousness.

"Ha ha—okay! Good, old Bryon, you're going to be just fine," I said, and Jade laughed. "Guardians of the Garden, thank you. I cannot repay you for your kindness."

The faces spun from one to the next.

"It is not us to be thanked. We are but servants to the Almighty. All glory and honor are His," they said in unison.

"Thank you, J.C.," I said, looking up to the sky.

"Dudes! This place is incredible! I could live here forever! I mean, look at this view!" Bryon spun in circles, slinging water around and pointing out past the mountain's edge.

The sky sparkled with stunning colors. It was as if the entire universe was in view, galaxies and stars alike. I must have been so focused before I hadn't truly noticed the grandeur of all that surrounded us. The cool night air brought upon by the abundant greenery and flowing waters cooled our skin. A gentle breeze greeted each of our senses. The silence that surrounded only to be broken by that of the gentle, flowing rivers watering the earth from the everlasting pond of life. A true Eden. We soaked it all in, taking every moment as it came.

"Rest, and regain your strength," the Guardians said, their voices softly going with the wind. "The path ahead will test your strength and faith alike. Drink and eat all that is in the Garden. Come sunbreak, you must be ready. Trust one another and walk in faith."

Their bodies were becoming transparent, slowly disappearing into the dark of night.

"Phew! I'm starving!" Bryon jumped for joy, high-stepping his way through the pond and running from tree to tree, grabbing all the food he could possibly carry, using his mouth as another means of storage like that of a squirrel.

Jade and I laughed in joy seeing our friend alive and well. I would never let that happen again. In all my memory, I've had no family other than Uncle. Jade and Bryon were my family now. Uncle has protected me all this time; now it is time for me to be the protector. I couldn't bear the pain if something happened to them. My strong demeanor slowly shifted...Abigail.

Jade took notice. "Hey, Dean. What's wrong?"

"Nothing, it's just...it's nothing," I said, moving along the mountainside. The trees hummed a beautiful tone as I slid my hands across their tall trunks. Each one a different note, like keys on a piano. I found my way to the mountain's edge and sat in the tall, swaying grass. The view of the stars was otherworldly. I hadn't noticed, but Jade had followed.

"What happened earlier?" Jade asked with sincere concern. "What did they tell you? I had never seen you like that before."

"They showed me something I didn't want to believe."

Jade was patiently listening.

"They showed me Abigail."

"What about her?" Jade asked. "I don't understand."

"I should have seen it sooner. Everything was so new to me. How was I supposed to know?" I said through quick breaths.

"Dean. What did they show you?" Jade asked, scrunching her brow.

"She is not who I thought she was..." I said.

"I'm not sure I follow," Jade said.

"I saw it with my own eyes. Her cousins, Flint, her father—it all makes sense now," I continued. "I've seen what she can become. She is one of them."

Jade was silent for a moment. With a spark of an insight, she said, "But she isn't yet. Right?"

"What do you mean?"

"I mean, free will. We all have it, right? Maybe she is one of them, okay, but from what I have seen, she doesn't know she is one of them just like you didn't really know what you were. She is kind and loving and a healer," Jade said, placing her hand on mine. I looked up at her green eyes; they were kind and honest. "Demons don't heal. They destroy. There must be something inside of her that is keeping her from darkness. You can't just give up on that. You can't just give up on her."

"The Guardians told me that if I pursued her, I would fail just as before. This isn't the first time we are doing this. Something happened a long time ago. I don't know what, but I think it was her. I think she was the reason I vanished," I said, dropping my eyes and moving my hand away from hers. I am torn by mind and heart.

"So then do it differently this time," Jade said.

"How am I supposed to do it differently if I can't even remember what happened?" I snapped back.

"Change the present, and you change the past. I believe in you," Jade said confidently. I looked over at her. Something about her was different. Her eyes seemed to twinkle in the starlight. Jade was a smart girl. A smile formed on my face.

I turned back out to the stars. "Thank you."

We stared off into the night sky, side by side, admiring the beauty of creation. The vast and endless universe that performed their cosmic play for those that watched. Bryon could be heard snoring near the pond, his belly protruding like that of a pregnant woman, stretching his jeans and shirt from all the food he so gladly indulged. The sound of the gently flowing waters accompanied by the soft orchestra of crickets playing their fantastical instruments gradually lulled us to sleep atop the mountainous peak among the clouds. No fear, no worries, only peace.

CHAPTER 16

A SOUL DARKENS

WITH THE RISING sun came a new day. The golden birds chirped and spread their wings, greeting the morning rays of light. Animals of all kinds made their way to the small pond to wet their whistles. The skies were clear and the air was cool, beams of light inching their way onto our sleeping faces.

We must have fallen asleep together looking at the stars. Jade's head was still resting on my chest with her small hand next to it. She looked so different, like I hadn't seen before. Beautiful. I moved slowly as not to wake her, stretching my arms and letting out a long, silent yawn. I softly placed her head onto the thick, pillowy grass. As I rose to my feet and took in all the beauty the Garden had to offer, my senses awakened. The light smell of roses and daffodils misted the air, and a cool breeze brushed my skin, greeted in return by excited goose bumps. Making my way to the pond for a morning drink, I moved carelessly, the sound of shifting rocks and crunching leaves coming with each step. Tranquility in every sense.

"CANNONBALL!" Bryon yelled at the top of his lungs, destroying the silence of morning as he ran toward the pond, jumped into the air, and pulled his legs into his chest. A wave of water came exploding out of the pond, drenching me from head to toe as I was about to lean in for a drink.

Bryon surfaced from the water, bobbing like a buoy at sea. "Wow, this water is cold!"

"Dang it, Bryon!" I shouted, slinging off water from my arms and wiping hair away from my eyes.

"Oh, shoot!" Bryon said, treading water. "Didn't see you there, Dean. My bad!"

I shook off as much water as I could with a look of amused annoyance directed at Bryon for ruining my calm morning.

"So, what do we do now?" Bryon asked. "Do we head back to town even though we don't have the sword?"

"What's all the commotion so early?" Jade walked over, rubbing her eyes. "And why are *you* wet?"

"Morning, Jade," Bryon said before diving under the water like a duck looking for fish.

"Morning, Bryon," Jade responded. "I see you're feeling better."

"Much! This water is intense. And the food here, I've never tasted anything like it! It makes me feel so…young!" Bryon said, climbing out of the water, opening his arms up wide, and back flopping into the pond.

"How'd you sleep?" Jade walked toward me as I attempted to dry off.

"Really great, actually, despite all that is going on," I responded, taking off and wringing out my shirt.

"So what *should* we do now?" Jade repeated Bryon's question.

"I don't know. I want to speak with the Guardians…I'll be back." I walked off down a narrow dirt path nestled between two rows of oak trees. Jade smiled and turned to the pond.

From behind me, I could hear Bryan call, his voice coaxing, "Jade! You getting in, or what?"

"What the heck?" Jade laughed.

I turned to see her run and jump into the pond. I am happy.

THE DIRT PATH was lined with beautiful, tall green trees filled with fruits of all kinds. Some that I had seen before and others that looked almost alien. The flowers were just as otherworldly, their colors almost metallic shining in the sunlight, glimmering as the gentle breeze acted as music for them to dance to. The sound of birds chirping and hooves trotting seemed elated to be alive.

Finding my way to the end of the trail, it was marked by a small, round patch of dirt encircled by the tallest of pine trees. In the middle of the dirt patch stood a child-sized stone with engravings that covered its entirety. It seemed to call for me, what looked like eyes drew me in like a black hole. I reached out, placing a hand on the stone, tracing the engravings along their path. I could feel the power and history from within the small artifact, so visceral and personal. This is where I had to be. I could feel it.

Kneeling in front of the stone, I bowed my head in respect. "Guardians of the Garden, I need your help. I know it is not your job to help me, but you are the only ones I can turn to."

"Turn your eyes to Him and all will be revealed," the voices echoed throughout the Garden, startling me. I looked around hastily. I listened and took a moment to refocus.

"J.C., sir. I could really use your help right now. I don't know what to do, and there are a lot of people counting on me…" I began. I sighed, rubbing a hand through my hair. "I know you have made me who I am for a reason, I just…I can't figure out how to do things right. I'm scared that I'm not pre-pared, that I'm not strong enough to do what has to be done."

The birds continued to chirp and the animals continued to trot. Silence had become a common response.

"Come on! I'm sorry for all the wrong that I've done, but I am trying to make things right. I am trying to be who or what-ever it is *you* made me to be. I just need a little help here. Give me a sign!" I yelled at the rock.

Silence surrounded me.

I rose to my feet and slammed my balled-up fists onto the stone in front of me. The stone became like a crystal, no longer gray and marked but clear and smooth. An image ap-peared—it was Abigail. She was sitting in a small, dark room with her knees to her chest and arms wrapped around her legs. The room was lit by a fading candle, and drops of water fell to the floor from the ceiling above. The cold stone walls were close enough to each other to shake hands. Abigail sat there nuzzled up, rocking back and forth. I watched as anger built within me.

"Dean..." she let out in a whisper. "If you can hear me...don't come back. Don't come back for me."

The crystal stone returned to its dull gray color, once again rough and covered in its ancient markings.

Hands still on the stone, eyes wide, I stared. Emotions flooded my mind. Thoughts fought each other like brother against brother. What to do. What to do.

"Ah!"

—§—

BRYON AND JADE were sitting on a small, grassy hill near the pond when I came bursting through the forest. Their focus turned to me.

"Whoa, what crawled up your pants?" Bryon asked.

I continued to walk toward them, fists balled, muscles flexed.

"Dean, what's wrong?" Jade stood.

"They have her," I said, pacing back and forth.

"What? Who has who?" Jade stepped toward me.

"Abigail. They have her in a jail cell. She's all alone. We left her there. All *alone*." I stopped pacing, staring at Jade. Her eyes dropped and quickly looked back at mine.

"Dean, we couldn't have brought her with us and you know that," Jade said. "She volunteered to stay back and find out more about what is going on anyway."

Bryon stood to join the conversation.

"We should have brought her," I said, annoyed.

"Who has her?" Bryon asked, walking close to Jade and me.

I placed one hand on my head and the other on my hip. "I don't know. But we need to go back. Now."

"Now? Right now? But it's so nice here," Bryon said as I stared him down. I was not asking. "Okay, okay, but what about the sword? What are you going to do without it?"

"Yeah, and I thought you said that she was not who you thought she was. That she is not fighting for us…" Jade said softly looking away.

"I know what I said. I'll figure it out when the time comes. For now, we need to get home and get her out of there. Now," I said, walking over to the edge of the mountain and looking out to the sky. "Guardians. I have one more request. We need your help."

The ground began to shake at my request. Bryon and Jade lined up on both sides, looking out to the open sky. In an instant, the Guardians materialized before our very eyes.

"State your request," they spoke in unison.

"Guardians, a friend of ours is being held against her will. We must return home. We have to help release her but cannot get there in time by the means in which we arrived," I spoke sincerely.

"The girl. She is not of your concern. We have told you this," their golden faces said, sparkling in the sunlight.

"Guardians, please! I know what you have shown me. I have seen it with my own eyes! But I cannot just give up on her. I cannot leave her to become what you believe her to be." I stared them in all sixteen eyes.

"What you request is foolish," the Guardians responded, faces spinning from one to the other. "Although you are strong and your faith is growing, you are not ready. Those waiting for you have grown immeasurably in numbers and strength. You will not succeed."

"I have to try—I love her." I said. Bryon quickly looked at me and Jade winced.

The Guardians took a moment, changing between man and ox, eagle and lion, gazing into my soul. "Then you must go."

"Thank you, Guardi—"

"But be warned, what you are about to embark on is of your own free will. There will be no one to protect you, and should you fail—darkness will rise," they said in such a tone that chills were sent through my body.

"I understand," I answered boldly.

"Very well." The Guardians raised their staff.

"Oh! And one more thing. We have this friend, Scott..." Bryon said.

MOMENTS LATER, JADE, Bryon, and I appeared out of thin air back in the old junkyard of AngelFire, New Mexico. The stench was not a happy welcome from the majestic mountain we were just on, surrounded now by buildings of cars and scrap metal, trash, and sewage. We should have just stayed there.

"Blehhhhh." Bryon threw up violently, bending over with his hands on his knees.

Jade stood leaning with one hand on a pile of garbage and the other on her stomach, finishing a dry heave and spitting on the ground.

"I am never doing that again," Bryon said, wiping residual vomit from his mouth. "I don't care how fast we need to get somewhere. I will walk across the world before I have to do that again."

"What about Scott?" Jade asked, standing up from her weakened position.

I stood strong and solid, showing no sign of sickness.

"Don't worry, I asked our tall friends to send him back to his plane yard as we were…teleporting? He should be there by now too," Bryon said, holding his stomach.

"Come on, let's go." I said looking for the exit and moving forward.

I started running toward the chain-link fence. Jade and Bryon shook off their teleport sickness and followed.

"Where are we going?" Bryon asked in between breaths as we jogged out of the skyscrapers of trash. We don't even know where they are keeping her or even *who* is keeping her."

Our feet echoed like that of a group of horses running through a forest. The smell of old gasoline and metal filled our lungs. Mud from a rain the previous night flew in every direction with each heavy step from the stampede of our galloping feet.

"I think I know just the person to ask," I responded through steady breaths.

—§—

THE FEELING OF loneliness became her.

Abigail sat alone on the cold, hard floor. The fear of her own thoughts filled her soul as the sound of silence became deafening. Time became irrelevant—how long she had been there escaped her grasp. Had it been simply an hour or a day, maybe longer? With no concept of sunrise or sunset, no clock to tell time, her mind spiraled.

Who was she really? she thought. All of her life that had led to this point, was it all a lie? Not knowing who her mother was, or what she was, ate away at her very being. Her father, the definition of a lie himself—is that who she was, was that what she was destined to become? Her whole life had been a battle between accepting what her father wanted of her and of what she truly wanted for herself. Sometimes she wanted to be causing nothing but pain and sorrow. While the other times, she detested the thought of hurting another living thing.

No. This was her throne to claim, her time to rise, not that wretched creature in the stone.

What about Dean? No, stop it.

The thoughts were a tornado of emotion and confusion within her mind and soul.

Pulling at her hair, she rocked back and forth with tears falling quietly from her face. The thunderstorms of her mind flooded her eyes and emptied like Hurricane Katrina itself to the floors below.

"AH! What is happening to me!" she yelled at the top of her lungs only to be met with silence.

Alone. She was alone.

CREAK.

The door slid open just enough to push in a tray of food, then quickly shut and locked once again. A plate full of the best filet mignon, potatoes, vegetables, and more. The food was a gesture not received. She didn't want food; she wanted to be released. She wanted her rightful place, her inheritance that was being ripped away.

"I'm sorry I have to do this to you, Abigail. But I cannot have that little…boy of yours ruining this for me. I have worked too hard." Mr. Li'Ved's voice came from the other side of the door. "I didn't want you to find out this way."

"Find out what? That you lied!" Abigail yelled from inside the cell. "That you never planned to give me the seat! That I'm a half-breed? That my whole life has been one big lie!"

BOOM! THE PLATE of food slammed up against the inside of the door. Mr. Li'Ved jumped back at the surprise.

"Abigail, I was trying to protect you. There is so much you don't know. Everything I did was to keep you safe. Those people out there, like your friend Dean, they just want to hurt us." His voice was soft.

"YOU'RE LYING! Dean would never hurt me," Abigail screamed back.

The room's temperature began to rise, the door turning red hot.

"Oh, my Abigail. You don't know him like I do…" he said, tracing a scar down the side of his neck. "He and his family, nothing but a bunch of self-righteous *brutes*. Once he finds out who you really are, there is nothing that will stop him from…well, you know."

"He wouldn't do that…" Abigail sobbed, her body could be heard sliding her back down the wall and landing on her butt.

"Don't be so naïve, child. You know what you are, and once he finds out…"

"WHAT AM I?!" Abigail screamed. Light from the bottom of the door emitted out onto Mr. Li'Ved's feet.

"You, my precious child, are the key to it all. And I can't have him taking you away from me. We are almost completed with the final phase. Your brother is almost home. And I am going to need your help to bring him here. Don't you want that? Don't you want to be a family again?" Mr. Li'Ved said with his cheek pressed to the door. Sniffling could be heard from within the cell, followed by a heavy sobbing. "Don't cry, baby. It will all be over soon. I promise." Mr. Li'Ved walked away. His steps could be heard making their way up the staircase.

—§—

ABIGAIL WAS ONCE again…alone.

"AHHHH!" she let out, weeping her soul onto the floor. "No…No…I won't let this happen. I will not be used like this—not like this," Abigail said, standing.

She looked around for anything, some type of opening or weak spot. Everything has a weak spot. She searched and searched every inch of the cell. There was not a crack, a missing stone, nothing. Unbreakable.

"Come on!" she yelled, slamming her fists onto the door. "Let me out of here!"

Her anger rose and rose, the room once again becoming hot to the touch. She could feel something within her growing, something she had never felt before. Anger. Hate. Fury. She had been lied to and kept around as an object, something to be used to procure a means to an end.

Had she really been loved at all by her own father, the one who cared for her? Was it out of love, or need? The thoughts floated around in her mind and moved like ghosts from cell to cell. Nerves firing off left and right.

The dark room oozed an even blacker shadow, blacker than black. An eclipse of all available light. Not even a shadow shone. Her blood began to boil as her pupils expanded to the edges of her sclera. Black as the night, her beautiful blue eyes became. The dark void that filled the room seemed to come from within.

Pieces of darkness assembled into what looked like miniature dragons the size of a finger, their skin the burnt color of the room. One by one they searched the room like ravaging dogs on the trail of blood. Making their way out of the room, one of the dark creatures took hold of the large steel-plated barrier that was locking the door. The creature lifted with all its might, and the lock slid above the brackets and fell to the ground.

A loud thud rang through the steel door, echoing in the room.

CREAK.

The door cracked open ever so slightly, letting in not but a sliver of light. Slowly like a mist, the darkness crawled in the presence of the stairwell light, absorbing it. The dark gloom grew from its point of origin: Abigail. Her eyes black, not a trace of color.

Abigail took in a quick, deep breath of air as she restituted a focused demeanor. A gasp grasping to life, life of the death from within. As she moved, the heavy barrier door opened as if kneeling in her presence. With no delay she made her way up the stairwell. Slow and with guile, she was not herself. Something from within moved her. Her skin pale, the veins around her eyes pulsed and spread like roots of a tree, her blonde hair now black.

Softly, meticulously placing each barefoot step, she hurried out of her jail cell.

The front door was close by, within reach when his footsteps were heard *click-clacking* on the hard marble floors. She commanded each movement, making her way for the exit like a lion from the zoo returning to the wild and away from the hell it had been kept. The sound of footsteps grew louder and faster. The darkness grew like an all-encompassing appendage, moving her forward, floating above the marble floors. The solid gold door swung open as she neared, as if it had been commanded. A blast of cold air came screaming into the castle, blowing her hair in all directions as she made her escape.

—§—

MR. LI'VED RAN DOWN the stairs to the holding cell, shoes clanking their wooden bottoms against the stone steps.

Reaching the bottom, he grabbed quickly for the opened door and poked his head in to see the empty room.

"ABIGAIL!" He let out a bloodcurdling scream as wind whistled into the castle. Mr. Li'Ved ran as fast as he could up the stairs and to the front of the house. "Abigail! My daughter! Look at you. You have never been more beautiful!" he yelled.

"I am not your daughter. Not anymore." Her voice had changed. Dark.

"This is what I have been waiting for! You are ready!" Mr. Li'Ved cried out.

"Goodbye, Daddy." She raised her hand to her father. He went flying through the air as if being hit by an invisible wrecking ball through the halls of the entire mansion. He smashed into the rock wall. Crippled. A ghost in the wind.

A smile from his lips.

—§—

Ding-dong.

The doorbell rang throughout the house. Footsteps could be heard running from the other side of the home,

"I'll get it!" a girl's voice yelled out. "Hello...oh...hey," Cherry said, opening the door after seeing my fake half smirk accompanied by two more half smirks on the two strangers standing on both sides of me.

"Hey, Cherry, is Abigail here?" I asked as kindly as I could.

The other two stood up straight, struggling to slow their breathing and not give away that they had ran to her house.

"No, she isn't..." Cherry's face twisted with confusion. "How do you know where I live?"

"Do you know where she might be?" I avoided her question—no time for small talk.

"No, I don't. Why?" Cherry asked, holding on to the door, ready to close it at any given second.

"I just *really* need to see her," I said. "It's about our school project we were working on together."

"The history one? Why would you need to see her for that; wasn't it due like last week?" Cherry was being smart—how odd. That wasn't normally a character trait she possessed.

"It...yeah...Anyway, if you see her, can you tell her I am looking for her?" I asked, a bit frustrated.

"Sure..." Cherry said, slowly closing the door. "Why don't you just go to her house?"

"Because I don't think she—"

Cherry shut the door.

"Why *don't* we just go to Abigail's house?" Bryon asked, scratching his head.

"Because that's not where she is. I saw her in some...cellar. It was dark and looked like a dungeon. I've been in her house, and I don't think there was a room like that anywhere," I said, looking around the forest neighborhood. The blizzard was growing again.

"You don't *think* there was a room like that, or you *know* there isn't a room like that?" Bryon answered back.

"Why would her own father put her in a dark jail cell? I have seen the way he treats her—she's his little princess. She's not there. Come on." I stepped off the front porch onto the dirt yard.

"Where are we going then? How do we even know she is here in town?" Jade said, still standing next to Bryon.

"Because she just is." I gritted my teeth.

"How do you *know*?" Jade repeated. "We could be blindly walking into a trap here. *Again*."

"I can feel it, okay? I can feel *her*—she is here. I just don't know where. You two are free to go anytime. I'm not making you do this with me. If you want to leave, then leave," I snapped, turning and walking away down the dirt driveway.

Bryon and Jade looked at each other and, for less than a brief second, considered the proposition. "Come on," Bryon nudged, making his way off the porch and following me. Jade followed too, and they caught up running along each side. The three of us exchanged looks, true friends running without direction into the tree-filled forests.

The smell of fresh pine needles was thin through the forming storm but still notable as it filled the air with a comforting aroma of home and safety. Clouds began to form in the sky, graying out the blue skies and white, snow-covered forest. The winds rose quickly, arresting our sense of smell and replacing it with the burning of frozen air.

"FIND HER!" MR. LI'VED yelled at Beth and Kip in his office, their heads bowed in fear.

Kip began to speak. "Master, we do not—"

"I don't care what you have to do! Bring her back to me!" Spikes came cutting through the shoulders of the back of his shirt, his face becoming dark and red.

"Uncle, please, we have tried," Beth said quickly and calmly in an attempt to speak reason into the ears of the devil. "Our seer cannot find her either. She is masking her energy from us."

"Enough. I do not want to hear these petty excuses. I have given you all you need to find this one. Little. Girl. Her power cannot be strong enough to block yours. Find her. And bring her back to me, alive. I am too close to let this SLIP OUT OF MY HANDS!" Mr. Li'Ved screamed, tossing his solid oak half-ton desk through the adjacent wall as if it were a toy made of feathers.

The two scurried behind each other in fear.

"She will not ruin this for me. I will not wait any longer for my throne. I will have my kingdom. I will have my glory." Dark black flames covered his body, his eyes red and black.

"Yes, master." The young demons complied and bowed their heads, exiting the room.

"AHHHH!" Mr. Li'Ved screamed as the flames exploded throughout the room, and disappearing into the cloud of fire and smoke, he was gone. Empty.

The room was wrecked and on fire as if a grenade had gone off in the small office.

The smell of smoke filled the air.

"WHAT'S THAT SMELL?" Jade said as she, Bryon, and I neared the Li'Ved castle.

"It smells like something is burning," Bryon said, looking over to Jade.

We changed gears and sprinted the last fifty yards, turning the corner to witness the house being consumed by the hungry flames. As we stopped in our tracks, the heat from the flames could be felt from down the drive. The once-gaudy castle was being reduced to ash. The stone lions that guarded the entrance melted to unrecognizable shapes. Not even the cold winds of ice could dampen the heat.

We were too late. I didn't listen again. I was too late.

"Abigail!" I yelled, continuing to run from where they had stopped.

"Dean, wait!" Jade yelled, chasing after me, stopping just at the steps of the castle.

I was moving as fast as I could, not thinking about the heat from the flames or the consequences of being burned. I made my way into the front door, flames spilling out the top of the door and wrapping themselves around the ceiling of the house. Smoke and soot filled the air, breathable oxygen was scarce. My vision was blurred by waves of heat and billows of smoke, soot, and ash cutting at the cornea of my eyes. Fireman level: Hell.

"Abigail!" I screamed, hoping for a response.

A deadly game of Marco Polo.

"Abigail!" I continued to scream in between coughs as my lungs attempted to clear themselves of the toxic waste that was lining their walls, threatening their lives. Clearing room by room, I made my way up the stairs, the heat unbearable, burning at my skin without even being touched by the flames.

The air itself was searing hot.

BOOM!

An explosion went off in the kitchen as the gas stove blew out one of the walls. The flames took to it like a sponge to water, expanding and growing as oxygen from the hole in the wall came sweeping in from the outside.

"Dean!" Bryon yelled. I turned, surprised to see him a few feet behind me. "Dean! She isn't here! We have to go!"

I heard him, but it didn't matter. I continued to call, "Abigail!"

"She *isn't* here! We need to go!" Bryon grabbed me by the shoulder.

I whipped around as fast as an alligator snapping on his prey and grabbed Bryon by the throat. As I stared him in the eyes with anger and sadness, Bryon's face began to turn red, lacking oxygen from my tight grip. Catching my reflection in Bryon's eyes, I saw my angered, heartbroken face reflected with the reds and yellows of the flames behind.

Releasing my grip, I dropped to my knees.

Flames surrounded us, and with not an ounce of mercy, they grew and grew.

"We need to go," Bryon said softly, once again placing his hand on me.

Timber fell all around us from the roof as it began to cave under its own weight. The construction was compromised, the frames were burning, and the support was rotting away as the flames moved like powerful waves against the shores of an island.

I stood with the help from my loyal friend. Slowly we rose together amongst the growing flames. In a daze of confusion and denial, I walked with my weight supported by Bryon, a zombie with no mind.

I could not accept the fact that she could be gone. That I was too late.

The two of us made our way back down the stairs into the ocean of flames.

BOOM!

Another explosion went off, tossing us like rag dolls about fifteen yards away. Burnt timber and glass flew in the air landing all around. My ears were ringing from the explosion, a war zone of twisted metal, rock and fire.

Groggy and weak, I attempted to push myself off the ground. My vision blurry and doubled, I looked to the house. Making it to my feet was no walk in the park. Standing of my own strength, I wavered with the night breeze and watched the flames as they devoured their prey.

Bryon and Jade slowly rose next to me, eyes wide in shock and awe, gazing at the dancing fires. Our faces and bodies were blackened from the war, clothes burnt and torn. Silently we stood. The sound of gentle crackling, as if a small fire, came from the house. An occasional pop echoed between the trees.

The pacifying sound of sirens could be heard off in the distance. As they grew closer and more distinct, Bryon snapped out of his daze. "Come on, we gotta go." He grabbed me once again. Jade complied and turned to leave.

I stood, in complete disbelief. Was she gone? Had I really lost her? My heart was in my throat. My stomach in shambles. I am numb.

"Dean," Bryon called again.

I snapped out of it. "Yeah. Okay," I said in monotone as I took one last look and turned to follow Bryon and Jade. The sirens were almost upon us, the red and blue lights decorated the trees. Two fire trucks pulled up in full force accompanied by three small police cars and a single red ambulance, the men got to work. The yelling from the response team was muffled and taken with the wind as they fought the all-consuming fire.

Emotionless I ran, no longer in a rush, simply running. My focus and motivation diminished with the growing flames. Running and running, passing one tree after the other, our feet pounded the ground. Breathing slow and steady like that of well-trained racehorses galloping along. The frozen air felt good against our still-burning skin, refreshing and healing. Snowflakes in the wind like miniature healers. Oranges and reds colored the sky, not from the sun—the sun had long since left.

After what seemed like a lifetime of running through the forest, over the rocks and snow, splashing through near frozen streams, we finally arrived home. There she stood, just as beautiful as ever with her strong wooden walls and colorful glass mosaics. Greeted by the familiar streetlamp, we stopped and stared, catching our breath. I was the first to move past the gate and toward the church. I was ready to feel some type of comfort, some type of safety. Creaking, the door opened as I pushed the heavy church doors into the main chamber. It was as if we had never left, everything exactly as it had been left.

"Dean, you okay?" Jade asked, breaking the silence. "We don't even know if she was in there."

I remained silent. Where was Uncle? Normally he would have greeted me with some smart remark.

"Yeah, man, she could have been somewhere else. Somewhere safe," Bryon added.

I moved about the church like a zombie with no purpose.

"We can keep looking in the morning. We should rest now," Bryon said.

"Rest?" I spoke. "Rest? You think those *things* are out there resting? You think if Abigail is even out there, she is resting!" I yelled.

"Dean, calm down," Bryon said. "That fire took a lot out of us. I mean, we almost died. We need to regain our strength."

"Gah! If we had just gone straight there, maybe we could have—"

Jade stopped me. "You can't do that. You can't play the what ifs. It will kill you."

"We shouldn't have left her. We shouldn't have left her all alone. She had no reason being here." I paced back and forth on the wooden planks.

Jade reached out. "Dean, you know why she stayed."

"We could have brought her with us and done all of this together," I responded.

Bryon sat on one of the wooden pews with his head in his hands.

"We can't keep going over this. We did what we did and that is that. We can't change the past," Bryon said with his head buried in his hands, rubbing his burning eyes.

"You want to just give up? Is that what you're saying?" I moved toward Bryon with my hands on my hips.

Bryon raised his head from his hands, staring me right in the eyes. "All I'm saying is we can't change the past. We need to rest now and start again in the morning. No one is benefiting from being angry and weak right now. If Abigail is still out there, she is going to need us at our best. If we go right now, we are not going to be of much help at all in our current state."

"Oh yeah, like you've even been much help at all," I muttered.

"What did you say?" Bryon stood up.

"Bryon, sit down," Jade said, moving toward the two of us. "Just let it go."

"No. No, I won't let it go. If this ungrateful bastard thinks that we haven't helped, then he needs to learn a thing or two," Bryon yelled. "We risked our lives just like you did. Even more! We don't have these awesome powers that you do! We put our necks on the line for you! I literally saved your life on that mountain in the desert! If it wasn't for me, you would be dead right this second!"

"If it wasn't for you, I wouldn't be in this mess in the first place," I responded, moving inches away from Byron's face. "I would have just continued living my life. But no, someone wanted to jumpstart their boring lives and try to get more views on YouTube!"

"What's all this commotion I am hearing?" Uncle Homer came out from his quarters behind the main stage. Good old J.C. loomed over us in his usual spot.

"Stay out of this, Uncle," I said. Uncle slowly made his way to us.

"You think that's why I did all this?" Bryon leaned in.

Jade moved to stand between us. "Okay, guys, just calm down. The smoke from the fire made us all a little crazy. Just take a breath."

Uncle Homer came closer. "Listen to the lady, Dean. Try to breath. And what am I hearing about smoke?"

"You think I did this for views? I risked my life to try to help you learn who you really are and where you came from, you prick! I wanted to help you just like I helped you that day on the bike! Ha, you probably forgot all about that, huh?" Bryon shoved me back a step.

I stared at Bryon, my eyes beginning to swell with tears. Bryon sat back down on the pew, his hands clasped together supporting his chin and covering his mouth. "Gah!" I turned and stormed off into my makeshift bedroom. I am the whirlwind of emotion.

"What in the world was all that about?" Uncle Homer tried to ask me as I stormed by.

I ignored him but heard Jade answer for me.

"He is just hurt right now." Jade sat next to Bryon. "Don't take it personally."

Bryon stood up and stormed off toward the front entrance.

I paced back and forth in my small, six-by-six room, no bigger than a large closet. Out of the open door, I could see Jade remained sitting on the pew.

The quiet room gently began to rattle, just ever so slightly that the water in the bowl for holy water formed small ripples. One after the other, hardly enough for anyone to notice. The rattling increased in measure, small pebbles on the wooden floor began to shake and move. Jade took notice first, looking up from where she was sitting. Then the pew shook once...then again a second later...and again...and again.

"Guys..." Bryon loudly whispered from the front door. "Guys...Dean?"

As I snapped out of my blinded anger to answer Bryon's call, the ground shook so hard I nearly lost my footing. "What was that?" I asked just as another shake came. I started to walk toward the front entrance. Jade was holding onto the pews with both hands. Uncle next to her.

The entire building began to move with each groundbreaking shake. They came in close waves like miniature earthquakes, one after the other.

"I think you're going to want to see this," Bryon said, looking out the front door. The terror in his eyes was obvious. Uncle Homer, Jade, and I came running to where he was and peered out the door.

"What is that?" I asked.

CHAPTER 17

READY OR NOT, HERE I COME

T HE TREE LINE shook in the darkening sky. Only the shadows of the pines could be seen wavering with each movement of the earth. The ground began to hop, bouncing our feet off the ground in intervals. We held on to whatever we could find, the doorpost and handrails of the rickety church.

A deep, rumbling voice came from the trees, shaking the ground just as the earthquakes themselves. "Oh, Deany-boy…ready or not…here I come."

My eyes widened, searching the trees.

"Uncle, any clue as to what that is?" I asked.

"Its energy is unlike any I've sensed. It is dark. It is very dark," he said, closing his eyes.

"Lucifer?" Bryon asked.

"No, not Lucifer. I know his energy anywhere. This is different. This is a new evil," he said as his eyes opened wide.

The forest's wildlife fled in terror. Birds screamed as they flapped their wings as fast as they could to get as far away as possible. The tall, strong trees began to wilt and shrivel as if delicate flowers under a fiery sun. Small fires began to sprout up left and right. A dark, black, dinosaur-like leg emerged from the tree line, landing hard on the ground and knocking us off our feet. Then another. Church windows broke under the violent vibrations spouted from each menacing step.

"I know you're out there—come play with me." The voice blew a strong wind against the church, my hair blasted back from the powerful hot air. There it stood like a modern-day Godzilla, black and tall, its eyes colorless, its fangs and tusks dripping a sticky, black tar. The spikes on its back were razor-sharp. Dragging its long, muscular, gorilla-like arms on the ground, it approached the church.

"Ah, there you are." Shit.

"D-D-Dean," Bryon stuttered. "Dean!"

"I'm thinking, I'm thinking!" I yelled back.

"Dean, take your friends and get out of here. I will deal with this," Uncle said, pushing us back as he took a step forward. He stood upright as if a young man, his muscles seeming to bulge.

"Ah. Hello, Homer. Don't you remember me?" the creature said, taking another step closer to the church. Its leg crossed the road, the dino-demon torso moved closer breaking the transformer lines that followed the roadway. Sparks flew as the transformer exploded on contact.

"You know him?" Jade asked.

"Asorath?" Uncle Homer said.

"Pardon my appearance, I have put on a few pounds since the last time we met. Maybe you remember this?" The creature changed its eyes to a bright bloodred and pretended to whisper to a tree. The image from the party flashed in my mind. The demon who whispered to the jock. I remember.

"How?" I uttered.

"He must have absorbed the souls of the damned. The six have joined into one. We didn't think it possible," Uncle

Homer said, pulling me up. "We need to get out of here. You aren't ready for this. None of us are."

"Homer remembers me too. How sweet." With that, his enormous monkey arm came sweeping in like a bullet train.

"Get down!" Homer yelled, tackling my two friends and me, flattening us onto the ground. The monstrous hand whooshed by with incredible force, smashing into the pillars holding the awning over the porch. The sound of exploding wood and concrete blasted throughout the quiet town.

"Move!" Homer yelled, pushing Bryon and Jade off the porch and rolling just as the overhanging roof came crashing down, narrowly avoiding our ant-like bodies.

Dirt and debris went flying in a cloud of dust rushing into the air.

Abruptly coughing up dirt, I yelled, "Jade! Bryon! Uncle!"

"We are okay," they said, pushing broken pieces of wood off from on top of them. Everything seemed like slow motion. Jade struggled to lift off what looked like the remains of the large front door. A line of blood trickled down Bryon's ear, his face covered in mud as he stood out of the glass shards. Uncle reaching his arms down to help lift Jade. I could not waste any more time. I am here. I am Dean Michael.

I ran over to them as fast as I could.

"Dean, get down!" Homer yelled as the other hand came flying in from the opposite direction. Jade pulled me down to the ground as fast as she could, just scraping past the punishing blow.

"You guys need to get out of here," I said. "I'll take care of this."

"I already told you that you are not ready for this, Dean. Don't you listen to me, boy? You'll be killed!" Homer said, grabbing at my shoulders. Asorath took another seismic step forward.

"We are not going to leave you," Bryon said, balling his fists and creasing his brow.

"Yeah. We are a team." Jade tied up her hair.

"How sweet. The humans want to help," the demonic voice bellowed.

"You are no good to me dead. Now get out of here!" I pushed Jade and Bryon as hard as I could, sending them flying a hundred yards away into a mound of fallen leaves. "Now, Homer what can we do?"

"Your sword—where is it?" Homer asked

"I didn't…" I couldn't finish.

"No." Homer realized I didn't have it. He stared at me. Strategizing. I looked at his eyes—I was more disappointed than he seemed to be. I let him down. I let everyone down. "Over here, you overgrown monkey!" Homer yelled, taunting the creature. "Save your friends. Find your sword," Uncle said, grabbing my arm before quickly moving out of the debris and closer to the monster.

"Two on one. No fair." Asorath's hand came swooping in to crush the ground where Homer was. He rolled and avoided it. Nimble for an old man.

"Pick on someone your own size!" Uncle Homer began swinging his hands around in a choreographed rotation. I couldn't quite make out what he was saying as he muttered something to himself. The ground began to shake, and the earth began to break and swirl around him. His body grew and grew, glowing a bright, white light, blindingly bright.

"Uncle?" I watched, shielding my eyes.

"Dean, go now," Uncle Homer said as he reached a size nearly matching that of the beast. His body glowing a bright and pure white. The two must have been over fifty feet tall.

Asorath frowned a gummy frown. "I see you still have some tricks up your sleeve, old man. No matter."

He rushed toward Uncle. The two clasped hands in a standstill of might. Asorath gnashed his teeth, trying to bite at Uncle's face. Uncle's eyes were strong and wise. The wrinkles around them seemed to be like fissures in the ground. His muscles pulsed, fighting against the creature. His arms the size of redwoods.

"You have broken the law," Uncle roared, tossing the demon into the ground. "You have upset the balance. I sentence you to death beyond Oblivion!"

"You think you can defeat me? The souls of millions surge through my veins. I am DEATH!" He freed his arm and swung, knocking Uncle off his feet. Grabbing him in the air, he slammed Uncle down into the ground. Pounding him blow after punishing blow. The earth shook with each hit, the crater under his head made deeper and deeper.

"Uncle! No!" I screamed, running toward him.

"Dean. You must. Survive. You must. Live," he spoke between blows.

His bright light begining to fade. Blood sprayed from his face. Bones shattered from the pummeling. I couldn't bear it.

"Enough! That's enough!" I yelled.

"You're right. That was too easy." Asorath picked up Uncle's limp body and tossed him into the air, so far I couldn't see when or where he landed. Asorath's focus shifted toward me.

"No!" I yelled. My mind went blank. My heart stopped. Heat. All I could feel was heat.

"Dean!" Bryon yelled from the distance. His voice could barely be heard over the siren of car alarms and terrified animals all swirled together by the rising winds. Dark clouds began to swirl overhead as if forming what looked like a hurricane above the building-sized demon. "We have to do something!" Bryon shouted at Jade, attempting to run toward me.

Jade grabbed his arm before he could move. "Dean is right. This battle is not ours. We need to find help." Jade and Bryon ran toward a nearby street, finding the first car in sight. The windows had been blown out from the earthshaking stomps.

"Get in!" Jade ordered.

Bryon ran around to the passenger side and jumped in. Jade reached in through the broken window and unlocked the door, then leaned under the steering wheel.

"What are you doing?" Bryon asked, keeping an eye on me. I was standing facing the Demon, prepared. The mouse and the pit bull. The car's engine roared. Jade sat up straight and revved the engine, and the two took off, peeling out from the street, tires screeching.

I LOOKED OVER with a sense of joy, glad my friends got out safe. I did not wish them to return. Just as I looked back to the demon, its hand came flying in once again, this time catching me off guard.

The hand hit with such great impact, my body went tumbling through the air, crashing through tree after tree, knocking them down like a wrecking ball through stone. It felt as if every bone in my body had turned to dust. About four hundred yards away, my momentum gave way to gravity, bringing me sliding through the dirt.

"Ha ha ha ha ha, you are weak, boy! I was told you had regained your strength. What a pity," Asorath said, turning his attention to where I had landed.

My body felt as if I had been hit by a train and reversed over and over and over again. By a tank. A heavy tank. Gathering my strength, I managed to rise up, digging one hand after the other into the dirt. I stood to my feet.

"Your father would be so very disappointed," Asorath said in his deep rumbling voice.

I stood, staring at Asorath, my blood boiling.

I was *not* a disappointment—I was strong. I was the one chosen to fight for the people. To protect them from evil scum like this. I will kill him for what he did to Uncle. For what he would do if I don't. My body began to heat, my mark glowing a deep red, running through my veins like neon strips of light.

"That's it. Get mad!" Asorath said, beginning to run toward me. My feet moved quickly on their own account toward the abomination, head to head, my small body not even the size of the demon's little finger. The moon lit our path through the tree-studded soil. The blizzard screaming all around us.

"Ahhh!" I yelled, inches away from one another. Only one instinct: kill. My body strengthened by rage, heat growing around in a visible aura.

WHACK.

Before I could get close enough, I was sent flying again by the truck-like hand, silencing me with ease. My face skidded in the earth, my body limp.

"You are weak, just like your mother," Asorath prodded.

Mom. An image flashed in my mind, too quick to catch. Was that her?

After a few moments of semiconsciousness, I lifted my face from the ground slowly, spitting up a cocktail of blood and dirt.

"J.C., I could really use some help right about now," I managed to say through busted lungs and a spinning head.

"Get up, you pathetic excuse for an Arch," Asorath yelled, shaking the ground.

Hail began to fall as the clouds tore open with a thunderous streak of lightning. I crawled like an army man under

barbed wires through the muddy, snowy ground. Hiding under a large cliff-like rock, I took shelter from the frozen water
and the ugly demon.

"Where, oh where did you go, angel?" Asorath said, searching from above.

I sat under the rock, rain tumbling in. My body weak and
sprawled out, I attempted to catch my breath. Touching my
tender ribs, I could feel some were broken. Groaning from the
pain, a drip of blood trickled down my face. I had been cut just
above the eye. Wiping the blood from my face, I bowed my
head. "I'm not ready for this, Father. I'm sorry."

"Ah, there you are," Asorath said, pulling the boulder from
the ground with simplicity, like a pebble from the beach, taking away my shelter from the rain. From pain.

I felt too weak to move. Asorath reached down picking me
up in his gargantuan hand. He held me like a baby holding a
doll, my head fell back, my arms trapped in the demon's grasp,
legs dangling. He raised me up high enough to reach eye level.
The demon's black eyes stared at my broken body, his mouth
oozing tar and blood. Hot air blew on my face with each exhale of the creature, vapor filled the cold air.

"With your power, I will be unstoppable," Asorath said,
opening his ugly snout-like mouth as wide as could, revealing
his hundreds multilayered razor teeth amongst his overgrown
tusks. Bringing me in closer and closer, he held me by my
shirt. I dangled, too weak to move.

"Abigail..." I managed to say with one last breath, just as I
was lowered down into the mouth of the demon.

"DEAN!" Abigail's voice screamed from the ground as she
came running up, out of breath. Was I dreaming? I couldn't
tell. My sight was blurry and my head was throbbing. I tried to
shake her out of my sight. She was still there.

Distracted, Asorath stopped. I hovered just inches above
his mouth.

"The girl," Asorath said, looking down at Abigail.

In a bright, hot flash of light something came flying out of the sky. Asorath's hand was cut off at the wrist, causing his hand to fall to the ground with my body still in its grasp.

"DEAN! NO!" Abigail screamed, running to where the hand fell from the sky.

"AH!" the demon yelled. The clouds darkened and the ground shook. He held his arm with the other in agonizing pain, staring at his nub of an arm where his hand used to be. He stumbled back into the tree line in shock.

The black, dinosaur-like hand smashed into the ground, forming a crater in the earth right next to the church. The old lamppost was crushed. Waterlines spewed water and waste into the crater and busted at the seams.

Abigail ran over to where I was still being held in the deadened hand. With all her might, she attempted to pry open the dead fingers and their stiff grip. Try as she might, she could not pull me free. Each finger had to have been the width of a tree trunk. She could barely wrap her hands around it. Still in a daze, it all felt like a dream. My mind didn't know what to think, to be happy she was alive or mad at the truth I now knew. I lay in mental agony. In physical pain. Was this Hell?

Tires came screeching in as Jade and Bryon skidded in the dirt, slamming on the breaks. The side of the car careened into the meat of the hand, smashing the remaining windows. Jade threw open her door and fell out, and Bryon followed, climbing over the center console and spilling out of the driver's door. Asorath was screaming in pain, as flashes of light burst in the sky like lightning contained in the height of the clouds, colliding with his face over and over again.

Jade ran to the back of the car and popped open the trunk. Bryon ran over to where Abigail was on top of the lifeless hand and its grip of death.

"We thought you were dead," Bryon said through heavy breaths, grabbing onto the large finger that Abigail was attempting to pry loose.

"It's a long story," she said.

The two pulled and pulled but could not loosen its grip. Their hands continued to slip in the heavy rain, the skies pouring down their icy tears. Jade ran over with an animal-skin pouch in her hand. "Here, give him this. Make him drink all of it…quickly!" She handed the pouch to Abigail, stood, and pulled an old wooden crossbow from her back. Loading it with an arrow, she aimed up at the pain-struck demon.

"How is that supposed to help again?" Bryon said, looking at Jade.

"*That* is the healing water from Eden…and this…is holy water," she said, nodding, motioning toward the bulbous, glass arrowhead's liquid contents sloshing around.

Just as Asorath began to reach down with his still good hand, Jade fired the arrow. Flying through the air, breaking through rain droplets on its path to the demon, it reached its mark. The glass from the arrowhead broke as it smashed into the side of Asorath's face, releasing blessed holy water onto the creature.

"Holy water…AHHHH!" Asorath screamed as his skin began to boil and rot off his ugly mug, exposing his back teeth and the muscle fibers holding his jaw together. Half demon, half skeleton, his face lit up in with strikes of lightning. Flashes of light appearing left and right, knocking the demon around like an annoying mosquito taking bites out of its victim.

Abigail moved her way around the fat, clawlike fingers and lifted my head into her arms.

"Here, drink this," she said, opening my mouth and pouring the contents of the pouch down my throat.

Swallowing the liquid, I began to cough as it spilled out the sides of my mouth. I could feel its warmth travel through my body. Strength returning. Focus returning. Power. My eyes began to flicker open and closed, the blurry vision of Abigail coming into view. It wasn't a dream. Snow from above made it hard to keep my eyes open while lying on my back, though she finally came into focus.

"Abigail?" It was really her sitting there in her red coat. Any anger I had toward her vanished. I could feel her heart beat, and mine. I am the foolish heart. Her eyes, though still beautiful, seemed different.

"Hey," she said, laughing through tears. "I thought I told you not to get into any more trouble, that I wasn't going to save you next time."

I smiled, coughing up more water.

"Guess I couldn't help myself," I said. Was I still in this disgusting hand? It held me back from embracing this dream.

"Hey, lovebirds, we kind of have a situation on our hands," Bryon said, still trying to pull open the hand. "Dean, I am going to need you to push as hard as you can on three, okay? Abigail, you ready?"

Jade fired another arrow into the sky—this one was blocked by the demon's good hand, burning a hole through it. "Any day now!" she yelled, loading another arrow.

"One…two…three!" Bryon yelled, prying with all his might, Abigail next to him doing the same.

"Ahhh." I pushed as best as I could.

The hand began to open.

"Keep going!" Bryon yelled through the rain.

"Rahh!" The hand peeled open just enough for me to wriggle out and slip down onto the muddy earth.

"Dean!" Abigail ran to where I had fallen on the ground, embracing me with a tight hug.

"We thought you were dead." I stood, wrapping my arms around Abigail. "We went to your house and…"

I was lost in her eyes staring back into mine. Gently I stroked her cheeks with my thumbs, pulling her lips close to mine. Closing my eyes, feeling every second, our lips softly met under the pouring rain. It was as if time stood still, the raindrops frozen in air, the creature like a statue of evil—we lived fully alive in the moment.

"Wait," Abigail said, pushing me away. "I can't do this."

I stared at her, confused to say the least.

She wouldn't meet my gaze. "I am not who you think I am."

"Abigail, I—"

"No. Dean, you don't know what I am. I am not good for you. I'm…" Abigail's eyes swelled, teary-eyed with a quivering lip.

"Abigail. I know," I said softly.

"No. You don't!" she said, moving to run away.

I grabbed her, stopping her from turning away.

"I know. I was shown in a vision. I know." I pulled her in close once again. "I know who you are, I know what you are, and I don't care…I love you."

"Dean—" Abigail started before I pulled her in and kissed her again. She melted into my arms and embraced my love. Finally.

"Guys! I hate to ruin your moment but…" Jade said, waving her empty quiver and dropping the bow.

As she did, the demon swatted in the air, knocking the flashing light to the ground so fast, like a missile from above, and grinding the earth down into a streak of torn mud and shrubs, the light flickered as it stopped near us kids.

"Nile? Nile!" I recognized my friend as I ran over to where he was lying. "Nile! What are you doing here? I thought you couldn't come back," I said as Nile attempted to get up onto one arm. The rain pounded down on us like waves of a tsunami accompanied by the frozen blizzard.

"Bryon called me…Ah," Nile said, grabbing his side. A metallic gold liquid dripped from his ribs—he had been injured. I could see Bryon grasping onto the necklace Nile had given him.

"Your father…" Nile said. "He would have come back himself, but…"

"But what?" I asked, leaning in.

"He sent your father on a very important mission. He could not make it," Nile said with all of us looking at him. We had quickly forgotten about Asorath in that moment until he reached his hand down, taking hold of Nile's broken body.

"You have interfered for the last time, angel," Asorath said, gripping Nile in his clutch and raising him to eye level.

"Nile! No!" I yelled, running as fast as I could toward Asorath.

"Dean!" Abigail yelled after me. By the scrap pile of a church they stood. Jade held Bryon back from chasing after me. I could hear their screams of pain and sadness.

My wrist began to glow a bright blue hue. I ran as fast as I could toward the massive demon. My legs, like spring-loaded machines, propelled me through the air as I jumped the entire height of the creature. With a strength from within, I screamed. "Ahhh!" I swung a fast right hook, landing square on the jaw of the creature.

The force from the blow was equivalent to that of a tomahawk missile hitting its mark. Dropping Nile from the unexpected bomb of a punch, Asorath went flying. His body destroying hundreds of trees as he crashed through them, feet dragging on the ground, plowing the soil.

I landed next to where my friend had fallen. "Nile."

"Dean…" Nile coughed up the golden biofluid.

"No, no, no, no. Ah. Nile. No. You're going to be okay…Jade! Get over here!" I yelled.

Jade came running along with the other two.

"Give me the water!" Abigail handed Jade the pouch.

"Give it here!" I grabbed the empty leather sack. "No, no. Where is the rest of it?!" I shook the bag in Jade's face.

"We only had enough for you," Jade answered, dropping her eyes.

I looked back down. "Nile." Something inside me felt like it was dying along with him. My heart was a punching bag, and it was losing the fight.

"It's okay," Nile said softly, looking back up at me.

"Dean," Bryon called to attention. "He is getting back up!" he said, looking over at the fallen demon.

"Dean, your father wanted me to give you this." Nile's shaky hand reached into a pocket on his silver utility belt around his hip. Slowly he pulled a golden chain from the pocket. It shone and sparkled in the moonlight with a brilliance like no other. At the bottom of the chain was an amulet, a small ruby stone encompassed by a twisted gold channel. Handing it over and taking a closer look, the same mark that shone on my wrist was engraved on the beautiful red stone. "It was your mother's . . . My sister's."

My eyes began to tear up. With not even a memory of who she was, what she looked like, smelled like, felt like...she became real. I looked quickly at him, having heard that last breath. His what? No. I couldn't lose another. Not before I knew him. Not today. Not like this.

I am the breaking heart.

"Dean!" Bryon shouted again. Vaguely I was aware that Asorath was almost fully up.

"That means you're my..." I said, crushing my eyelids together, tears squeezing out.

"Yes," Nile said with a soft voice.

"I can't lose you too," I struggled.

"Never lose your faith. No matter what happens, we are with you always." His words slid off quieter and quieter as his eyes lightly shut. Without saying a word, I laid Nile easily to the ground.

I reached over and shut Nile's eyes completely—at rest he shall lay. Nile's body began to glow a glorious white light. So bright, myself and the others were forced to shield our eyes. His body began to fade away into a million firefly particles floating up to the sky and disappearing into the dark night. The cold night rain showered our bodies with icy temperatures. He was gone, and so was a piece of myself.

"Ah, ha ha ha ha ha!" Asorath laughed, standing to full height. "That's more like it!" He began running back toward us at full sprint.

Still kneeling in the cold mud, I raised his eyes to meet Asorath's. "Stay here," I commanded Abigail, Jade, and Bryon. Step by step, I spooled up into full speed matching that of the demon's. Puddles of water and mud splashed with each landing footprint. The still-standing trees shook their pine needles loose with the vibrating ground, and rocks bounced as if rubber.

Like the breath of a dragon, Asorath let out a deep rumbling growl, sending a torch of flames into the air as he reared up his good fist. Closer and closer we came. I jumped once again into the air, fist cocked back like a piston ready to fire. *BOOM*! The sonic boom from the punch shook the ground, creating a force wave bending the surrounding trees, and stopping the rain from its downward descent.

Asorath hit the ground once again, this time waking up quicker, turning his head to look back up to the sky. I landed on top of the demon's face with rage in my eyes.

"Yes, yes!" the demon mocked.

"You…" I punched his ugly face again with brutal force, shutting him up. "Killed…" Left hook. "My…" Right hook. "FAMILY!" Left hook.

The demon's face was being pounded so hard into the ground, it formed a crater around his head, growing deeper and deeper with each unforgiving furious fist. Every dark bone in his face, completely destroyed.

"You are weak," Asorath whispered through a broken jaw, barely moving his mouth. "You will watch your friends die, one...by...one. He is coming for you. You will not stop him." Asorath's eye wobbled in its socket, looking over to me. Out of breath and losing strength, I stood on the creature's jawline, taking hold of the abomination's oversized tusk. "You cannot defeat me. I am death," he said, weak and beaten, his body limp on the ground as I stood on his face. Like a piece of meat that didn't know it was already dead.

Violently, I tore the creature's tusk from his mouth, raised it high above his head, and looked him dead in his black eyes.

"Go to Hell." I drove the razor-sharp tusk down with all my might into the demon's mindless skull, drilling a hole so far through it pierced the ground below. The lack of acoustic resonance. The creature's body lay there, lifeless and limp. Dead. Like a modern-day dinosaur in size and stature, its body quickly decayed. Melting away its flesh and bone became an oozing lake of tar and blood. To oblivion and beyond.

I stood covered, like a grease monkey at battle.

Jade, Bryon, and Abigail came running over.

"Dude! Yes! That was incredible!" Bryon ran up to me, wrapping his arms around my bruised body. "I knew you could do it! These two doubted you, but I knew it."

"Good work." Jade took her turn and embraced me in a warm hug. Then Abigail approached. Her soft, porcelain skin shone beautifully in the white moonlight. Her blue eyes sparkled like the stars in the sky.

"I thought I lost you. Twice." Her eyes locked with mine. "Don't do that to me ever again."

"Abigail, I—" I began before she pulled my face into hers, completing the kiss she had so abruptly ended the first time.

"I love you too," Abigail said, staring deeply into my eyes, into my heart and soul falling harder and deeper with each passing moment. I am loved.

"Isn't that just precious?" A voice came from behind a lonesome tree, accompanied by obnoxious clapping.

Quickly I turned. I knew that voice.

Kip and Beth emerged from behind the lightning struck tree. Clapping his hands together, he moved into the light in his dark purple suit and tie and leather shoes. Beth came out almost gliding on the ground, her long black hair lying flat against her black flowing dress. Her white face paler than a ghost.

"What are you doing here?" I asked, pushing the others behind me and preparing for a fight.

"Oh, don't you worry. We are just here for our little cousin," Kip said, moving clockwise around my friends and me. "Uncle wants her back. We will deal with you later."

"You're not getting near her," I answered.

"Don't make this harder than it has to be." Kip continued to circle the group. "That big hunk of meat," he said, pointing to the tar and blood that I was standing in, "he broke the rules. He tried to defy my uncle's rule. He was weak. He had no…real power. Replaceable. You did us a favor, honestly. Uncle wanted me to kill him after we got the girl back anyway. So, thank you."

I kept my eyes on both Kip and Beth as they circled in opposite directions around the group.

"Oh yeah, sorry about your little buddy too—what was his name?" Beth slithered. "Nile, that's right. Pesky little worm, serves him right for interfering. Guess he won't be around to save you this time, huh?"

I became enraged, my wrist glowing a dark red feeding into my fast-beating heart.

"Getting a little angry, are we? Good. You're gonna need it." Kip lunged toward me, tackling me to the ground with lightning-quick speed.

We began to wrestle on the ground for control. Kip ended up on top, pinning my arms to the ground. "My uncle gets what he wants, one way or the other." His voice felt dark and evil. His eyes nearly popping out of his head.

"Get off of him!" Bryon came running in toward Kip.

With one fluid swipe, Kip swatted Bryon away, sending him flying flat against a large boulder, instantly knocking him out.

"Ahhh!" Jade ran toward Kip next with a bat-like stick in swing position. She went flying with another swift swat from Kip, hitting the same rock Byron did, sitting there unconscious side by side.

"Bryon! Jade!" I yelled, struggling to get free. Kip's grip was unparalleled.

"Like I said, I will deal with you and your little degenerates later," Kip said, looking over to Beth and giving her the go-ahead. She disappeared in an instant, vanishing into thin air. Kip looked back over. "See you later, lover boy," he said, blowing a kiss. He vanished as well, gone into the night air. I jumped to my feet. Jade's head rested on Bryon's shoulder. The two were unconscious but breathing—I could see their chest rise and fall. I ran over to Abigail, who stumbled in place.

"Are you okay?" I grabbed her by the shoulders.

"Yeah, I'm fine," she said.

"What was that all about? Why did they just leave?" I asked, as if Abigail would know the answers.

"I don't know, I…"

"Abigail?" I looked at her with concern. "What's wrong?"

She looked uncomfortable and confused.

"I just…" she said, looking at me and tilting her head. She grabbed her stomach and then her chest.

"What is it?" I asked.

"I don't feel so good." She looked up at me, her eyes scared. "Dean?"

Abigail went flying backward at unearthly speeds. Her arms and legs flying in front of her as if she was being pulled by the waist from behind. Nothing was there—she was flying through the air.

"Abigail!" I screamed, running after her.

She was moving so fast that I began to lose sight. Faster and faster, she was pulled through the air. Pure adrenaline pumped through my veins. My legs moved faster and faster, so fast they could not be seen like the blades of a fan. My arms pumping faster than a hummingbird's wings, I could feel them sliding into a remarkable upward cadence. I ran after her, losing all sense of thought, all sense of self, of law, of rules.

My body moved out of pure instinct. Muscle memory. It was as if I was becoming myself again. Someone I had once been, someone forgotten.

Memories flashed through my mind, memories I could not recognize. They all came so quickly, like a slideshow set on hyper speed. Images blurred together. Though they were un-recognizable, my body saw them. My body felt them. Emotions of all kinds flooded my being, only to be overcome by the thought of her. The feeling she gave me. When her lips touched mine for the first time. The sound of her sweet voice saying those three words I could never unhear.

The falling rain began to sting as I ran faster, each raindrop hitting my face like endless bullets from the clouds arsenal of dihydrogen oxide. The pain was numbed by the feeling of anger. Anger toward whoever was behind this. Anger toward Uncle's pain. Anger to those who took Nile. My mother. And now taking away the one person I loved, the one person who loved me. I would not let it happen. I ran faster and faster, so fast I streaked the sky invisible to the naked eye.

I began to catch up to her. Getting closer and closer, she was within view. Fifty yards away now. The ground began to shake, more violently than before.

My mind flew backward to a fateful day. My birth, I could remember the rain, the screaming, the feeling of fear, the feeling of losing something I once loved. I could remember the earthquakes. The planet on which I now lived shaking as it rotated on its invisible axis, floating in space, tracking the gravitational pull of the sun.

Trying my hardest, I focused on running and nothing else. Placing one foot after the other was more difficult with the shifting plates below me. Twenty yards away. I've almost got her. Lightning lit the night sky left and right, the electrons collided like a massive highway pileup one after the others. The whites and purples bounced off my face.

Ten yards away. She is so close.

Five yards.

I reached out my hand. Her eyes—the fear in her eyes—it broke me.

"Abigail!" I screamed, reaching my hand out, stretching it every inch I could.

The ground began to crack and rip open forty yards ahead. A deep fissure formed in the earth. So deep, bubbles of molten magma from the planet's core spouted out from the canyon like angry volcanoes.

"Grab my hand!" I could feel her fingers touching mine—I've almost got her. She was being pulled so fast through the air.

"Dean," she whispered.

I was too late.

Her soul—torn from her body—exited in full form. I could see the life leave her physical eyes, the fear transferred into the eyes of her translucent soul. Time reached slow motion. Her body fell just inches from the cliff's edge, landing in my arms.

I slid to my knees, pushing pebbles and rocks into the bottomless fissure. Her transparent hand reached desperately for mine as I watched her being dragged down. Down into the depths of Hell. I couldn't reach, desperately as I tried.

Holding her soulless body in my arms, I could not move. The heat from the fiery depths licked my face like the tongue of a dragon as the cold rain pounded me from above. My mind went blank. No fear. No anger. No love. Nothing.

I felt...nothing.

Then...tears.

Tears formed in my lost eyes, dropping like the rain that fell from above. Rage flooded my being. Every cell in my body. Rage. Blood and rage pumped through my veins. I could feel my soul ripping from its seams. My heart pounding out of its cage. My skin began to feel hot, smoldering hot. I could feel my skin tightening as my muscles expanded.

I was completely aware. Completely in control.

No longer bound by the rules, I let myself go. I bowed my head. "Yeah, though I walk through the valley of the shadow of death...I will fear no evil."

Ripping through my skin like razors, they emerged. The length of twenty-five yards on each end, half a football field in total, they unraveled in all their glory. Like the wings of an eagle, they spread. Stretching and spreading my feathers, I placed her empty shell of a body on the soft earth below. Leaving nothing behind but fear, I dove in. The blistering heat scorched my face.

Ready or not...here I come.

ABOUT THE AUTHOR

Luke Valen, born and raised in small town America, grew up on green chili and hot desert days. After attending New Mexico State University, Luke embarked on his life journey in the direction of Los Angeles, California. He has had the pleasure of sharing the television screen with some of the best. From network shows of TNT, CBS, TBS, and more, Luke has expanded his skills from script to screen. Though a more true flame burned within; the fires of an author. Having always had a passion for creating, writing was no stranger. In fact, creating alternate worlds from pen to paper has always been his number one art form.

"I can't wait for my daughters to enter the world of books, to enter the world of Angelfire."—Luke Valen

Having now completed his debut novel, book one of three in the ANGELFIRE series, the invisible war is becoming visible. Luke lives in Los Angeles, California with his wife and daughter (and another on the way).

—§—

Follow Luke at:

www.lukevalen.com
www.instagram.com/lukevalen
https://www.facebook.com/LukeValenOfficial/